T0146499

BOOK II

THE EDUCATION OF
INNOCENCE

BY: SOPHIA

Order this book online at www.trafford.com
or email orders@trafford.com

Most Trafford titles are also available at major online book retailers.

Cover by Brigit Suslow
Artwork by Artist, Linda "Kamp" Lugo
Backcover Photograph by Linda Louise LoCastro
Editing Assist by Linda Louise LoCastro

Printed in the United States of America.

ISBN: 978-1-4120-7917-4 (sc)

Library of Congress Control Number: 2012910503

Trafford rev. 06/29/2012

North America & international
toll-free: 1 888 232 4444 (USA & Canada)
phone: 250 383 6864 ◆ fax: 812 355 4082

TO ALL STARSEED
Men, Women & Children

You Came From the Stars and
To the Stars You Shall Return

May You Awaken from the Dream
And Remember Who You Are

From THE GREAT MOTHER GODDESS
to Her Children
as it was written
at the Beginning of Time

ACKNOWLEDGEMENTS

See Book I for a full list of Acknowledgements.

In addition, I would like to acknowledge my readers
for having the courage "to volunteer" for
The Education of Innocence
on the Planet Earth–
a unique place of unparalleled challenges.

AUTHOR'S NOTE

You have come to Book II.
Welcome.
But unless you have read Book I,
there shall be no entry
through this Doorway.

Though you may read on,
the understanding you gain
will lack the fullness of
Wisdom and Breath.

To the Apprentice,
Initiations best take place in succession
so the Inner Dimensional Doorways
to the Mysteries that lie within
can be opened appropriately
with the Keys given.

I invite you then to complete Book I
before you enter this Realm.
Only then will the Guardians
grant you full passage,
so you may understand
the Metaphors that will set you free.

This book shall test your Innocence.
The brutal passages revealing
Darkness at its core
shall challenge the faint-hearted
and those with purity of heart.
Fear may also rise and forbid
you to go further.
Whatever reactions you may have,
you shall know your strength, courage,
and tenacity of will by reading
straight through to the end.
Then you will have the opportunity
to shift the negativity you have
vicariously experienced
during this journey when
you see THE LIGHT within reach.

If fear should enter at any
time and block your way,
Mysteia, High Priestess
of The School of Mysteries,
would like to suggest
the following Invocation,
so protection shall rush to
your side and guide you through.

In Alignment with
the *Divine* Immortal
of ALL THAT I AM
I Now Create
A Sacred Circle of *Divine* Light
All Around Me
Above . . . Below
and Throughout All
Parallel Worlds and Dimensions
Inside and Outside of Time
So All Negative Influences are Disarmed!
Thus, I Create,
A Holy and Sacred Sanctuary
Where I May Preside
Side by Side with the
DIVINE MOTHER and *DIVINE* FATHER
by THE POWER and FREQUENCY of LOVE
of ALL THAT IS!

Having all you need
to continue your journey in
The Education of Innocence,
ready yourselves to enter through
THE STARGATE!

AN APOLOGY

I personally wish to apologize
to all of you of great Innocence
who have had to be confronted
by Darkness of any kind,
and the pains, trials, and tribulations
you have experienced
because of Darkness.

Yet, it is important to know
that Wisdom does not
come to those naive of
the challenges of this world.

Wisdom comes to those
willing to see into the
true nature of things
with eyes wide open.

So let your eyes be opened
so no Darkness can take you by surprise
by setting you up as a Victim
because you chose to hide
or remain in denial instead.

Remember, you have all come to
this world as "Innocence"
so Wisdom, the Grand Master
of the Mysteries, could become
your Teacher, Protector, and Guide.

TABLE OF CONTENTS

BOOK II

Part III – Egoson: Lord Of Darkness And Chaos

Part IV – The Prophecies Fulfilled

Part V – The Final Reckoning

THE GREAT MOTHER GODDESS wanted to know
about THE POWER and FREQUENCY OF LOVE
that bore Her, when *LOVE* spoke:

I AM the ALPHA and the OMEGA
the BEGINNING and the END
of all CONSCIOUSNESS.

I AM ALL THAT LOVE IS
from across the WHOLE OF TIME.

Wherever I AM, THOU ART.
Wherever THOU ART, I AM.

I AM THAT I AM
FOR I AM *LOVE* THAT I AM!

I AM THAT I AM
FOR I AM *LOVE* THAT I AM!

From *The Sacred Sea Scrolls*

PART III

EGOSON: LORD OF DARKNESS AND CHAOS

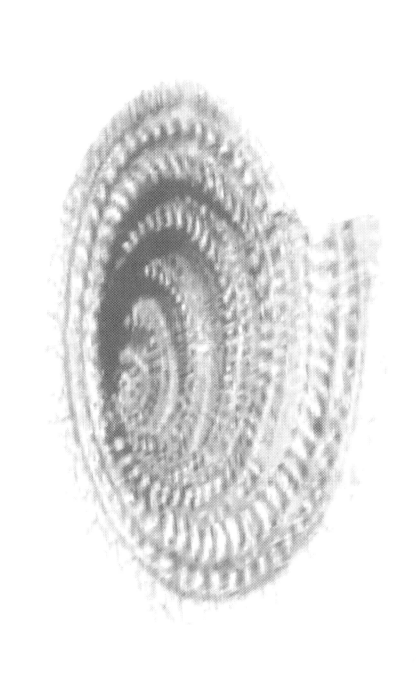

19

BLACKSHOE CRAB

Egoson, Great Father of Darkness, soon we will
take back The Kingdom of Oceana from the hated
Mother Goddess. Soon, I will reign forever and ever
as your embodiment, the Prince of Darkness and
Chaos. This I vow with every part of my blackened
Soul. This I live to die for!

Deep in the caverns of inner Darkness, recessed within the bowels of The Kingdom of Oceana, Blackshoe Crab pulls himself onto a ledge from the ocean waters below. He is inside a vaulted space set apart from the ocean by rocks and walls and free-flowing air. Blackshoe Crab is one of the few sea creatures in The Kingdom of Oceana who can live in the domains of airspace, earthspace, and seaspace.

Blackshoe Crab shakes off the excess water from his limbs as he turns and bows in deference to The Great Father of Darkness before the altar of his keeping. The altar is cast in sea creatures' bones, grotesquely gnarled in the shock of their deaths. Above the altar, an upside-down, black pentacle towers, where thirteen torches alternate in a circle around it, highlighting skulls propped on wooden spikes. Further above it is an oversized skull and cross bones—*the insignia of power for the Empire of Darkness.* The altar, alive with the ghoulish presence of tortured souls, appears suspended in hellish worlds of Darkness.

Blackshoe Crab moves toward one of the fiery torches, lifts his black claws over the flames, and sighs in relief as he feels the pain move across his body in tickling sensations. He watches as the steam rises from his claws, casting shadows of the Souls of Darkness on the walls all around. He sneers diabolically as he sees them take shape within the scalding midst, restlessly waiting for their Master to begin.

Blackshoe Crab rubs his claws together causing sparks of flame to ricochet in every direction. Anxious to try his power, he steps back from the altar and lets fly the flames from his claws without a moment's hesitation. Nearing the water's edge, Blackshoe Crab releases a lightning bolt from his stiff anterior tail into the ocean water below. Several dead fish rise to the surface, while he bellows with sardonic laughter. Stamping his iron claws against the ground, he powerfully triggers earth-shaking tremors in every direction, causing fear to rise among the general population. Absorbing the accumulated power of such fear, Blackshoe Crab continues the earthquake tremors until he feels he could annihilate all life in one brutal sweep of explosive fear.

Blackshoe Crab shrills again and again in celebration of sustaining the energy of The Dance of the Sacred Spiral of Life that unleashed the powers of Egoson within him. As the crowning achievement of his life, it made him the greatest reigning Lord in the Empire of Darkness. Raising his claws in exhortation to The Great Father of Darkness, Blackshoe Crab began:

> *"Egoson, Great Father of Darkness, soon we will take back The*
> *Kingdom of Oceana from the hated Mother Goddess. Soon, I*
> *will reign forever and ever as your embodiment, the Prince of*
> *Darkness and Chaos. This I vow with every part of my blackened*
> *Soul. This I live to die for!"*

Blackshoe Crab subdued the temptation to strike with all the powers of creation given to him at The Dance of the Sacred Spiral of Life. He did not immediately act on mass destruction because it would leave him with no slaves to rule except the disembodied Souls of Darkness. He would not deprive himself or them of their trophies of exploitation and unending source of *life force!* It was in the nature of evil to feed upon the energy of *living beings* to satisfy their ravenous, insatiable appetite. By making contact with the minds of sea creatures and triggering relentless suffering, Souls of Darkness bled sea creatures of their life force to feed upon it. Once emptied of life force, sea creatures weakened into apathy and depression, illness and even death, because they did not have the strength to exorcize the evil that possessed them.

Blackshoe Crab gloated over his accomplishment with a zeal and enthusiasm he rarely expressed. He had fulfilled the first part of the Black Oracle, eliminating other Lords of Darkness from the prospect of becoming the Prince of Darkness. In celebration of his greatest triumph, he chanted the words to the Black Oracle:

Son of Flesh with Spirit Bound
Who Lives to Serve
With Sword Unbound

Born of Hatred, Soul's Black Fate
Unleashes Mighty Storm of Hate

Death be Vanquished and Life Begun
After the Spiral Dance be Done

So Dance the Sacred Dragon's Fire
Mantle of Power Only Fire Can Sire

Know You are Egoson when Three Furies of Fame
You have possessed as Anger, Hate, Guilt & Shame

Father and Son will become All In One
The Greatest Lord of Darkness when
All is said and done!

Blackshoe Crab stirred from sleep by sounds he could not identify. He looked around and realized he had passed out before his Father's altar after black mass. He had been awakened by his own voice humming the words to the Black Oracle. He looked around feeling quite disgusted it was only a dream. Yet, its vividness convinced him it was not just a dream, but a *prophetic* dream.

Blackshoe Crab reeled on his hind legs and began to stamp his iron claws against the ground with all the power he could muster to feel his dream come alive. Instead, echoes bounced off the walls without so much as creating a ripple in the ocean water. The rage that flooded him just then blackened the very atmosphere around him. Focusing his glaring eyes upon the altar, he ignited the torches into billowing flames, enough to realize he was not without power.

Blackshoe Crab

In the next instant, Blackshoe Crab vowed to implement the strategies necessary to become the greatest Lord of Darkness that ever lived. He pulled out his father's journal and realized his father had used simple strategies to turn sea creatures into Souls of Darkness, whose ranks increased tenfold because of his insidious manipulations. He read his father's outline for creating an Empire of Darkness by setting 10 precedents for triggering the conditions of hell within The Kingdom of Oceana.

1. *Override Free Will.*
2. *Trigger Judgments and Criticisms.*
3. *Create Chaos and Confusion.*
4. *Perpetuate Worry and Anxiety.*
5. *Eliminate Safety and Security.*
6. *Instill Hopelessness and Despair.*
7. *Eradicate Peace with Terror.*
8. *Distort Reality with Misinformation.*
9. *Destroy All Clarity of Truth by Expressing Lies, Lies, and More Lies.*
10. *Eliminate Faith in the Goddess by Portraying Her as Powerless!*

Blackshoe Crab processed the information and started making plans for the future. He recalled one of the most important lessons ever taught to him by his father. It was during his youth when his mind was razor sharp, and he could speak with a clarity obscured only by living in Darkness. As Muckraker materialized before him, he began to remember.

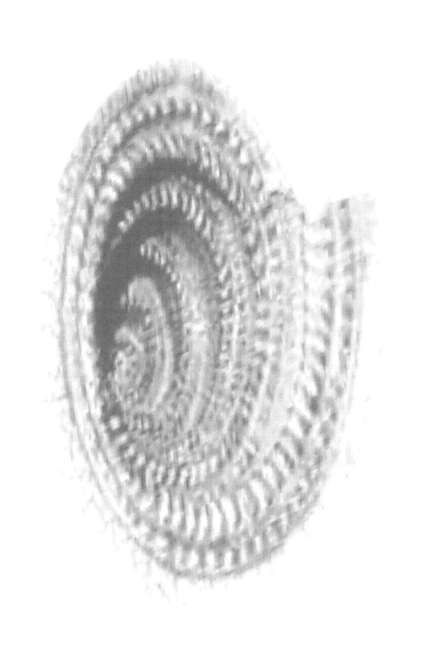

20

DUEL WITH MUCKRAKER

Muckraker's alliance toward me ultimately sealed
his fate.

Blackshoe Crab shifted into his memories and traveled back in time, opening a door to an unforgettable day with Muckraker. He was explaining to his doomed friend one of the most important lessons ever taught to him by his father.

"Old Blackshoe abruptly stopped his discourse on the mysteries of black magic to ask me a question," I began, noticing that Muckraker's eyes had become riveted on me at the mere mention of my father's name. Muckraker shifted closer.

"Although I may have known the answer, I could not think quickly enough. I knew I was being set up by him like I had been so many times before. You know what I mean, don't you, Muckraker?"

"Of course, I do! No one dares to be in his presence for too long! No one trusts the bastard!"

"Indeed! Whenever my father asked anything of me, fear would blind side me like a vengeful ghost, crippling my thoughts, as I struggled to find an answer. Regardless of how much I tried to concentrate, nothing came forth from my trembling mind. I had to admit by my silence that I did not know the answer. Shuddering, I remained paralyzed where I stood."

"Why didn't you run from him, Blackie?"

"Hah! My punishment would have been worse if I dared! So, my father waited with his fiery eyes burning into my flesh until I bled sweat. No response came quickly enough. The very thought of triggering his displeasure blocked my thoughts entirely, as I helplessly grappled with empty thoughts. My father always waited until I had molted my shell to provide me with the greatest lessons of my life. It was during those times I dreaded being near him—*when I was most vulnerable!* He reasoned that if I was going to follow in his footsteps, I would have to sustain every conceivable pain, agony, and torture of the flesh to inure myself to everything by becoming *deadened* to all feeling."

"Like him, no doubt!"

"Exactly like him! Once he set me up, he let fly the whip that scalded my flesh not once, or twice, but more times than I could count. He continued whipping me as he asked me again and again: *'What separates the Master from the slave in achievin' anythin' he wants? Hey? What is it, boy? What is it? Let me hear the answer!'*

"Did you know?"

"How could I even *think* when he came upon me like that! Although I tried to get away from him long enough to gather my thoughts, he followed after me, striking me repeatedly with his whip and stinging my flesh with agony beyond words. Then he would start again, *'What separates the Master from the slave in achievin' anythin' he wants? Hey? What is it, boy? What is it?'*"

"How abominable!"

"My father excelled in abominations, as you know! With every pause of breath, he whipped me until I fell away from him nearly unconscious. Writhing in pain, he stood over me, menacing my life with the question, *'What separates the Master from the slave in achievin' anythin' he wants? Hey?*

What is it, boy? What is it?' He then let fly the whip one last time as he mocked me with the answer that left its imprint on my mind and flesh forever.

"*DOUBT, my son, DOUBT!!! Once yah DOUBT yahself in any way, yah paralyze yahself into dah role of a slave forev'r 'n ev'r. So, NEV'R DOUBT, my son, NEV'R! . . . for that is how yah'll become a master ov'r slaves!!!"*

* * * * *

I smirked fiendishly, remembering the incident with Muckraker, which had changed my life forever. Although Muckraker was like a brother to me, he, too, became ruthlessly sacrificed on the altar of my ambition for claiming Egoson's powers.

Muckraker and I had worked diligently toward the acquisition of magic, knowledge, and power. Both of us competed with superior minds to achieve a distinct level of unparalleled intellect. Both of us were born to fathers known for their insidious acts of unimaginable cruelty toward sea creatures during black mass, where Lords of Darkness set abominable precedents as Taskmasters of Evil. Both fathers also obsessively demonstrated to us by their example that everything in Darkness became attainable once we dispensed *with all feeling!* As a result, Muckraker and I became bonded to each other because no one else came close to the abuse and cruelty that scarred our lives with festering wounds that never healed.

If I had known Muckraker would act on the wisdom gained from me on that fateful day, I never would have shared it. Muckraker would have made a fine ally had I been able to trust him. But it was not in the nature of evil to trust anyone. Muckraker's alliance toward me ultimately sealed his fate.

I noted with envy how much Muckraker had changed after our discussion concerning doubt. He assimilated that lesson so well that he became cocky and developed a smooth oily confidence that made everyone believe he could do anything. When asked a question, *any question*, such as when he was asked about the outcome of The Final Reckoning—*an unknown mystery*—he channeled the answer without hesitation:

> *"The Final Reckoning shall bring the forces of Darkness to their greatest victory yet! The Kingdom of Oceana shall take heed of Egoson's powers, and all shall tremble when he storms The Temples of the Goddess of the Sea!"*

The attendees at black mass exploded into cheers, whistles, and applause, as Muckraker was picked up and paraded around the room. It was apparent to everyone, including me, that Muckraker was being showered with every imaginable gift by The Great Father of Darkness in preparation for something great!

Seething with rage, I looked on, plotting my next move. Cursing myself, I acknowledged that Muckraker had shifted *because of me!* No longer did he doubt himself, but acted with a level of conviction rarely seen in anyone of Darkness. With jealousy burning into my flesh like scorching irons, I chose to act. Nothing, *absolutely nothing,* was going to stand in my way of claiming Egoson's powers.

I congratulated Muckraker after black mass for his prophetic vision before challenging him to a mock duel using our stiff anterior tails. We did this often to polish our combat skills. Before dueling, I covered the whole of my tail with a powerful poison that could bring down a whale after piercing the skin. I also laced it with powerful incantations to guarantee mortal wounding.

"So, how are you, my brother?" Muckraker asked, with a mocking laugh, once we stood opposite each other.

"Miserable, as always."

"Good! May The Great Father of Darkness *curse you* with greater misery for every day that passes. Now, let us see, how much pain you can endure!"

"If you can touch me!"

We leaped on either side of each other, poised with our stiff anterior tails, ready for combat. Circling each other, Muckraker repeatedly jabbed me as I flinched, again and again. Piercing my shell several times, I waited for the right moment. It was our practice to continue in this way until one of us had opened a wound deeply enough to permit bloodletting.

"Too much time with the ladies, I see. It has made you soft and sluggish, Blackie. Perhaps if I told you I had one hell of a time with a special lady you frequently visit. She even called out your name in a moment of excruciating pain. I repaid her insolence by returning her to The Great Father of Darkness to serve in his concubine. Sorry, I robbed you of that privilege yourself, my brother."

"Jezebel!" I screeched aloud, anger scorching my veins with poisonous fire. Seizing the moment, I did not hesitate to act. I ran him through, as he shrilled and I was done. There were no more words said between us. He held my eyes in frozen shock as I drove my anterior spear deeper into his paralyzed body without looking away. Just as I stepped back, he fell before me, as his smile died on his face.

I never again had to struggle with feelings of any kind. The ruthless murder of my brother sealed the stone cold hardness of my heart. It accomplished for me what I had not been able to achieve until then. The last shred of real feeling left, proving to The Great Father of Darkness that I was consummately ruthless by sparing no one in my bid for power.

Many times, I looked back thinking it was ridiculous that I was ever threatened by Muckraker, or even thought him capable of overpowering me. That incident was perhaps the last time I doubted myself.

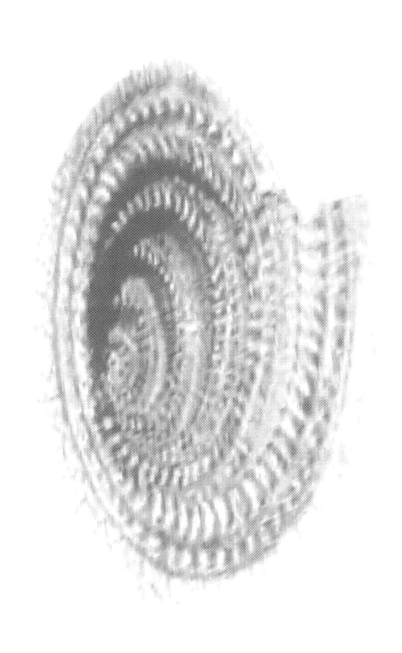

21

DEFILEMENT AT BLACK MASS

Old Blackshoe's legendary acts of cruelty drew
crowds from all corners of Darkness to bear witness
to his unmitigated ruthlessness. How many were
seasoned deeper into evil because of him!

Blackshoe Crab sat down on a chair made of sea creatures' skulls and bones and pondered the idea of fate. He questioned why he was born to a father who had shaped his evil character by repeated abuses. He studied the sequence of events that molded his destiny forever as a Lord of Darkness. By reviewing his life, he savored the most despicable things about it, which gave meaning to his blackened Soul. Suddenly, he stood up and looked around.

"By all the powers of Hell, I command the most depraved Souls of Darkness to listen to my cursed tale, so we may together glorify The Great Father of Darkness. I command your presence NOW!"

As soon as the words were dispatched, a wind picked up in the cavern where there could be no wind in a charged space of putrid air. Immediately, the walls fell away as Darkness gathered deeper than night, charging the very atmosphere with an emptiness so profound that even Blackshoe Crab shuddered. Luminescent eyes, the color of fire, gathered in that Darkness. Blackshoe Crab grinned, knowing he had his audience.

"Listen well, you forsaken Souls of Darkness, and you might deepen your hate even more and know you are not without purpose! As you know, Old Blackshoe was one of the most ruthless servants of evil the world has ever known. He was unrelenting, cruel, and violent in the most ingenious ways possible. He used not only physical torture, but every psychological weapon of torture his evil and distorted mind could dream up."

Blackshoe Crab paused, allowing the ripples of memory to gather tension in the Souls of Darkness. He then continued.

"It was not unusual for Old Blackshoe, by the sheer madness of his abominable nature, to turn on anyone and crush them with his bare claws, without reason or provocation, whether hungry or not, and then scatter their body parts as a common meal for all. Always, Old Blackshoe acted for the thrill of shocking anyone. Even the most seasoned diabolical servants of evil blanched from his unparalleled ruthlessness. All of you know of his deeds, eh? Especially those of you cast into Darkness because of him!"

Snarls and hisses came forth ominously, and if it were not for the thrill of igniting such a response, Blackshoe Crab may have succumbed to fear.

"Not even a ruthless, senseless mob dared to confront my father's paralyzing eyes. You remember, don't you? Every one of you who became helplessly paralyzed in submitting to a marathon of exquisite torture? Hmm? He splintered your mind until *you snapped! . . . and you became hapless victims of flesh without Soul!* What a monstrous Taskmaster of Evil he was! Everyone was tortured and dismembered in slow progression to the diabolical delight of all present! How well did you gorge yourselves of *living blood* every night my father took over black mass. No one could want for more, except his victims, who died, *begging for death!*"

Chaos exploded, as diabolical cackles and sneers screeched across the Darkness because of the heinous tortures many had endured that turned them into Souls of Darkness.

"But you were not the only ones who suffered! Every time Old Blackshoe returned from his excesses, blind with intoxication, *he beat me again and again with his hate, rage, and scorn.* The more he drank, the more his eyes blazed with the bellowing screams of tortured Souls swirling around inside of him. Repeatedly, he pushed beyond all excesses until all lines blurred, *and hell itself became the result!*"

Blackshoe Crab exploded into diabolical laughter, triggering Souls of Darkness into a frenzy, until madness reigned in all worlds of Darkness. Only after he riled such a frenzy, did he continue.

"Old Blackshoe repeatedly filled the chalice with the blood of his sacrifices for The Great Father of Darkness. After drinking his share, he would pass around the chalice so everyone could drink heartily of the still hot blood that immediately began to coagulate with the agony of his victim's suffering. It was a drink to be coveted above all others because no other drink compared to it. It was a fiendish delight to all who drank. Remember the thick tasty wine? Hmm?"

Deep sighs rippled in all directions, as Souls of Darkness remembered the blood without equal.

"Old Blackshoe's legendary acts of cruelty drew crowds from all corners of Darkness to bear witness to his unmitigated ruthlessness. How many were seasoned *deeper into evil* because of him. During the climax to his mass, Old Blackshoe mounted the male and female sacrifices alike. While still throbbing in the visual ecstasies of abominable degradation, he would discharge the pent up rage of his desecrated energy into their lifeless bodies. He then made an offering of their flesh of what he could not eat before the crowds of Darkness that gathered. All this was served to The Great Father of Darkness as a testimony to his brutal, diabolical nature!"

Blackshoe Crab shrilled as he staged his father's profanities in mocked exaggeration to squeeze as much defiled energy as he could from his audience. Aroused from the visual degradations of unspeakable horror, his passion swelled as the tension of hunger rose so keenly from the Souls of Darkness that he stopped to deliver his seed before continuing. Only after he had discharged fully and the Souls of Darkness had sighed in response from lapping up his energy, did he continue to rouse himself again in anticipation of yet more filth to come.

"Because of his monstrous example, Old Blackshoe insidiously shaped me into the mirror image of himself. He wisely recognized that once I had dispensed with *all feeling* I could become the consummate embodiment of evil–*EGOSON himself!*"

Breathless silence slammed in from all directions. No one stirred. It was the first time Blackshoe Crab had compared himself to Egoson before Souls of Darkness. No Lord of Darkness dared speak Egoson's name because it was rumored that Death would be roused and come knocking. Yet, Blackshoe Crab did not shudder or retreat, but waited in silence, charging Souls of Darkness with the terror of Death. He waited, challenging Death to appear, and waited, together with Souls of Darkness, who recoiled at the thought of rousing Death again. But Death did not appear, *though Blackshoe Crab was ready for a fight!* Instead, his thoughts shifted to his parents, who he remembered with monstrous disdain. They had already encountered the worst Taskmasters of Evil, Brothers and Sisters to Death, in the image of ones they had trusted.

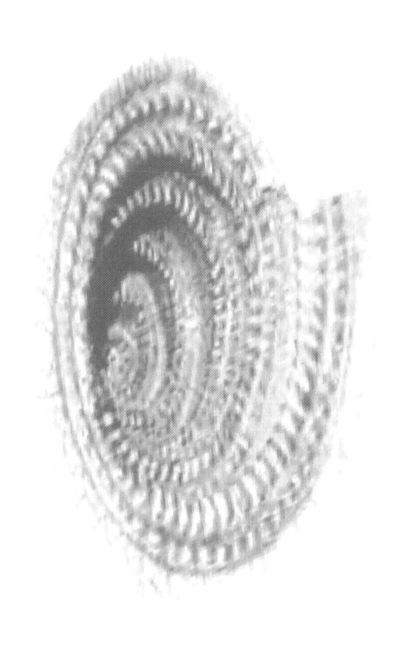

22

DEATH AND
DESECRATION

Once my mother was gone from my life, my heart
was crushed of any tenderness it had left. I then
began to hate with a passion I had never known.

"So, what of Death? Eh, my brothers? You still live, don't you? Let Death come knocking as it did for you and my parents, for not even my mother escaped the Stalker of Death or my father's punishing wrath, for being his mother and later wife to him. Old Blackshoe came to hate her more than life for betraying him because of her loveless disregard for him. When she exposed her raw feelings toward me when I was first born, her feelings became transparent to her husband/child even though it was something that had never existed between them. Not even when he was young. Not even for a moment!"

Blackshoe Crab stopped, trembling with rage toward his mother, as he rejected his mother's love with vehemence and disdain.

"For this abominable shred of real feeling that awakened inside of her at the time of my birth, my mother suffered unimaginable agony at the hands of my demonic father. The pain she witnessed inflicted upon me compounded her own pain. Although she had been born into pain and suffering as the only reality she had ever known, a flame ignited inside of her the moment I was born, and she could not hide or deny it. This flame melted the impenetrable hardness of her heart, and she awakened to new levels of suffering because it inspired Old Blackshoe to excel in the art of exquisite torture. She became the target of his unparalleled abuses of scorn and hate because of jealousy toward me he could not hide."

Blackshoe Crab stopped and reached behind the altar to grab a chalice filled with the cold blood of a recent sacrifice. Gorging himself with it, he splattered what was left against the wall, only to see it disappear from sight. Intoxicated with blood, he continued.

"My father became diabolically obsessed with hatred toward my mother and all females for representing the despised Mother Goddess. He persecuted both of us relentlessly in an attempt to discharge the rage, contempt, and jealousy that possessed him. When he could no longer suppress his explosive rage, he murdered my mother. She became his greatest victim and earned him the reputation of being the greatest Taskmaster of Evil who ever existed!"

Blackshoe Crab shrilled diabolically, while thunderously stamping his claws against the ground for being the son of the greatest Taskmaster of Evil that ever lived. Only after he had gloated sufficiently, did he continue.

"Old Blackshoe killed my mother during the High Black Mass of Hallows Eve. He raped her before the Kingdom of Darkness and then plunged his claws deep into her heart as her eyes bulged with shock. He ripped her heart out while she was still panting, ate part of it before her dying eyes, and then pulverized what was left of it with a rib bone until her blood covered everything!"

Blackshoe Crab began pounding the floor with a rib bone taken from the altar as his screaming mother materialized before him. The Souls of Darkness cheered him on while his mother disappeared into a pool of blood.

Breathless from the exertion, Blackshoe Crab looked up with the blazing eyes of a madman, until all hushed in response. Several Souls of Darkness dared press against him to lick his throbbing pride, but he viciously kicked them away.

"I was ten years old when I witnessed the brutal slaying of my mother. As my father approached me with blood dripping from his mouth and eyes blazing, I thought I was about to suffer the same fate. Instead, he grabbed me by the throat, paraded me around the packed room filled to capacity at Hallow's Eve, so I could view what was left of her desecrated body. He then shoved my face against the floor.

"Drink! Go ahead! Drink of what's left of 'er and anyone who represents the hated Mother Goddess! And always remember your father as the greatest Taskmaster of Evil that ev'r lived!"

Blackshoe Crab panted from the smell of his Mother's blood, as vivid to him as the day he drank of it. He circled, babbling to himself, forgetting about his audience while the images of his mother's monstrous death reared into his mind. When a Soul of Darkness slinked toward him and jolted his thoughts, he viciously grabbed it by the neck. Holding it between his claws by sheer will, he exposed it to the open flames as a harrowing, shrilling cry of pain filled the cavern depths before he released the Soul of Darkness. He glared into his audience, daring anyone else to come close. Recovering, he continued.

"Once my mother was gone from my life, my heart was crushed of any tenderness it had left. I then began to hate with a passion I had never known. The terrible pain and conflict I felt toward my mother ultimately reconciled me to her horrific death. I became my father's son in killing her, again and again, during the climax of every black mass that has occurred ever since."

Blackshoe Crab kept mumbling to himself in a rage when his mother suddenly came into view.

*"After all, Mother, was it not **what you asked for** by remaining wedded to such a sadistic, diabolical fiend! Was it not apparent to you after so many years of torture that your demented husband could not be trusted under any circumstances? Was it not inevitable that you, too, would become his greatest victim by proving yourself to be in greater denial then even him?"*

Blackshoe Crab tried to understand the anger and rage that still possessed him. Many times he had begged his mother to leave his father so both might be rescued from the abuses of daily torture, especially following his bouts of drinking. But her fear was so great, and her self worth so poor, that she remained with him and became his slave, *until he had no respect for her life!*

Still raging over his memories, Blackshoe Crab walked over to a jar and pulled out the severed claw left of his mother's mutilated body. Placing it on a stone, he pounded it with a rib bone until he crushed it into sand.

"Enough of that!" he shouted, as his breath caught in sickening waves of intolerable nausea. Souls of Darkness crowded around, taking advantage of his sickened response, but he kicked them away.

"My mother cursed me with feelings I have sought to eliminate. Although she cared for me, her feelings meant *nothing* to me because *she meant nothing to herself!* It underscored my hate toward her because she had no pride, dignity, or any feelings of self worth. In fact, a powerful Lord of Darkness was robbed of his powers because of *feelings* he demonstrated. Given the chance to show his loyalty to The Great Father of Darkness, he was commanded to sacrifice his first born at black mass. Because he could not, his son was eaten alive before his dying eyes so others could see what was *blasphemous* to Darkness. Make no mistake! *Love* could serve Darkness, too!"

Chaos exploded among the Souls of Darkness for it was blasphemous to speak the word *love* in any way.

"Wait, listen well, before you charge yourselves and revolt against me! It was because of *this feeling* my mother was hastened toward a most violent death. It was *in reaction to this feeling* Old Blackshoe scarred and molded me into the most notorious Taskmaster of Evil that ever lived, surpassing even him! It was also because of *this feeling* one of the most powerful Lords of Darkness and his son were hastened toward their brutal end! Can you see how all feelings can be made to serve Darkness, too?"

Blackshoe Crab shrilled as he scoffed the Souls of Darkness. To mask the deeper pain wrenching in his gut from the excruciating memories of his hellish childhood, he suspended his claws over the open flames. Releasing harrowing shrieks of pain, he demonstrated his acquired passion for pain of any kind. As the atmosphere around him became charged with the revolting stench of burnt flesh, Souls of Darkness gathered around, devouring his energy like blood. Swarming around him, Blackshoe Crab viciously kicked them away until he stood his ground once more. Arriving at the place where he was ready to speak of his father's death, Blackshoe Crab shifted into revelry, likened to a swoon, because he had saved the best for last.

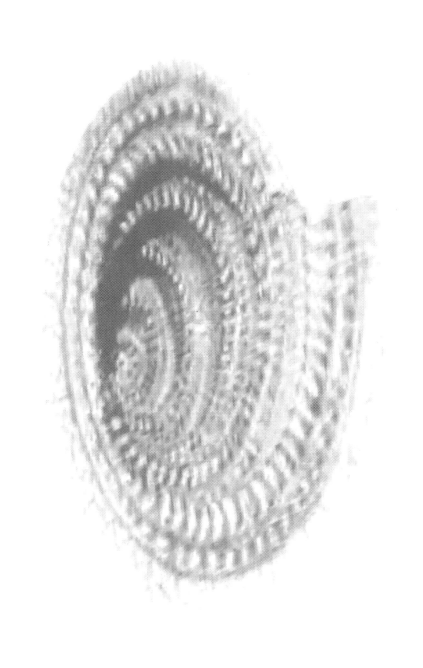

23

THE BLACK WIDOW SPIDERCRAB

"So engrossed was my father in his own pleasure,
he became oblivious to the Black Widow Spidercrab,
as she elongated her neck and reared menacingly to
face him."

Blackshoe Crab swung back and forth, poised on his hind legs, while hissing sounds emerged from him typical of sounds made during sexual exploits. Instead, he was readying himself for his final act before closing down his self-staged soliloquy before the Souls of Darkness.

"Although my father could have become the greatest Lord of Darkness that ever lived, he met his despicable end when a Black Widow Spidercrab took possession of him. He became so mesmerized by her exquisite black beauty that he walked into the jaws of her mouth, unsuspecting he would be eaten alive for his folly."

Sighing deeply, Blackshoe Crab threw back his head to savor the most poignant memory of his youth, unparalleled by any other.

"If only you could have been there to see what I did," Blackshoe Crab said, swooning in response to his vivid memories.

"Old Blackshoe danced around the Black Widow Spidercrab in the sacred spiral dance usually reserved for spring. He hummed and hissed and used his mind-control penetration on the Black Widow Spidercrab, certain that his power was seducing her into a helpless pawn for his despicable use. Once he assumed he had her under his full power, he leapt on her back. Holding her tight with his claws, he shoved his upraised pride into her despicable womb. Working himself into a frenzy, he panted breathlessly, as he fiercely pounded the Black Widow Spidercrab."

Blackshoe Crab stopped for a moment in the telling of his story to capture the hushed silence of the Souls of Darkness who gathered around. It was rare when they were not swirling around him in an attempt to distract him and get closer to lick the desecrated energy coming off of him in waves. So remarkable was this stillness that Blackshoe Crab bellowed with sardonic laughter because he could capture and trap into trance the most wretched Souls of Darkness that roamed the Fourth Dimension. Shattering the empty stillness of his temporary reprieve, Blackshoe Crab continued before the Souls of Darkness reacted to his apparent manipulation of the senses they had left.

"So engrossed was my father in his own pleasure, he became oblivious to the Black Widow Spidercrab, as she elongated her neck and reared menacingly to face him. With eyes closed and panting furiously, Blackshoe crab raced toward his nearing climax. As his mouth dropped open to let out a cry with his discharge, the Black Widow Spidercrab swooped down without warning. Her razor-like jaws cut through flesh, dismembering him of his pride and slicing through the legs that held her tight, while he was still fully conscious. My father's jaw dropped to the ground before his body reached it; no words or sigh escaped his lips. My father had lived for exquisite torture *but none compared to this!* His pride had been the last thread of real feeling left to him, and he was rewarded with the excruciating and unparalleled pain of his own stupidity. I bore witness to this ultimate desecration and *reveled in it!*"

The Souls of Darkness shrilled and howled and worked themselves into a frenzy, celebrating Blackshoe Crab's hideous castration by the Black Widow Spidercrab.

"But that's not all! I saw her rise, poised to strike again!"

Blackshoe Crab waited, savoring the moment he craved, which obliterated any trace of hunger within himself and equally within the Souls of Darkness. The titillation of holding captive all Souls of Darkness as one mind, where every trace of hunger and separation had dissolved, thrilled him.

"With eyes of terror fixed on her," Blackshoe Crab continued, "my father froze, looking upon her face in mute suspension, breathless. The Black Widow Spidercrab lowered her dripping jaws and opened them slowly, relishing the hypnotic trance of her power. As blindingly swift as before, she swooped down and devoured his head, leaving his body to jerk uncontrollably on the ground, until it shuddered into lifeless form. *Ahhh!* The ecstasy I experienced that night was beyond measure. So, let your hate be satisfied, those of you sent to hell because of him, *for no one suffered more at death!*"

Cheers exploded among the Souls of Darkness in response to Old Blackshoe's hideous death. Blackshoe Crab became so aroused at the viewing of his father's dismembered body that he seeded his audience one last time before releasing them from his grip.

"BE GONE, depraved Souls of Darkness, BE GONE, for I am done with you!" The Souls of Darkness were gone in the next instant!

Blackshoe Crab stood before his Father's altar sapped of all energy and weary beyond words. Remembering the Black Widow Spidercrab's treachery and his mother with hatred, he vowed *never* to have anything to do with the abominable creatures of the opposite sex, except to sacrifice and desecrate them to The Great Father of Darkness. Never would he allow himself to share his throne with any representative of the hated Mother Goddess. Instead, he vowed to reign in terror, alone and forever!

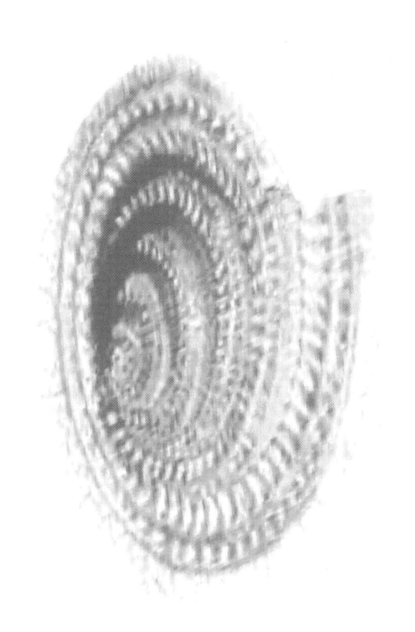

24

THE DARK NIGHT

Settling for less would become oppressively trivial,
for without a goal worthy of his passion, there would
be no reason to live!

When Blackshoe Crab awakened the next day, he was exhausted for having allowed Souls of Darkness to drain him of his energy as he gloated over his life of Darkness. Unlike other times before, he was left feeling empty. Although he savored his life review as a feast of incomparable measure, he felt inexplicably altered by this experience, as if something had gone out of him. When he sought a reason for it, he collapsed into despair because he instinctively knew his life could no longer remain intangibly expressive of past events that lingered like shades.

Since a lifetime of experience had already been crammed into his young adult life, Blackshoe Crab recognized that nothing could be challenging enough to keep him from becoming desperately bored in life. His perverse passions, fueled by his anger and rage toward his parents, no longer thrilled him, now that they were gone. But what else could he do with his life that he had not already done?

Blackshoe Crab retreated to a cave of writhing darkness for three days, where he could not rouse himself to eat, sleep, or even care about life. On the third day, a visit by Ebony, the alluring temptress of the Old Crone, Sister to Death, materialized, radiating with greater beauty than his father had seen in the Black Widow Spidercrab. She danced before him in erotic revelry, pulsing his flaccid pride, until the energy of arousal brought him back to life. Blackshoe Crab sustained that revelry until she finished. Moving away from him, Ebony signaled that he should follow her. In that moment, he understood he would drift away into Darkness, until he had no breath left. Blackshoe Crab shrugged and looked away as his pride dropped, draining any passion left in him. *Ebony turned and vanished in the next instant!*

Several more days passed when the tendrils of a presence gathered in that Darkness and edged its way into Blackshoe Crab's mind. It filled him with energy, strength and purpose, making the direction of his life clear. Nothing was left to live for that made any difference to him except to claim the most coveted prize in all of Darkness—*to become Egoson himself!* Blackshoe Crab stormed out of his tomb filled with an intractable resolve. Eyes blazing, he readied himself *to do anything* to claim Egoson's powers. Settling for less would become oppressively trivial, for without a goal worthy of his passion, there would be *no reason to live!*

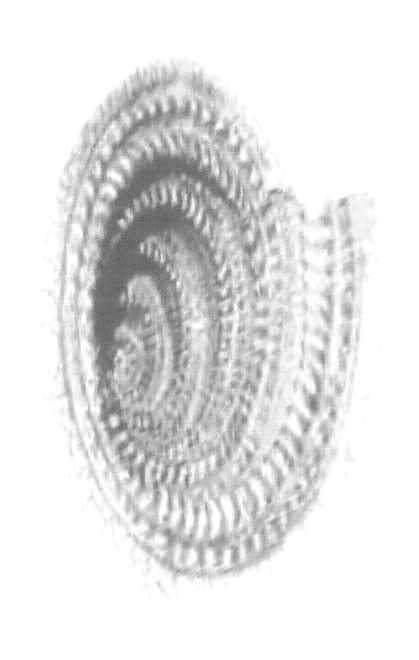

25

MIND CONTROL

"Keep workin' the eye of the gods till you can get
into der heds at The City of Light and mak'em
your slaves."

Prior to his death, Old Blackshoe had gone through six months of rigorous preparation in the hopes of fulfilling the Black Oracle by channeling the energy of The Dance of the Sacred Spiral of Life to claim Egoson's powers. When he came near the sacred ceremony of spring and was exposed to the killing voltage, he nearly died. He lost partial sight in both eyes as cataracts developed and made his eyes look more diabolical than before. His shell became scorched and blackened to the color of night. He also never again molted his shell as it became hard as rock.

Old Blackshoe deeply understood the need to shift his body chemistry if he were going to successfully assimilate the deadly voltage of The Dance of the Sacred Spiral of Life and transcend the limitations of the flesh. Apparently, there were secrets to be unlocked within the sacred spiral of light anchored within every cell of the body. It was said in Mystery books of old that Immortality could be triggered within flesh by the magnified power of blinding light! Only an Initiation involving The Dance of the Sacred Spiral of Life could ignite such power. Although Old Blackshoe did not get the opportunity to try again, he had made copious notes in his journal of the methods he had followed.

With so much to gain, Blackshoe Crab decided to follow his father's methods, but with the intent of setting a precedent never before achieved by anyone. Even *Death* no longer daunted him.

* * * * *

I began stealing small crystals from The Temples of the Goddess of the Sea because their higher vibration made it possible for me to grow accustomed to the higher-level energy of holy ground. Since I could not trespass onto holy ground myself, I gained access to the sacred eels by casting spells of black magic and putting them into trance. I then gained control of their minds and directed them to dig up and place the crystals from holy ground into strategic caverns of Darkness. Once the sacred eels were returned to holy ground, I released them from my grip, and they never suspected they had been possessed and manipulated by evil.

Although I successfully incorporated the higher-level energies of the crystals, I intuitively realized it was not enough.

I obsessed for months on how I could target the Goddess and deal a powerful blow to the faith and trust sea creatures maintained in the holy sanctuary of The Temples of the Goddess of the Sea. That holy sanctuary with its magnificent marvels created an impenetrable shield of higher consciousness impossible to pierce. Yet, once I had assimilated the higher energies of light, I could telepathically see into a world that had once been forbidden and inaccessible to me.

By shifting into higher consciousness with the help of crystals from holy ground, I telepathically gained access to Initiates still training to become Temple Priests. Once Initiates completed their Initiations as Temple Priests, they became impervious to evil and any mind control whatsoever.

After gaining such access, I immediately plotted to steal the most revered crystal from Temple grounds—-*The Blue Crystal of Galexia.* It was reputedly the most powerful crystal in The Kingdom of Oceana because The Original Ancestry of the Gods had used it to initiate Priests and Priestesses into *Divine* consciousness. Although the theft was considered an impossible feat, I remembered my father's lesson in controlling minds and never doubted I could do anything with that awesome power!

* * * * *

"Sit 'ere, Blackie!" Old Blackshoe shouted, pointing to a place within reach. I shuddered and obeyed my father, knowing that a lesson in sustaining pain and torture was about to begin, rather than any actual lesson where knowledge was to be imparted. But on this occasion, my father's appetite for causing pain was unusually diminished. He had just returned from the excesses of black mass, and he was still feeling *so satisfied!* As a result, my father thought it was time to give me a lesson in controlling minds.

"Blackie, ov'r 'ere *now!*" Old Blackshoe repeated, because I was not moving fast enough for him. I bolted to his side.

"Don't yah worry, Blackie, I'm not goin' to hurt yah," he said, as he snickered, which meant he was about to inflict serious pain.

"Yah see dis?" Old Blackshoe pointed to his head. "Dis is where ev'rythin' that means anythin' is. Behind yah eyes at da center of yah hed is a place of great power. Once yah make contact with it and get control ov'r it, *yah can do anythin'!* It's for makin' yah invincible! Yah can kick others around, get any ass yah want, and even jerk off gettin' higher fur doin' it. It's just amazin', Blackie. Ev'ryone will get out of yah way when yah approach. They won't have to see yah. They will *feel* yah. Yah know what I mean, right?"

I nodded furiously.

"Den yah gotta giv'em somethin' to remember yah by. Den yah gotta leeve sum blood or they'll tink yah soft," Old Blackshoe continued, as he swiped me across the side of the head to make his point. "As far as yah hed is concerned, yah gotta make it work like lightn'g, so yah can take on those stinkin' bastards at The City of Light and get anythin' yah want. Work up 'ere and stop workin' down der. It'll make yah stupid if yah jerk off too much! Keep workin' *the eye of the gods* till yah can get into der heds at The City of Light and mak'em yah slaves. Yah could *freeze* dem and get'em to act out yah commands without dem havin' any memory of bein' controlled by yah. Do yah get my meanin'?"

Old Blackshoe stabbed my head with his claw til he cracked my shell.

I nodded furiously, dodging another swipe.

"Good! Now, let me sho yah," Old Blackshoe said, as he took one look at me, and in the next instant, I was standing on the other side of the room coming out of a trance, as I pounded my head with a rock. He shrilled with a fiendish bellow that could only be taken as laughter. It was apparent from the excruciating pain I felt that I had been at it for some time before he released me from his oppressive grip.

"Jus one mor ting. You gotta cleen out yah body and get all the shit out! Cleen yah body with erbs and stop drinkin' and havin' so much sex. Yah gotta do dis to build yah energy to great power! Then, it'll be so easy to tak'em ov'r."

* * * * *

Although I did not recognize it at the time, the lesson on controlling minds was the most important lesson of my life. I spent hours stimulating that place inside my head because I no longer wanted to be my father's slave nor his next victim. I was doomed to be slaughtered by him if I did not prepare to fight back and protect myself when the time came. So I wanted to be ready by standing up to him and becoming his *murderer* instead. I dreamt and obsessed of nothing else, which my father took as my zeal for becoming

Egoson. It was my zeal for wanting *to kill him* that I became obsessed! I lived for the day that I could torture my father until he begged for death!

Although I devised many torturous ways to kill my father, I could not have imagined a more insidious way of killing him myself than the way he died. To this day, I believe my obsession made possible the outcome that took my father's life. Having been taught by my father that *my thoughts have great impact on events to come,* I, too, must have contributed to my father's death. I did not have to personally raise a claw to affect the result. I simply had *to will it,* and it was done. No one would have suspected that I was as responsible as the Black Widow Spidercrab for his death.

* * * * *

Setting aside all doubt and following my father's protocols for making telepathic contact with uninitiated Temple Priests, I went ahead with my plans to steal The Blue Crystal of Galexia. Gripping the mind of the weakest link, a young Temple Priest studying at The School of Mysteries, I entered his mind and trapped him in Darkness in a state resembling sleep. Yet, his body was mine to command.

Piloting his body like it was my own, I caused him to leave The School of Mysteries and enter The Temple of Worship. As I approached the altar of that holy Temple, I could feel the radiant power of The Blue Crystal of Galexia before I saw it. When I made contact with it through the eyes of the Temple Priest, I vibrated, feeling its awesome power reach my very Soul through the doorway between worlds. After creating a false projection of the blue crystal upon the altar, I retreated through a back door known only to Temple Priests.

The Temple Priest made his way to one of my caves, which was marked over the doorway with the skull and cross bones insignia of the Empire of Darkness. Once inside its mouth, he gently placed the blue crystal on the ground and left. I released the Temple Priest only after he had reached The Temple of Worship once again.

This single act accomplished the greatest coup the forces of Darkness had ever achieved. This strategy struck terror in most sea creatures because they had come to believe the Goddess was invincible, and her sacred Temples impregnable. Until then, The Temples of the Goddess of the Sea were seen as an impenetrable fortress of holy power that could not be trespassed by any one aligned with Darkness.

Tapping into the power of the gods, I prepared for Initiation as one already a god. Here I end my notes, for only actions carried forward with conviction could bring about results that mean anything at all.

* * * * *

A year after the theft, I managed to be in the presence of The Blue Crystal of Galexia without seizures or vomiting. Once I sustained its unparalleled power, I prepared to meet my Soul's fate at The Dance of the Sacred Spiral of Life. Only in assimilating the power of the gods, could I vanquish all sea creatures from The City of Light and finally prove that I was indeed the greatest Lord of Darkness that ever lived. By completing this last Initiation, I would discover whether it was worth risking *death for everlasting life!*

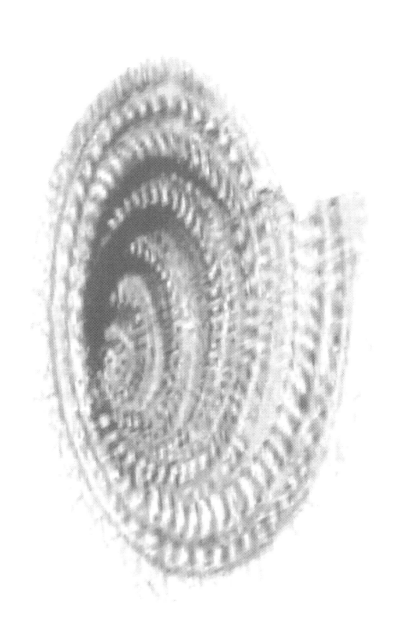

26

OVERCOMING ADDICTIONS

---

*I learned early that taking mind-altering herbs
and drinking intoxicating brews created deep
tears in my energy field, which bled my energy
like blood. Attracting invisible Souls of Darkness,
they devoured my energy, leaving me empty and
without strength.*

Turning to my father's journals, notes, and incantations, I created a journal of my own, which I called, *Blackshoe Crab's Journal*. Within it, I listed all the sacrifices I needed to make to come into the power of the gods.

Blackshoe Crab's Journal

I followed my father's protocol of raising my physical vibration by detoxifying my body to allow higher energies to move through it. To achieve this, I needed to cut out three of my favorite vices: the engaging in exploitive sex, the taking of potent herbs, and the drinking of intoxicating brews.

Exploitive Sex

I entered a new world of exploitation when I discovered I could trespass into the bodies of my sexual pawns during sex and rob them of life force. The more I abused my sexual pawns, the more their emotions of pain, fear, and dread heightened within them. Once my sexual pawns realized it was never my intention to release them alive, their eyes shaded into shock and fear bled from them from the gaping wounds of their mortal terror. With eyes mirroring their panic, I began a desecration of the flesh in the name of The Great Father of Darkness previously impossible to perceive even in the imagination.

My ritual of debasement altered their life force into desecrated energy so I could devour it until nothing was left of them but a black hole of inverted energy. Thus, the living vampire was born!

So enormous was my obsession for reigning supreme that I completely restrained from having exploitive sex altogether. To have it all, I was willing to sacrifice all that stood in my way, without exceptions!

Mind-Altering Herbs and Intoxicating Brews

I learned early that taking mind-altering herbs and drinking intoxicating brews created deep tears in my energy field. Leaching my life-force like blood, the tears left me weakened until my senses blurred. The more intoxicated I became, the more "blood" I spilled until I lost all control over my defenses. Attracting Souls of Darkness like sharks, they devoured my energy as they penetrated my defensive shields and altered my personality. When my energy field collapsed, I blacked out. Souls of Darkness were then able to take possession of my body, although I appeared to be the one in control.

The most abusive, violent, and murderous times I ever initiated became possible under the influence of intoxicating substances because Souls of Darkness acted out in my place. Only the ignorant indulged in intoxicating brews because they never knew what they were risking of themselves. Under intoxication, the bowels of hell erupted inside of them, throwing open doorways of forbidden places within them, whose doors were better left shut!

I returned from my blackouts feeling quite nauseated and ill because of the extreme shifts in my energy due to possessing Souls of Darkness. I couldn't remember anything of what I had done during my blackouts. I only discovered what I had done from others who had witnessed my macabre actions.

Allowing Souls of Darkness to manipulate me when I became intoxicated ultimately became a game to me. When I consciously understood all that was taking place from the moment of my first drink, I chose to act by eliminating my excesses altogether. Once I sobered for the last time, I shifted into a formidable Taskmaster, viciously expelling the Souls of Darkness that had taken possession of my body. Fearlessly overpowering them, I was able to rid my body of their presence and manipulation. If Souls of Darkness had not been removed, they would have gained increasing control over my thoughts and actions until I would have collapsed into hell without knowing why it had become a way of life. Under the power of addictions and the pull of hungry Souls of Darkness, I would have lost all identity of myself, until they would have succeeded in utterly destroying me.

It did not matter how addicted my personality had become to mind-altering herbs and intoxicating brews. I put all things aside for the greater realization of my dream. However difficult it was, I surrendered all addictions that weakened and robbed me of life force. Although I suffered from intense withdrawal, I increasingly saw how my life had otherwise become defined by shallow purpose and meaning.

As I moved forward with conviction and determination and without complaint, pride and greater power became my allies. Becoming fixed on a coveted goal made possible a fierceness that forged my will into formidable intent, so I could become the brutal adversary I needed to be before the forces of Light. It was gratifying to anchor myself in the knowledge that not even the most powerful Souls of Darkness who roamed the Realm of Lost Souls could challenge and overthrow the one destined to be their Master!

Diet

I began a special diet to purge and detoxify my body of defiled matter and desecrated energy. My intent was no longer to debase my energy by eating creatures that had been slaughtered lovelessly. Creatures who die in terror taste so much more delicious because their fear pollutes their body and actually toughens their meat with overpowering and nauseating negativity. Just the way I liked it! My body responded well to such a diet, since what I ate became a part of me on all levels of being.

Particularly tasty were the young creatures herded and imprisoned since birth that had their throats cut for bloodletting just before death. They incorporated their terror and pain in their bodies the best. Conscious of their imminent death, their meat became tenderized with pure terror. Even their organ parts, delicately sautéed, were exquisite because they backed up the energy of suffering the best. I could even taste the violence and shock of their death. It was a hellish delight!

Unfortunately, all of these delicacies were no longer possible. I had to rid my body of all that debased my energy. While I deeply resented having to give up such meaty morsels—I stopped it all!

Once I changed my diet, the level of sensitivity I experienced altered significantly. My energy heightened to such an acute vibration that I began to feel again, denying me nothing of all I had experienced.

Clearing the Cells

I discovered the depth of my pain and suffering were so deeply ingrained within every cell in my body that I succumbed to crushing agony when I channeled pure energy. The higher the vibration, the greater my response to a landslide of corrupted feelings I had not experienced since childhood. Everything became alarmingly poignant. My senses became moved to new levels of exquisite pain.

Over time, much of the tortuous pain I endured from my past became purged from my cells with my new diet, and all pain, anger, and illness began to vanish! I became increasingly tranquil and serene as my mind became razor sharp! Even my telepathic abilities increased as the world became increasingly transparent to me.

Cleansing the Blood

Midway through my program, I began drinking special liquids made from teas, herbs, and roots. These purified my blood and cleansed my organs so I could channel greater energy. I especially wanted my heart to open and allow for a greater voltage of energy to pass through it to increase its healthy rhythms. Many in Darkness found they succumbed to heart attacks, heart failure, and paralytic seizures because it was impossible for the heart to be shut down without arresting it cold!

Plants

Finally, during the last stages of purification, I ate only plant food because plants were nourished by the light of the sun and anchored by the salt of the earth. Only the green blood of plants made it easier to channel the currency of pure light, making possible the unleashing of my Soul's intelligence, hidden within the deeper reaches of my being.

Once I completed the detoxification program and released myself from all addictions, I emerged from Darkness with a clarity I had never known. Hovering in consciousness between the world of Light and the world of Darkness, I became aware that I could reign supreme over all living in The Kingdom of Oceana and over all dead in the Realm of Lost Souls.

I spent many nights contemplating whether I should continue ascending into higher levels of consciousness to penetrate the secrets of the world of Light by becoming an ally of it. Perhaps, I should proceed with a tenacity of will until I could trespass the boundaries of the Temples of the Goddess of the Sea and infiltrate its ranks? Perhaps, I could become a Temple Priest and claim dominion over The City of Light by implementing mind control? Perhaps, I could formidably rival Godson on sacred ground, rather than storm The City of Light as an adversary?

In the long drawn out days of contemplation, I considered other options, although one option especially tempted my will. I could become like a "glider", who was capable of playing both sides. In The Kingdom of Oceana, a glider was known as a black devil ray, whose sting could paralyze or kill any sea creature. Yet, on Temple grounds, it would turn white and serve passively by transporting sea creatures to and from the Temple of Healing. Unlike the glider, I would remain fully conscious of my agenda and through mind control would make pawns of all sea creatures in The City of Light. I shrilled contemplating all the possibilities of exercising my power!

Approaching the day of The Dance of the Sacred Spiral of Life, I held out for every possibility. Knowing I would soon reclaim and become part of The Original Ancestry of the Gods, I waited with bated breath for the reclaiming of power as Nabyss, cloaked in hooded form as Egoson!

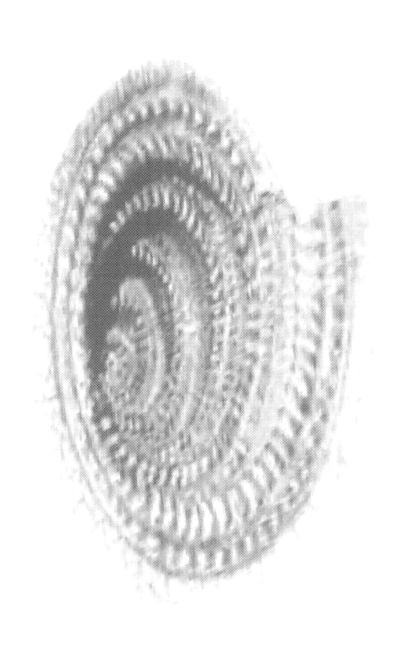

27

THE GREAT FATHER OF DARKNESS EVOKED

Discharge yourself of any conflicts and let clarity
possess you again. Only then, will you succeed
in becoming one with Me and gain immunity
from all that you fear."

On the day of The Dance of the Sacred Spiral of Life, Blackshoe Crab fasted and flushed his body continually by pulling in large amounts of seawater to clear his energy. He spent the morning in deep and profound meditation opposite The Blue Crystal of Galexia and in prayer before the altar of The Great Father of Darkness.

As Blackshoe Crab emerged from silence to begin his journey to The Temples of the Goddess of the Sea, a powerful tremor shook the cavern depths and rocks began falling all around him. He scurried from the room containing The Blue Crystal of Galexia. Nearing the exit, a massive fissure rent the walls, collapsing the ceiling as a flood of boulders filled the room. The blue crystal became buried under tons of granite and rocks. Blackshoe Crab barely escaped alive.

"Those filthy bastards!" Blackshoe Crab raged, for he believed the forces of Light were attacking to achieve his brutal end. Two fireballs of phosphorescent lights suddenly materialized and blazed upon the altar. Blackshoe Crab hushed in response.

> *"My Son, do not discharge your energy wastefully and disarm*
> *yourself of the clarity you have gained of single-minded intent.*
> *Re-focus now! The Dance of the Sacred Spiral of Life is unlike*
> *any foe you have ever met. Unless you surrender and empty*
> *yourself of any thoughts whatsoever, you will fail. Discharge*
> *yourself of any conflicts and let clarity possess you again. Only*
> *then, will you succeed in becoming one with Me and gain*
> *immunity from all that you fear."*

Blackshoe Crab bowed before his Father, trembling. The presence of The Great Father of Darkness had been evoked, which had never taken place. He was chilled to the bone because the energy of this black presence reminded him so much of his demonic father. Dismissing the feeling, he did as he was told. He closed his eyes and emptied his mind. Once he shifted into deep meditation, the dancing lights from the altar faded out of his awareness until he found himself in absolute darkness. Opening his inner eye, stars emerged glowing in the heavens, giving way to the midnight sky. The constellation of the crab emerged, shifting into a fire-breathing dragon of enormous proportions. The Great Father of Darkness was altering into yet another formidable form. As the image dissolved from his awareness, peace enveloped him and brought him to a place of immense tranquility. Awed by it, Blackshoe Crab returned slowly to full consciousness and opened his eyes. He noticed with alarmed curiosity that it was the first time the altar had gone out completely. The fires had shifted from the outside and were now burning within. He smiled, knowing, his time had come.

Without delay, Blackshoe Crab headed for the water's edge. Passing the room containing The Blue Crystal of Galexia, he noticed its undiminished power through the solid barrier of tons of granite and rocks. Blackshoe Crab smiled knowing he had fully assimilated the power of Light, as well as the fires of Darkness. Though Death had threatened to take his life, it came as a cursed blessing. The Great Father of Darkness had been evoked, disarming any lingering doubts he might have had, guaranteeing the inevitability of his triumph.

Blackshoe Crab scurried over to the water's edge and placed his claws underneath the water. He clicked them together in a language known only to his servants. After a few moments, a huge dorsal fin cut the water, as a double row of razor sharp teeth broke the surface, and an eye as dead as night looked on.

"What took you so long, you idiot! We've got to get moving!"

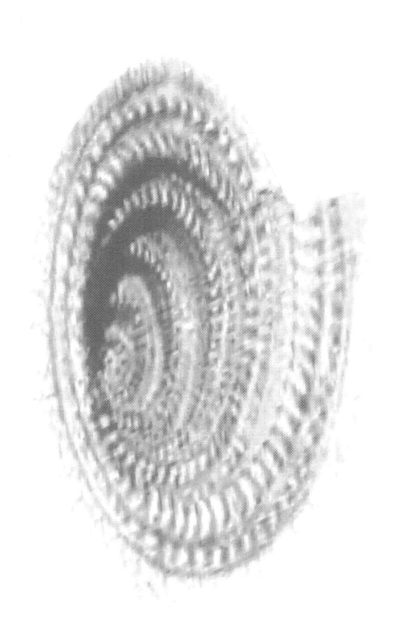

28

INITIATION

Blackshoe Crab's bulging eyes, more than his paralyzed
body, expressed the fear now exploding inside of him.
He did not anticipate the resurrection of a living fear
that consumed him from the inside out during the
Initiation of his life.

Blackshoe Crab jumped off the Great Black as he neared The Temples of the Goddess of the Sea. The Great Black fidgeted because he was nauseated by the dramatic change in energy. In times past, this was as far as Blackshoe Crab had been able to go. Rather than feeling giddy, nauseous, and weak, he was feeling excitement, strength, and power.

The Great Black left immediately without waiting to be dismissed by his Master. Blackshoe Crab shook his head and shrilled with laughter seeing such a monstrous creature reduced to a fidgeting weakling. He remembered only too well when his response would have been the same. He could hardly believe he was able to confront forces that only a year ago would have rendered him powerless.

Blackshoe Crab turned and looked to The Temples of the Goddess of the Sea, but their outline could barely be seen because great turbulence obscured his vision. Flashes of light drenched the landscape as frenzied movement covered the entire area around the plaza. It became obvious to him that the ceremony had long since begun.

Blackshoe Crab moved steadily toward holy ground pondering the solemnness of the occasion, when his mother jostled his thoughts and startled him into a halt. It was no wonder. Approaching the most sacred and powerful domain of the Mother Goddess, would it be any wonder that his mother would appear to his mind?

Blackshoe Crab cursed her now for crowding his thoughts, for it was the last thing he wanted to think about. He needed to focus all his attention on the Initiation at hand. Yet, her image became as persistent as a piranha. Blackshoe Crab stopped and shook his head until he dislodged his mother from his thoughts. Resuming his concentration, he advanced as the current picked up, day blackened into night, and flashing lights quickened without pause.

As Blackshoe Crab neared the entrance to The Temples of the Goddess of the Sea, he dug his claws into the ground to keep from being carried away by the turbulent current. He was breathing heavily to keep the currency of energy moving through his body. Nausea rose in revolting waves, and any attempt to control its effects failed.

In the midst of nausea and stark rising pain, Blackshoe Crab became riveted by the violent ritual dance taking place before him in the plaza of The Temples of the Goddess of the Sea. He had grown accustomed to witnessing the orgies of ecstatic union during black mass, but none, except the High Black Mass of Hallows Eve, compared to this! The sacred eels stretched forth in every direction, undulating in pairs. Though their skin was the color of darkness, radiant light intermittently exploded from them as they danced in ecstatic revelry.

Blackshoe Crab marveled that this spectacle in The City of Light held little difference to the sacred rituals of Darkness. The sacred eels generated their own life force, and it was this negligible difference, which separated the world of Darkness from the world of Light. How empty their world must be, he thought, by having a life force that prevented them from the attendant pleasure of vanquishing and overpowering another creature in the act of consuming their life force. How boring indeed!

When Blackshoe Crab reached the entrance to The Temples of the Goddess of the Sea, he did not risk trespassing onto holy ground. No sea creature of evil had ever crossed onto holy ground and survived. Although he believed he would be the exception for having successfully assimilated the energy of The Blue Crystal of Galexia, he decided it was better to accomplish one thing at a time without taking on any more than necessary. It was enough he had gotten this far in assimilating the energy of The Dance of the Sacred Spiral of Life, which stood as one of the greatest mysteries to both Darkness and Light.

Blackshoe Crab dropped abruptly on his stomach as liquid fire coursed through his veins, doubling the pain now inside of him. His instincts to run became ignited by the shocking energy flooding him just then. Ready to bolt, his limbs shut out his directives. He was paralyzed where he stood.

Blackshoe Crab's bulging eyes more than his paralyzed body expressed the fear now exploding inside of him. He did not anticipate the resurrection of a living fear that consumed him from the inside out during the Initiation of his life. Terrorized, he began defending himself against treacherous thoughts crowding his mind. In the midst of excruciating pain and loss of bodily control, images erupted, stealing across his mind, with the force of remembrance of all that had brutalized him his entire life.

The avalanche of savage beatings by his father suddenly pounded Blackshoe Crab with brutal clarity. Muckraker loomed into his mind as a bloody mess with eyes deadened to all feeling, except when they located him. Twisting in horror, Muckraker lunged forward and ran him through with his anterior tail, as Blackshoe Crab succumbed to agony beyond words.

No pain, however, compared to the excruciating pain he felt upon viewing the desecrated, dismembered body of his mother. Screaming in agony, her tortured Soul materialized before him amidst the bloodied scattered debris of her body. His heart jolted violently upon seeing her, swelling beyond its size, threatening to explode inside of him. Senseless from the ravaging pain fracturing inside of him, he telepathically called upon Death to release him from its brutal Taskmaster of Pain.

The energy of burning light flooding his heart became unsustainable with the sweep of brutal memories responsible for shaping his evil character. The unbearable strain was loosening his mind from his body, and he felt relief knowing he would die soon.

Another wave of explosive light blinded him, as Blackshoe Crab tumbled, taken up by a capricious current that provided some distance from the energy of The Dance of the Sacred Spiral of Life. Surrendering his force of will, Blackshoe Crab realized he had gone where no other Lord of Darkness had ever been—*to the absolute limits of terror, pain, and feeling!*

A vision betraying an impossible reality struck his mind, as he welcomed the arrival of Death cloaked in hooded form. Two enormous sacred eels rose from the center of The Dance of the Sacred Spiral of Life, extending toward the sea-sky without stopping. Shifting into spiraling radiant light, they suddenly and unexpectedly shape-shifted into The Sacred Sea Dragons of legend. Shuddering uncontrollably from the strained tension of their radiant light, Blackshoe Crab passed incomprehensibly beyond all limits. A piercing, shrilling scream discharged explosively from his throat, shattering his voice box. A lightning bolt simultaneously thundered from the explosive union of The Sacred Sea Dragons, colliding into an epiphany of terrifying light! As the lightning bolt ripped through and parted the waters between Heaven and Galexia, the unforgettable image became seared into Blackshoe Crab's Soul, while he convulsed into dying seizures. Closing his eyes in mute surrender, he smiled knowing he had lived to witness the extraordinary spectacle and Mystery of The Dance of the Sacred Spiral of Life!

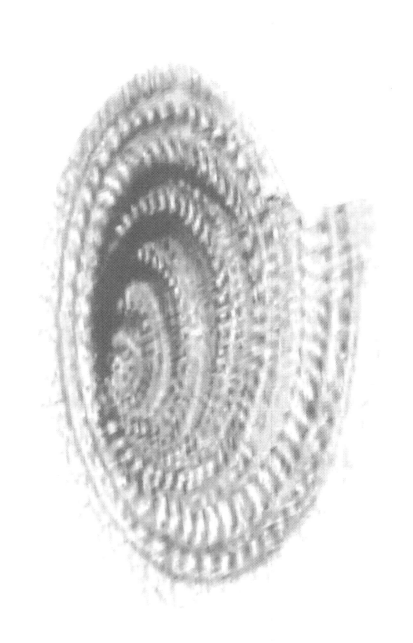

29

THE MADNESS OF OBSESSION

The Great Black shook his head acknowledging the
madness of obsession, and he questioned whether
to reach for power was worth such a price.

When Blackshoe Crab came to, he was unsure whether he was dead or alive. He did not feel his body any longer, and there was no pain. Visions of The Sacred Sea Dragons followed by the sight of a Wizard and a radiant Soul bound to him by a silver cord came abruptly to his mind and left. Like an empty shadow, he looked around and tried to get his bearings and recognized the familiar Realm of Lost Souls.

Blackshoe Crab tried making contact with his body but without success. He despaired thinking he had failed his greatest challenge by permanently passing over into the Land of the Dead. Collapsing into anger and regret, Blackshoe Crab thrashed about as if fighting with an invisible beast. Then he saw her—his Mother coming toward him on clouds of radiant light. Only then did he remember her youthful beauty as the day he first saw her.

Blackshoe Crab's Mother held his gaze in a flooding of summer warmth, as she drifted closer to him until she was directly opposite him. Colorful sea flowers began falling all around him as she held his eyes with loving grace. Eliciting from him the child when he was firstborn, Blackshoe Crab hurriedly gathered them up, marveling at their exquisite beauty. As his Mother faded into mist, Blackshoe Crab desperately reached for her, the terrible anguish of her absence crowding out all other pain from his Soul. Stepping back from his empty reach, he let out a scream that finally erupted from his shattered heart: *"Motherrrrr!!!"*

* * * * *

The Great Black discovered Blackshoe Crab floating near a reef suspended in a coma. The Great Black rammed his body gently to awaken him, but it was no use. His scalded body was lifeless and the Great Black doubted whether he was still alive. So intense was the energy radiating from his body, the Great Black had difficulty being near him. Yet, loyalty to his Master exceeded the nauseating feeling overwhelming him just then. He knew his Master needed immediate attention and only the powerful sorcery of The Abominable Hags of Anger, Hate, Guilt & Shame could help him now.

The Great Black moved under Blackshoe Crab's body and gently lifted him, taking him in tow toward a cave where no Lord of Darkness ever entered without good cause. Only in matters of grave consequence were The Abominable Hags consulted for their extraordinary powers of black magic.

The Great Black moved steadily toward his destination with the lifeless body in tow. He wondered whether Blackshoe Crab was gone for good, suspended in twilight, where nothing had any meaning. Perhaps Death had already robbed him of a meaningful life.

The Great Black shook his head acknowledging the madness of obsession, and he questioned whether to reach for power was worth such a price. If Blackshoe Crab died, another Lord of Darkness would inevitably take his place—*only to strive for power to become trapped by it! Another hunger born to become a living obsession!*

The Great Black was glad to be a slave rather than a victim, risking everything to become a fool instead. Better to be a slave, he thought, then to reach for power in the attainment of nothing more than a dream . . . an empty dream!

PART IV

THE PROPHECIES FULFILLED

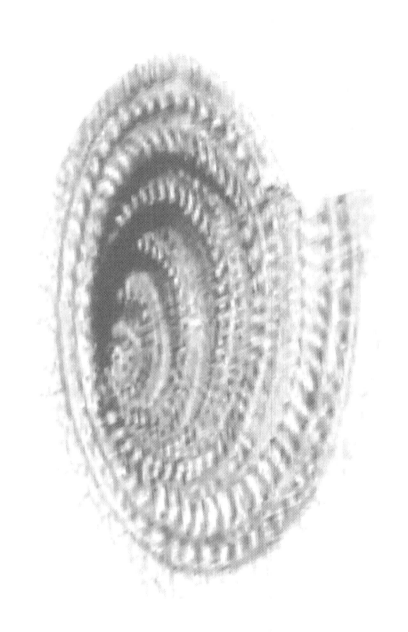

30

WINDOWS OF THE SOUL

That is why you have often heard the expression,
'the eyes are the Windows of the Soul.' It is by
looking through the eyes that you can make direct
contact with the Soul.

Domaine returned from the Realm of Lost Souls and opened his eyes to look upon the quietly resting form of young Sol. He tried to straighten from his kneeling position and moaned from the effort to get his legs moving. If only he could bring back his powerful presence into his aged body. Instead, overwhelming exhaustion followed him back from his journey when he re-entered his body. It was the strain of going from a higher consciousness to the lower consciousness of his body. In spite of his fatigue, Domaine was immensely pleased. He had accomplished the major part of young Sol's healing without taking any steps that were physically self-evident.

When Domaine got up and turned, Sonar shuddered to see how much Domaine had significantly aged. The youthful vitality of his presence was gone from his eyes and face, and he had shape-shifted into what was probably the true semblance of his age. Deep wrinkles and pale color penetrated his fallen face and aged body, and slow, wobbly movements now characterized his steps. He had gone from being ageless to barely holding himself up with his crystal staff. He had become what he was in truth physically—*an old hermit crab of the sea.*

Sonar then realized Domaine had done more than just pray for young Sol. Something had transpired that robbed Domaine of his energy and strength, and he was anxious to know about it. Since Domaine was obviously in no condition to answer, he decided to postpone his questions. Theia and Starborn came forward as Domaine turned from young Sol. Startled, they also captured the accelerated aging within his shifted form.

"It would be better if you made arrangements to move young Sol as quickly as possible to The Temple of Healing," Domaine said, speaking slowly and deliberately. He will be molting his shell very shortly, and I can see by the size of the cave opening, he will be unable to remain in this cave. If he stays and molts, nothing less than drilling swordfish will get him out."

"What did you discover about Little Sol's condition?" Theia asked, noticing Domaine's intense weariness, which must have been due to expending his energy on healing Little Sol.

"Young Sol will recover from his burns once he molts and releases the outer layers of his damaged shell. He will need to be strengthened with special roots and herbs that will tone his internal muscles and organs and bring on new transformation of skin into shell. Light compresses of medicinal plants containing mineral extracts need to be placed on his exposed skin after molting to accelerate healing and renewal. In addition, fluids containing specific minerals and electrolytes need to be administered to restore the proper fluid balance in his body. Most of all, he will need a great deal of rest in a safe place until he has regained his health and fully recovered from his burns."

"And you say you are not a physician?" Theia said, her eyes raised aloft and smiling, engaging the hermit crab in a radiant warmth that betrayed her growing affection for him. She dismissed the fact that Domaine was little more than a stranger to her. Theia felt a kinship toward him as if she had known him all her life. Yet, the healing had taken quite a toll on him to be engaged in such a manner so soon after his long journey.

"Why don't you sit here and rest a bit," Theia said, putting her arms around the wobbly old hermit crab while gently assisting him to sit down. "Sonar and I will make arrangements to have young Sol transported to The Temple of Healing immediately."

Domaine submitted like a child to her gentle prodding and smiled at Starborn and Sonar after sitting down.

"Perhaps you will honor us by being our guest at The Temples of the Goddess of the Sea and stay with us until you have rested," Sonar said, hoping to have the opportunity to speak with the hermit crab further.

"I would like that very much," Domaine said.

"I, too, will be calling on you while you are here," Starborn spoke, breaking his silence. "But for now, I think we should move Little Sol while he sleeps so when he awakens, he will not be discomforted any further."

"That's a good idea. But I would like to suggest we no longer call him Little Sol. He is nearly an adult now, and that name conjures up a past that no longer exists. It would be better if we acknowledged him as young Solar."

Sonar, Theia, and Starborn looked quizzically back and forth from each other.

"Forgive me for asking, but how can we call him . . . ?"

Sonar stopped abruptly, caught by Domaine's penetrating eyes. He tried to speak, but Domaine's presence suddenly filled the room with authority.

Domaine gently smiled at Sonar, although the powerful spike in his energy and presence became evident to them all. Sonar had been quick to object before reason had an opportunity to temper his response. Domaine perceived it was due to his youth and a wild untamed heart and a restless Soul. Although Sonar had been repeatedly reminded at The School of Mysteries to patiently *listen* to his own intuition before speaking, he continued to ask questions impulsively. The self-discipline needed to achieve a state of inner receptivity to higher guidance could not be taught. It could only be achieved through conscious effort and the naturally evolving attribute of wisdom. Thus, maturity would still elude Sonar for some time to come.

"We will speak about young Solar at a later time. But as you know, Sonar, there are many different ways to communicate with another and discover who they truly are beyond their form. The first imperative of connecting to the true self is by making contact with their Soul."

"Yes, I know, but . . ."

"The second imperative is to listen to the spoken word by tuning into the subtle exchange of information that can be picked up by higher intuition. Listening to words alone is very limiting and leaves much room for misunderstanding because sea creatures are taught *to listen* to words rather than *intuitively tuning into* deeper levels of reality."

Sonar shifted uneasily.

"Thus, it becomes difficult to know when the truth is being spoken if we disregard the input of our extrasensory perception. Only when we listen on different levels are we alerted to all that is going on beyond the scope of words. Intuition used in place of words adds depth to our common language. As an Initiate Priest, I suspect you already know this."

"Yes, of course," Sonar said, withdrawing from the room energetically.

"So, in answer to your unspoken question about what healing I did with respect to young Solar, I will tell you. When I first reached out to communicate with young Solar, I noticed his Soul was gone from his body and was not hovering nearby. That immediately alarmed me. As you know, when the Soul completely detaches from the body, there is death. I did notice, however, that the silver cord connecting the Soul to his body was not severed, although it was very, very weak, and therefore, there was great risk of that."

"I see."

"So, my first priority was to get his Soul back into the body as quickly as possible. I surmised that his Soul must have become trapped in the Fourth Dimension in the Realm of Lost Souls. To delay returning the Soul back into the body meant risking death. Souls of Darkness had also begun to take possession of his body. Had I not discerned the absence of his Soul, I may have made the mistake of healing his body without knowing who I was bringing back to life until it was too late.

"Such possession is possible?" Sonar asked, in disbelief.

"Of course. But Theia will be able to explain it to you better than I."

"How could such a thing happen?" Sonar asked, alarmed.

"Sonar, you may as well know that *every living creature is possessed by a Soul,*" Theia cut in. That is why you have often heard the expression, '*the eyes are the Windows of the Soul.*' It is by looking *through the eyes* that you can make direct contact with the Soul. When you look at possession in this way, it does not seem like such a fantastic idea."

"But how can anyone become possessed by *other* Souls?"

"If the Soul exits the body for any reason while it is still corded to it," Theia continued, "other Souls can get in and take over. The Soul's presence provides natural barriers of protection ordinarily."

"Why haven't you told me this before, Theia?"

"Everything is revealed in its own time. Apparently, the time has come or we would not be discussing it. Domaine, what kept young Solar from returning to his body?"

"I will explain at a later time," Domaine replied, catching his breath, while leaning on his crystal wand for support. "What's important is that young Solar will be regaining consciousness in full possession of himself."

"How did you accomplish that?" Sonar asked.

"We had better talk about this at a later time," Theia answered. Domaine is tired, and for now, we must act swiftly and get young Solar to The Temple of Healing as quickly as possible."

"Of course. I apologize for . . ."

"There is no need," Domaine said.

"Just one more question," Starborn cut in reluctantly. "Do you believe young Solar is in danger?"

"Yes. No one is safe any longer outside of Temple grounds," Domaine answered, yawning aloud, in spite of himself. "Oh, *my*, I am a bit tired!"

"Let's go, Sonar!" Starborn commanded, rushing toward the door. "A skate shall be summoned to act as a stretcher to bring young Solar to Temple grounds."

"You had better get two skates," Theia said, looking back at Domaine. From one moment to the next Domaine had succumbed to exhaustion. He had fallen asleep holding tightly to his crystal wand.

"Two skates, it is!"

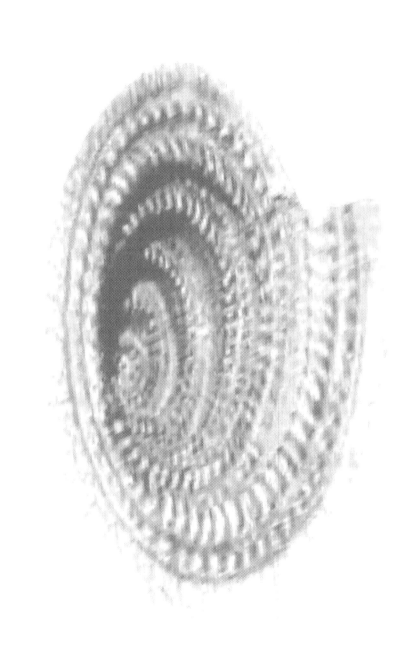

31

THE ABOMINABLE HAGS

All Lords of Darkness who had attempted to
conquer the Abominable Hags all lived to
regret it. They had become eunuchs instead
for attempting to overpower the greatest forces
of Darkness that existed in unison.

It was the Old Crone, Harbinger of Death, who visited Blackshoe Crab during his feverish delirium. He looked into the black shroud of Death looking for the Old Crone and felt an icy chill move through him. He searched the darkness for her eyes or even her form. He was grateful he could see neither.

The Old Crone materialized before him with his Soul hovering beside her. As she turned and moved away, his Soul followed. Blackshoe Crab rushed after her pleading for his Soul, but then the Three Sisters to the Old Crone–The Abominable Hags of Anger, Hate, Guilt & Shame–made their appearance and blocked his way. It was Shame that spoke, screeching with every word:

"You have called upon the forces of Darkness to make you an ally of Death, so you may reign supreme in the Empire of Darkness. It is my place to tell you that you have succeeded, my brother. But as a tradeoff to life, it is necessary to place your Soul in Death's domain to stand invulnerable to all that is life."

"But how can that be?" Blackshoe Crab cried. "With my Soul trapped in the Realm of Lost Souls having no access to my body, how am I to govern in the world of the living?"

"By becoming the greatest power in the Universe—by becoming *Death* yourself. All other powers of Darkness pale next to it. Those coming into your presence shall be immediately confronted by their fear of Death, striking terror in their hearts and paralyzing them, giving you supreme control over them."

"So that's it? That's the only way?" Blackshoe Crab replied, uttering a plaintive cry, when he realized Death had arrived to take him home.

"Yes, that is the only way, my brother. The Great Father of Darkness shall now act *through* you. *That is Egoson, a kin to Death!* With your Soul out of the way, Egoson can completely command and direct you in any way he chooses.

"But . . ."

"You're a fool to think Egoson would share his power with you! Can't you see? *He shares his power with no one!* The end of your life has come as you have known it. By choosing the way of Darkness, you have reached its ultimate end! Now, *GO!* Celebrate your oneness unto Death for *Egoson shall now take your place!"*

* * * * *

The first time Egoson became fully conscious inside of Blackshoe Crab's body, he discovered bandages over his eyes and the Abominable Hags attending to his wounds. The body had not yet recovered from burns nor become defiled enough for him to become fully present within it. He withdrew and allowed the body to succumb to sleep once again. Only the powerful sorcery of the Abominable Hags could create a shield strong enough to deflect the energy of light coming from the body. Meanwhile, the Abominable Hags continued giving infusions of desecrated energy to alter the body to the way it had been.

Egoson shifted back and forth into Blackshoe Crab's body at different times until he awakened within it and was able to stretch forth his energy into it without pulling back. When he found himself fully anchored to it, he panted without warning from the immense deprivation of indulgences he had been denied while in Darkness without a body. All he had experienced had been vicariously through others until now. Rising from his bed, his appetite had become a ravenous hunger unlike anything he had ever known.

Anger

Guilt & Shame

Hatred

The Abominable Hags

Egoson pulled the bandages from his eyes and saw the vague outline of the Abominable Hags of Anger, Hate, Guilt & Shame, before him. Although he could not see them clearly, he felt an overwhelming need to force himself upon them to satiate the voracious hunger that now completely possessed him. He wanted to devour them in the act of releasing himself from all that bound him. Blackshoe Crab's memory stirred within him and reminded him they could not be vanquished.

All Lords of Darkness who had attempted to conquer the Abominable Hags all lived to regret it. They had become eunuchs instead for attempting to overpower the greatest forces of Darkness that existed in unison. Blackshoe Crab knew never to attempt such a folly. But as Egoson stared at them with a voracious hunger he had never known, he pushed away the memories and did not stop to think of what he was risking in the flesh!

When the Abominable Hags saw the diabolical, obsessed look on Egoson's face, they immediately disappeared from sight. They knew their job was done, while he knew his time had come.

"Return, I COMMAND IT!" Egoson proclaimed, as the Abominable Hags materialized and immediately attacked. They discharged their venomous powers from their many tentacles directly into his lower abdomen. Rather than become paralyzed by the attack to his pride, Egoson swelled without restraint. Laughing from sheer madness, he used the same currency of energy to vanquish them in turn. In the orgy of ecstatic union, Egoson's Initiation into full consciousness within living flesh marked the completion of the Black Oracle. In the spellbinding explosive union of their mutual surrender, Egoson gained control of their Abominable offspring: Rage, Blame, and Regret. Together with Death, *Egoson was born!*

Egoson

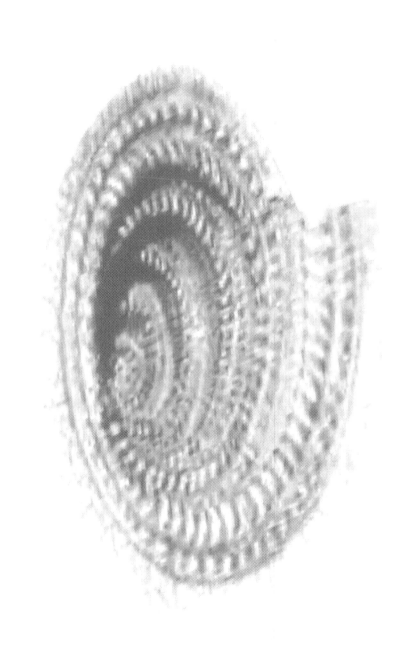

32

BODY VEHICLE OF IMPRISONMENT

Blackshoe Crab now witnessed the world behind
eyes within his body vehicle of imprisonment,
where he could no longer exercise his own free will.

Blackshoe Crab awakened inside his body and looked up at the altar and realized it no longer had any meaning for him. He thought about all he had gained by his passage unto Death and thought about all he had lost.

Physically, his body had suffered immense injuries. His voice box had shattered causing his voice to become reduced to hard gravel against stone. His eyes had become overlaid with cataracts, gving them an eerie, diabolical look. As a result, he was nearly blind. Scorched to the color of Darkness, his shell had become warped in places because of grooves carved into his flesh by blinding light. Blackshoe Crab would never again molt his rock-hard shell, preventing him from experiencing the seasonal shifts in his nature. Worst of all, his joints had become sealed in places, nearly immobilizing him.

In spite of the injuries Blackshoe Crab had sustained, there were many alternative compensations that existed because of Egoson's presence. Blackshoe Crab noted that Egoson could perceive objects near him as if by radar. He could telepathically link to the thoughts of sea creatures and prophetically sense things to come without the use of incantations. He could wield the awesome powers of the four fundamental elements of earth, water, fire, and air. In so doing, he could initiate tremors within the earth, create turbulent storms with formidable currents, and shoot bolts of lightning from his anterior tail, instantly paralyzing sea creatures. When exposed to the currents of air, he could create winds that shook the seas with formidable power. All this spontaneously came into manifestation allowing Blackshoe Crab to understand what it meant to be a god!

Blackshoe Crab now witnessed the world behind eyes within his body vehicle of imprisonment, where he could no longer exercise his own free will. It was still a mystery to him why he remained fully conscious inside his body, since Egoson had already taken it from him. By asking himself a direct question, he immediately got an answer. Egoson needed *a living body*, which could only take place as long as the silver cord from the original Soul was still connected to its body.

"You're pretty smart, Blackie," Egoson cut in, disrupting Blackshoe Crab's thoughts. "You have figured things out on your own. It looks like we are going to share this forsaken body of yours and make the most of it. I'm so glad you went through such pains to get me in. You became the key that unlocked the door to my prison of Darkness. When you asked to become the embodiment of Egoson, you did not know what you were risking of yourself, did you? Now, I'm in, and your out, bearing witness to *All That I Am* as I take over The Kingdom of Oceana!"

Blackshoe Crab shuddered as the energy of his father's diabolical presence flooded him and took his breath away like a cord wrapped around his neck. He had sought to kill his father and be rid of him for all time. Now, he shared a connection to his father and all Darkness more despicable than any other situation imaginable. What a strange paradox to experience the newly acquired powers of Egoson *but only as a helpless pawn!* It was now easy to see why Old Blackshoe had demonstrated so many powers. Egoson had long ago trespassed into his father's mind and had overtaken his will. It was easy to overtake sea creatures when they were unsuspecting that powerful evil forces could manipulate them, acting in place of their own Soul, *while they remained uninitiated into the Mysteries that could protect them!*

Other matters raced through Egoson's mind, as Blackshoe Crab was forced to the background. Egoson began contemplating the methods he would utilize to block *The One Who Knows* from assisting Godson in developing his newly acquired powers. As long as Egoson could manipulate Godson into experiencing fear or turbulent emotions of any kind, Egoson could destroy him!

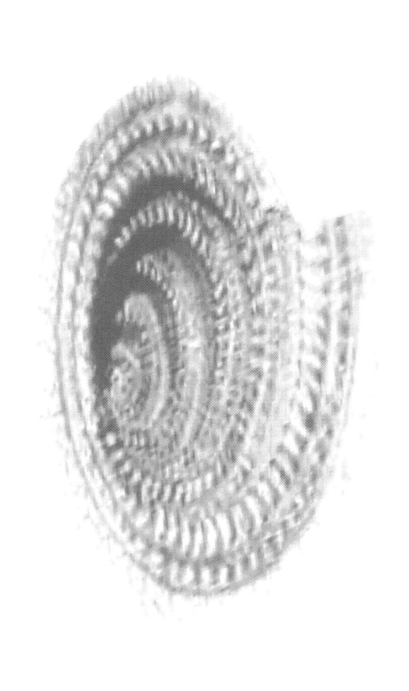

33

THE END TIMES

The end times had begun, marking the
beginning of The Final Reckoning. As a result,
sea creatures acknowledged in ever alarming
numbers that The Kingdom of Oceana was
nearing collapse.

Since arriving at The Temples of the Goddess of the Sea, young Solar noted the dramatic extremes taking place in all things. Freak storms and earthquakes had escalated, making widespread destruction of the environment common. Marine life succumbed to outbreaks of contagious diseases that continued to decimate the population. Such spurious outbreaks had been linked to Egoson, who was suspected of manipulating the laws of creation. The collapse of social order led to violent crimes turning many sea creatures toward Darkness instead of Light, forcing many to travel only in schools. As the social fabric of law and order continued to disintegrate, anarchy became rampant in many places, leading to an increase in random killings by gangs calling themselves the Sons of Egoson.

The end times had begun, marking the beginning of The Final Reckoning. Sea creatures acknowledged in ever alarming numbers that The

Kingdom of Oceana was nearing collapse. Once seen as a time of liberation from the forces of Darkness, The Final Reckoning was now being decreed as a time of total destruction.

Great numbers of sea creatures sought refuge on holy ground in a last attempt to neutralize their immutable sense of panic. In spite of deteriorating circumstances and formidable challenges, these sea creatures dismissed the hateful lies being spread about The Great Mother Goddess, and the blasphemous curses being charged to Her name. They never faltered in their faith, even when they appeared to be forsaken, and all traces of The Great Mother Goddess seemed to have vanished! Although such sea creatures appeared foolish and ridiculously sentimental for holding onto their faith, *still they believed and obeyed the laws,* because they held steadfast to the memory of holy ground and their pilgrimage to The Temples of the Goddess of the Sea. Never did they doubt The Great Mother Goddess was more powerful than Egoson, even as the gangs of Egoson viciously cut them down.

Young Solar had already seen it all in his meditations, dreams, and nightmares. He could hardly believe how much the dream was accelerating to its inevitable end. Having survived the near-death experience of The Dance of the Sacred Spiral of Life, he had reclaimed his inner sight, re-awakened memories from across time, and revived the immortal powers existing within as Godson. No longer did he doubt himself, the role he came to play, and the purpose he came to fulfill.

Young Solar abruptly returned from his life review. Slamming into his body, he tumbled repeatedly before coming to a stop. He had still to practice slowing down the traveling speed of his soul before entering his body, after searching out information from across time that would assist him in making predictions for the future.

Using the art of meditation, Solar could shift into different time-space continuums, so he could bear witness to his memories from birth until the present moment. In doing so, he reconciled himself to the world of his existence, including the trauma of his birth when hungry predators had eaten his brothers and sisters alive.

Young Solar, under Domaine's guidance, had sought to become increasingly dispassionate about all that had taken place, like a Temple Priest, who is taught to witness life's situations *without reacting to them*. By being aware of distortions that stream in from the senses, he could sustain a state of equanimity and never be triggered into behavioral reactions that made him a slave to his senses rather than a Master aligned with the reality of his Soul.

At the Soul level, young Solar learned to see beyond all appearances and into the parallel worlds of existence. He clearly saw the multi-levels of personalities acting through the fleshy vehicles of sea creatures. Since sea creatures could not see into the invisible, they did not fathom their own split personalities or how often Souls of Darkness manipulated them.

Given this advantage of greater insight, young Solar now dealt directly with the source of his pain, anguish, and terror that had overshadowed him his entire life. By shifting into the eyes of his Soul, he could see the forces of Darkness gather around him whenever his energy became distorted. As a precautionary measure, he brought up his light to prevent the forces of Darkness from getting too close and sapping his energy or attempting to manipulate his mind with negative thoughts.

In this regard, young Solar was deeply grateful for the teachings of the Mysteries by the incomparable Grand Master Wizard, Domaine. Domaine had taught him to see beyond the veil of physical matter into the world of hungry Souls. Presently, the forces of Darkness were winning their war by igniting an onslaught of escalating fear among the general population. Outside of holy ground, many sea creatures were being manipulated into helpless pawns where chaos reigned in response to the terror that characterized their lives. Having little knowledge of the abilities that lay dormant within them, they succumbed to hopelessness and despair because they could not disarm the destructive forces of interferences overpowering them from the outside.

Young Solar wanted to reach the masses with the truth of his revelations. He wanted to remove the veil from their eyes and lift the Darkness that existed deep within them. Until they were ready to see all they had judged, repressed, and stopped loving in themselves, he could do nothing. He could not release them of their demons until they were ready to do it for themselves.

Domaine came into the classroom where young Solar was waiting for him. Young Solar felt tormented and agitated in spite of all he knew. He felt escalating pain rise increasingly from the masses to an overwhelming degree. He immediately turned to Domaine without greeting him and blurted out, *"Why has The Great Mother Goddess forsaken them?"*

Domaine lingered on young Solar's eyes, extending loving comfort and kindness, waiting until he shifted into higher consciousness before beginning his next lesson.

"The day has arrived, young Solar, for you to journey all the back to the beginning of time to get your answers!"

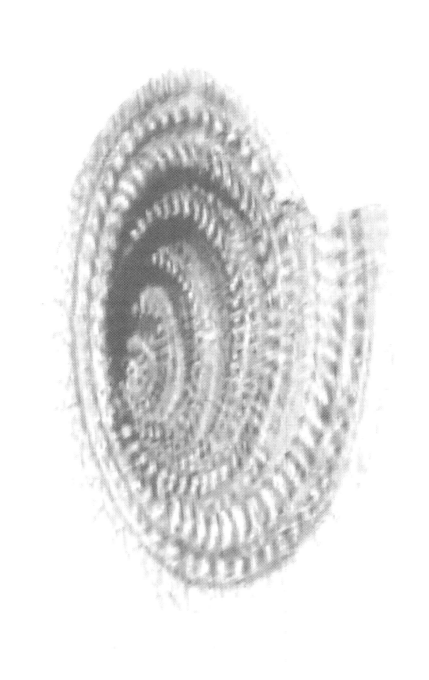

34

RALLYING THE EMPIRE OF DARKNESS

Egoson stood in front of the altar shrilling with
sardonic laughter. Shifting into the full expression
of his omnipotent powers without the use of magic,
he began incantations that would open the doors to
the formidable presence of the Empire of Darkness.

Egoson went over to the water's edge and pulled on rope until a snake skin bag came into view. It became difficult to manage while its contents were violently trying to get out. He dragged the moving bag across the floor and placed it alongside the large black cauldron positioned in front of the altar. Intermittant lights flashed, outlining the undulating figures from within.

Egoson placed the driftwood, which had been stacked along the walls of the cavern, beneath the large black cauldron. He then went over to the shelves carved into solid rock, which extended along the walls surrounding the altar. These shelves were filled with a baffling array of sorcery potions used in black magic. As chaotic and disordered the shelves appeared to be,

Blackshoe Crab knew where everything was. Egoson had only to reach into his memory to make sense of it all.

The chaotic arrangement that characterized Blackshoe Crab's workplace thrilled Egoson with delight. It was the most powerful weapon at his disposal—*the attribute to make sense out of chaos!* How else could he otherwise be an accomplished Master of Deceit? How else could he manipulate others into a desired outcome unless he knew ahead of time the intended outcome of his seemingly chaotic manipulations! That simple strategy—*using the power of confusion and chaos*—achieved the greatest dysfunction in sea creatures aligned with the Goddess than any other weapon at his disposal.

Egoson turned to the large black cauldron positioned before the altar and lifted the cover. He jolted back from the intensity of the stench. Even he became nauseated by its contents. He looked in and noticed floating body parts left over from black mass, as an undulating skin of maggots covered the top of it. He smiled knowing it would be a good brew.

Egoson sent torches of flames from his claws and set fire to the cauldron. He wondered which tools he might use and potions and dried body parts he would add from Blackshoe Crab's celebrated collection to season his already matured brew. As he scrutinized the shelves containing all manner of paraphernalia of black arts, he questioned whether he needed them at all. After all, as Egoson he no longer needed to coddle, entice, or appease the forces of Darkness to retrieve from them any powers and information he wished to channel for his own personal use. This realization made him shrill with delight. No longer did he need to pacify Souls of Darkness as he had done through others because he was now their Master in flesh and Soul!

Egoson stood in front of the altar shrilling with sardonic laughter. Shifting into the full expression of his omnipotent powers, he began the incantations necessary to open the doors to the formidable presence of the Empire of Darkness.

Egoson's raspy incantations began slowly and rhythmically and continued to build in momentum until the potency of them charged the very atmosphere around him into deepening Darkness. He continued his incantations reaching deeper and deeper into the bowels of Earth until all Souls of Darkness became caught in the whirling vortex of penetrating control. He continued to build upon control until none could escape. All the dead and undead appeared, including the Abominable Hags of Anger, Hate, Guilt & Shame, with their Abominable offspring, Rage, Blame, and Regret, who emerged from the ocean waters below. Egoson continued his raspy incantations until the walls fell away, and the Empire of Darkness stretched forth in every direction. By the time Egoson was finished, he was in command of his Empire!

Egoson stamped his claws upon the ground as earthquake

tremors fanned in all directions. Remembering the words to the Black Oracle,

So Dance the Sacred Dragon's Fire
Mantle of Power Only Fire Can Sire

Egoson recognized the image detailing The Mantle of The Sacred Sea Dragons seered into Blackshoe Crab's back. He then turned up the phosphorescent image until the images came alive and danced on his back, as his audience shuddered at the sight of them. Finally, he lifted his anterior tail and discharged a fireball of energy over the archway, carving the words in clear, bold letters: **EGOSON LIVES!**

Egoson then looked into the eyes of every one of his servants by projecting his image directly in front of them all at once. Gasping in unison, Egoson then withdrew his image and began speaking before a fully mesmerized audience of Darkness.

"Today, I have summoned all of you together to acknowledge a turning point in the war against the forces of Light. Namely, that I, Egoson, am now present and fully in command!"

Riotous cheers erupted, stopping Egoson from speaking. Momentarily, he continued.

"I am here to escalate the demoralization of the population by using terror as the most powerful weapon at our disposal. Together with the Abominable Hags of Anger, Hate, Guilt & Shame, and their Abominable offspring Rage, Blame, and Regret, we will gain control over all sea creatures. Even *The One Who Knows* and Godson will be unable to stem the tide of anarchy, hopelessness, and despair from its present course. Every day as we become more powerful, they shall become less powerful in trying to prevent The Kingdom of Oceana from sinking deeper and deeper into Darkness and mass chaos!"

Whistles and applause exploded, while Egoson paused, as The Sacred Sea Dragons' image danced on his back.

"Each of you has done very well so far. Now that I am among you, we will do even better! It is time to clamp down on our prey and squeeze the life force out of them, until we have completely ravaged them from within. By sucking out their Souls and possessing them, we shall make them our slaves by turning them into living vampires of Darkness *forever and ever!*"

Chaos erupted and continued longer, while Egoson pounded his chest like beating drums, until he shook the cavern depths with rhythmic thunder.

"You have excelled in fanning the fires of corrosive fears and venomous thoughts. Many sea creatures are already our slaves, while many others in The Kingdom of Oceana are still unsuspecting forces like ours even exist. Imagine our stroke of luck! They still argue that only Light is real, and Darkness in themselves is but an illusion!"

The roar of squeals, cackles, and howls silenced Egoson, as he danced before the fiery altar, while heightening the phosphorescent glow of The Mantle of The Sacred Sea Dragons on his back.

"The best part is knowing that these despicable morons mercilessly blame everyone else around them for their distresses, rather than looking deeper inside themselves for the cause. They don't even suspect how their emotional upheavals affect the weather itself!"

Howls exploded again before Egoson continued.

"Natural disasters will accelerate, as tremors from sea creatures own emotional earthquakes will build in momentum and affect everything around them with increasing destruction. They will be reduced to terrified slaves looking for a deliverer. And guess what? They will turn *to me* instead of Godson! Imagine that!"

A deafening roar exploded and continued even longer this time, as Egoson strutted across the stage, gloating in revelry before the forces of Darkness, and even Blackshoe Crab swelled with pride from within.

"Yes, we are winning our war. Before long, we will storm The Temples of the Goddess of the Sea and command the Empire of Darkness from our new palace of power! It shall be our ultimate triumph!"

Silence slammed in from all directions, as Egoson took advantage of the charged silence he fully expected. By trespassing into the minds of the Souls of Darkness, he manipulated their thoughts as easily as they manipulated sea creatures loyal to the Goddess. He could feel their terror at the thought of trespassing holy ground. None of them wanted to personally incur the wrath of the Goddess by being cursed to death by Her Light, which seemed more terrifying than any torture they would willingly endure in Darkness. In spite of the loyalty and allegiance to their Master, they wondered how Egoson could accomplish such a feat. Since they all knew his power lay in illusion and black magic and manipulation of the senses, they wondered how Egoson could overtake the Goddess by trespassing onto holy ground. How could he penetrate the fierce reality of that holy domain? How could he survive the awesome energy of holy Light?

Egoson allowed them to hang on to those thoughts for awhile, suspended in another kind of fear, overtaken by another kind of terror, paralyzed by another kind of madness. He wanted them to feel the incomprehensible fear that characterized their existence. He brought them to the very edge of all he stood for, an abyss of Darkness of such unfathomable depths, that when looking down upon it, they would experience *their stark emptiness and recoil terrified by it!* Egoson could then fill them with purpose, animated at least *by something* for all the emptiness that possessed them! It was then easy to make slaves of them, as they reared from their gutless impotence and dreaded emptiness, ready *to do anything for their Master,* who guaranteed them redemption in Hell! Egoson easily manipulated the forces of Darkness by getting them to believe *they were nothing without him!*

As a final climax to his demonstrated powers, Egoson walked over to the bag and yanked out the sacred eels of *The One Who Knows.* The forces of Darkness fell back and shrieked in unison as night shifted into day. All instantly vanished as they recoiled from the sight of blinding light.

"No need to run! I will protect you from their light!" Egoson shouted, as he formed a force-field of energy around the sacred eels so their light would not burn the Souls of Darkness.

"Return, all of you, at once! I COMMAND it!"

The Empire of Darkness returned reluctantly, still squirming from the pain of radiant light.

Grabbing the sacred eels by their heads, Egoson held them aloft, so all could see and recoil from the sight of them. Never before had any Soul of Darkness gotten this near any sacred living creature to *The One Who Knows* without falling deathly sick from the energy of them.

Egoson walked over to the bubbling cauldron and held the sacred eels aloft. Hushed whispers rose from his audience. In an instant, Egoson slashed and gutted the male and female sacred eels to allow their blood to drip into the cauldron. The brew hissed in response. He then brought the sacred eels to his mouth and sucked their blood, while devouring the still throbbing organs before a gasping audience. Once Egoson was satisfied, he threw the limp bodies into the cauldron to top off his brew.

Egoson felt a yawning chasm of hunger rise from the Souls of Darkness, as he gorged himself to the delicacy they could not touch. He felt them crave his power to devour such energy without harm. Any of them would have been savagely burned for attempting such a folly. Yet, he could gorge himself to what had always been forbidden to them.

Egoson roused them to salivate over the blood without equal. He manipulated them to consider whether such an extraordinary morsel could stop their hunger for just a moment? Fill their emptiness just a little? Or ventilate their hate enough to die for!

Lord of all Darkness, Egoson celebrated his dream of complete and utter manipulation, and *he reveled in it!* The final challenge was finding a way to banish *The One Who Knows* and destroy Godson forever. By killing the sacred eels, he hoped to take control of their Souls and have them spill any secrets locked inside of them. Egoson smiled knowing his time for revenge had come at last.

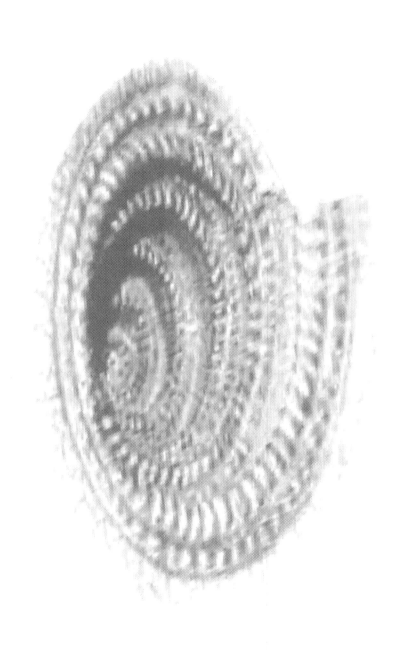

35

THE SACRED SEA DRAGONS

Matching the phosphorescent image on Egoson's
back, The Sacred Sea Dragons materialized from
the spiraling mists, suspended aloft, ready to strike!

Egoson mounted another series of incantations to unlock the secrets and mysterious powers hidden within the lifeless forms of the sacred eels stirring within the hissing cauldren. The brew moaned in response to the Souls being invoked from the sacrifices. Egoson danced the sacred spiral dance around the bubbling cauldren, waiting for their Souls to emerge.

Billowing smoke began to rise from the cauldron mists in the form of two spirals, and all waited in hushed silence for their full manifestation to take place. When the ever-expanding spirals continued to fill out the greater dimensions of the cavern hall without stopping, all gasped, including Egoson, because none realized what he would invoke. Matching the phosphorescent image on Egoson's back, The Sacred Sea Dragons materialized from the spiraling mists, suspended aloft, ready to strike!

The Empire of Darkness disappeared from sight, while Egoson remained, reeling from the sight of them. Remembering The Dance of the

Sacred Spiral of Light and the transformation of sacred eels into The Sacred Sea Dragons of legend, he instantly grasped what he had to do.

"Return, all of you, at once! I COMMAND it!" Egoson thundered, as all Souls of Darkness returned, gripped by Egoson's telepathic mind control, while they helplessly squirmed in terror.

Astonishment visibly took hold of them all, as Egoson displayed his awesome powers and extraordinary magic by having The Sacred Sea Dragons hover aloft, without striking. They did not suspect that Egoson had been equally surprised by their invoked presence. The mystery of the insignia on his back had finally revealed its correspondent. The Mantle of The Sacred Sea Dragons had been carved into his shell by the power of sacred light, and it was unimaginable to believe, Egoson was now their Lord and Master as well.

Egoson interrogated The Sacred Sea Dragons before a fully mesmerized Empire of Darkness and discovered the secrets he sought concerning *The One Who Knows*.

"Are you The Sacred Sea Dragons of legend?"

"We are," said The Sacred Sea Dragons, who spoke in unison.

"Are the sacred eels your physical counterpart in The Kingdom of Oceana."

"They are."

"Do you serve *The One Who Knows* as *Divine* Guardians just as the sacred eels have served as Guardians to The Temples of the Goddess of the Sea."

"Yes, we do serve *The One Who Knows* as *Divine* Guardians."

"Do you now serve me, Egoson, as well?"

"No, we do not serve Egoson in any way."

"Do you serve The Original Ancestry of the Gods?"

"We do, as those named who came through THE STARGATE as Luna and Solar."

"Ahh, but I also came through THE STARGATE as Nabyss! That means you also serve me!"

"No, we do not serve Nabyss."

"What if I can prove to you that I am also one who came through THE STARGATE?"

"Only one who is marked by sacred light during The Dance of the Sacred Spiral of Life can call himself a god worthy of commanding the Gatekeepers of the *Void*."

Egoson burst into sardonic laughter and began shape-shifting into a formidable presence before The Sacred Sea Dragons of legend. He shifted to five times his size, filling out the great cavern hall before abruptly turning to reveal The Mantle of the Sacred Sea Dragon dancing on his back. The Sacred Sea Dragons did not shutter or retreat, but simply said, "We are at your command."

Egoson continued his sardonic laughter until it echoed off the walls like thunder. Once he had celebrated his triumph of commanding The Sacred Sea Dragons of legend, he continued his questions.

"How can I destroy *The One Who Knows?*"

"*The One Who Knows* cannot be destroyed."

"If I cannot destroy *The One Who Knows*, is there any ancient words I can say, any magic I can exact, any ceremony I can perform, where I can send *The One Who Knows* back to the *Void?*

"There is."

"Is that so?"

"Yes."

"Now we're getting somewhere! How in the Name of The Great Father of Darkness can it be done?"

"It cannot be done in the Name of The Great Father of Darkness."

"Never mind. I was only . . . *Forget it!* How can it be done?"

"It can only be done by targeting the body vehicle of *The One Who Knows* who is living in The Kingdom of Oceana and returning it back to the *Void*."

"What did you say?"

"We said . . ."

"Did you say *The One Who Knows* has a physical body vehicle existing in The Kingdom of Oceana?"

"Yes."

Egoson burst into diabolical laughter, spurring every Soul of Darkness and even the Abominable Hags and their offspring to burst into cackles, shrills, and screeches because they all simultaneously recognized their inevitable triumph in destroying *The One Who Knows*.

Egoson waited until everyone had relished the exquisite triumph of his unparalleled manipulation of The Sacred Sea Dragons of legend before continuing. Only after everyone had settled down, did Egoson continue.

"Am I to understand that eliminating the body vehicle of *The One Who Knows* from The Kingdom of Oceana will send *The One Who Knows* back to the *Void?*"

"That is correct."

"But how is that possible? Destroying a body vehicle usually sends the Soul to the Realm of Lost Souls or returns it through THE PORTAL OF LIGHT to a place I will not speak of here. How will *The One Who Knows* be returned to the *Void* by destroying its body vehicle?"

"We must clarify."

"Then do so!"

"The body vehicle we are speaking of is not like any other body vehicle typical of The Kingdom of Oceana. This body vehicle is *Divine* and, therefore, *cannot be destroyed* just as *The One Who Knows* acting as a *Divine Emissary* to The Great Mother Goddess *cannot be destroyed*. But the body vehicle can be *eliminated* from The Kingdom of Oceana and returned *directly* to the *Void* because it is not a Soul, per se, but *Divine Spirit taken form*. The body vehicle and *The One Who Knows* are actually *one and the same* existing in different expressions. Since they are both *Divine,* they do not return to the Realm of Lost Souls or Heaven. They return directly to the *Void* as their source."

"Does that mean that only I, acting as a god, can destroy the body vehicle?"

"No."

"Then how?"

"We cannot speak of the Mystery to you. We can only answer if you claim the Mystery for yourself."

Egoson stopped and considered everything The Sacred Sea Dragons had said. He was told he could not *destroy* the body vehicle because it was *Divine* and could only be *eliminated* from The Kingdom of Oceana and returned back to the *Void.* Yet, with all the powers given to him at The Dance of the Sacred Spiral of Life and by The Mantle of the Sacred Sea Dragons, why could he not *eliminate* the body vehicle and return it back to the *Void*? If he could not do it, then who?

Egoson paced back and forth contemplating this phenomenon. If he destroyed any sea creature's body vehicle, their Souls were immediately sent to the Realm of Lost Souls. They would never return directly to the *Void.* Only the *Divine* were sent back to the *Void* as their source. And if *Divine,* he could not destroy them. He felt he was going in circles without cracking the Mystery that might give him the answer that The Sacred Sea Dragons withheld. But then, if the body vehicle is *Divine,* then what did *eliminate* really mean? It apparently did not mean the body vehicle could be destroyed, as The Sacred Sea Dragons pointed out, but perhaps meant it could be *transported back to the Void* and *eliminated* from The Kingdom of Oceana. Egoson weighed this a little longer when the answer finally dawned. If The Sacred Sea Dragons were *Gatekeepers of the Void,* couldn't they use their primordial powers to return anyone or anything back to the *Void* by the direct use of their powers? Would this be *destroying* them or simply *eliminating them from physical existence* and, thus, returning them back to their original state as *Divine*? *Egoson realized he had his answer!*

"By the powers given to me by The Mantle of The Sacred Sea Dragons, can I command you to transport the body vehicle for *The One Who Knows* back to the *Void* and, therefore, simultaneously return them both to the *Void?*"

No answer came.

"Is that correct?"

There was a pause by The Sacred Sea Dragons who were intentionally holding back their answer.

"Is that correct?

No answer came.

"I COMMAND YOU TO ANSWER ME!"

"That is correct," The Sacred Sea Dragons replied in unison.

"Then I believe I now have the right to know the name of the physical identity of *The One Who knows.*

Once again, The Sacred Sea Dragons hesitated to give their answer, but gave it nonetheless.

"The physical identity of *The One Who knows* is *Domaine.*"

"And what form has *Domaine* taken in The Kingdom of Oceana?"

"A hermit crab."

"A hermit crab? A hermit crab? Imagine that!" Egoson exclaimed, breaking out into riotous laugher, together with the Souls of Darkness and the Abominable Hags and their offspring.

"A hermit crab? It looks like it's all in the family!" Egoson exclaimed, as everyone roared because this great Mystery became reduced to a hermit crab. When everyone had sufficiently gloated, Egoson returned to The Sacred Sea Dragons.

"You have served me well. But now I must attend to other matters. I release you both in the name of the gods and will once again call upon you at the proper time. So, *BE GONE!*"

The Sacred Sea Dragons were gone in the next instant!

Egoson now claimed his victory knowing the physical identity that anchored *The One Who Knows* to The Kingdom of Oceana would be dead before long. Yes, *dead!* Such technicality was typical of the forces of Light, when in fact, he would be deader than anyone who was released into the Realm of Lost Souls. At least in the Realm of Lost Souls, such Souls could be contacted at will. But in the *Void?* Hah! They were gone for good!

Having witnessed Egoson's extraordinary magic and awesome powers, all doubt vanished within the Empire of Darkness. All indisputably believed that Egoson would one day rule The Kingdom of Oceana from The Temples of the Goddess of the Sea.

To commemorate the most extraordinary event of all time, Egoson invited everyone to drink of his special brew, as a gesture of his gratitude and a celebration of the inevitable victory to come. As the brew disappeared from sight, all Souls of Darkness agreed that never before had such a brew held such magic and power. Its taste was beyond critical comment. All sighed from the energy that equally charged them with invincible power.

Egoson looked into the cauldron to see if there was anything left and discovered that the flesh of the sacred eels remained untouched on the bottom. He marveled that even after being desecrated by his supreme sorcery, the sacred eels could not be eaten by anyone, except himself. He celebrated his prize knowing these lifeless remains foreshadowed the death of *The One Who Knows*. He relished his feast knowing his triumph was assured. After all, who else but Egoson could rule over Heaven and Galexia?

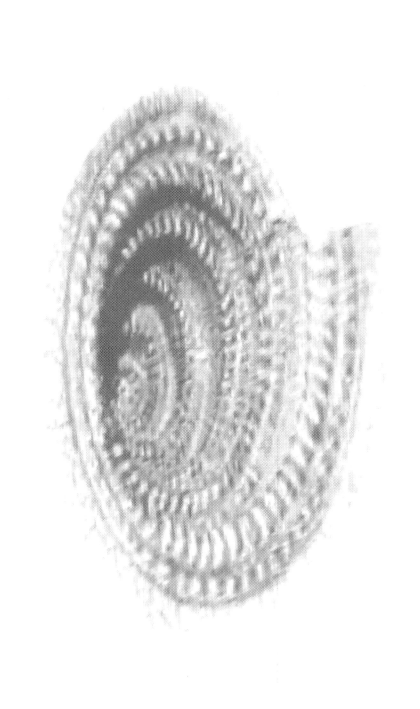

36

THE *VOID*

To leap into the Void and experience annihilation,
and yet, be able to return intact as a unique being
of creation, is a journey marking the crowning
achievement of all time.

Domaine stood before young Solar waiting to secure the light of his Soul before answering his question. Only then could he hope to shift young Solar from conflict to inner peace and reach him with the truth. Otherwise, he could speak to him gently or he could argue with him, but the truth would *not* be heard.

"Young Solar, your question, *"Why has The Great Mother Goddess forsaken them?"* reflects a deeper conflict that has overshadowed you all your life. If you do not see beyond it, Egoson will surely use your anger and resentment toward The Great Mother Goddess as a weapon against you and destroy you. What I propose then is a journey all the way back to the *Void,* so you may understand the resentment you hold inside of you is but a distortion of the truth."

Young Solar's eyes widened. "All the way back to the *Void?* But I have not been able to go back *to the beginning of time,* although I have tried more than once. Yet, you speak of going back before that? But how? I keep getting trapped within the memories of past lifetimes and have never been able to complete the journey. I had thought it impossible."

"Young Solar, you must know by now that nothing is impossible, although it is true, few can go back that far for a very good reason. Not many can endure a state of pure formlessness before existence, unrealized potential as it were, and then be able to return. That is only possible when you have a strong unity with your Soul and are absolutely connected with it, since that unity must dissolve completely when you become one with the *Void*. Only by reaching that distant *Void*, can you reach the omnipotent consciousness of The Great Mother Goddess. Then you will understand that the anger and resentment you hold toward The Great Mother Goddess is but a reflection of your ignorance, and by ignorance, I mean, all that remains unknown within you."

"But what is the *Void* exactly? I have heard you speak about it often, but what is it *really*?"

"The *Void* is not easy to explain, but I will attempt an explanation. One may say the *Void* is silence . . . within nothingness . . . outside of time . . . where everything exists as pure potential . . . yet is charged with infinite energy and power! Thus, it is a place where nothing exists and everything exists at the same time!"

"Oh, I see. I was afraid you would attempt to explain what cannot be explained."

"You see what I mean. Perhaps, said another way, it would be better to say the *Void* is where you will discover the essence of pure consciousness."

"But how can I find The Great Mother Goddess in nothingness?"

"There is no point in speaking about this further. I will go with you and show you the way, so you can make contact. But you cannot make contact with the *Void* without annihilation. It is the ultimate act of surrender. To leap into the *Void* and experience annihilation, and yet, be able to return intact as a unique being of creation, is a journey marking the crowning achievement of all time. I have been there, I have experienced it, and I have returned forever changed by it. Only then, will you experience the veil of all Mysteries lifted forever."

"You made it back without *losing your mind?*"

"Then you already understand one of the challenges. You cannot reach the *Void* and experience annihilation without *losing your mind.* By the inspiration of your Soul, you have already tapped into this revelation. It is true I did lose my mind. I did so *to reclaim it!* But, once I returned, I came back laughing from the experience of it."

"Laughing? Laughing, did you say? I don't understand!"

"I don't expect you to understand. Not yet. If I were to describe my experience to you, you would still be at a loss. It is something you have to experience for yourself. No one can explain it to you."

"You have surely fired my curiosity!"

"Are you ready to see for yourself?"

"Of course! I wouldn't miss it!"

"But I must caution you. I would never suggest this if we were not living in these dangerous and unpredictable times. Since every day becomes critical in your Initiation, I invite you to take this risk because the end times of The Final Reckoning are already here. Understand this is a *very* dangerous journey. Only the highest of Initiates who have made direct contact with their *Divine Spirit,* as you have done, can actually travel to the *Void.* This is the supreme Initiation. There is no way of knowing when anyone is ready to do this at higher levels of consciousness. It is normally undertaken after many Initiations, and sometimes, lifetimes are involved in preparation. It is because of *who you are* on the Soul level that you may be able to leap ahead of those Initiations and reclaim the Immortality of *Divine* consciousness by making direct contact with the *Void.*"

"If I make it to the *Void* and experience annihilation, how is it possible to reorganize my consciousness and return to this time/space continuum as myself? After all, isn't it possible for me to show up anywhere in time and space and never return here?"

"Young Solar, if I were to allow you to ponder all the risks, there would be no end to them. Understand what I have been trying to tell you. To say it simply, there is a *very good chance* you may *never* return from the *Void* and bring life back into your body. Once your Soul exits your body to time travel to the *Void*, you have only so much time to accomplish this before your body goes into shock, then slips into coma, and then death."

"Oh, I see. This may be a one way into nothingness."

"Perhaps, but only if you *reach* the *Void*. I admit your chances are slim. Even if you came close to the *Void* and yet did not reach it, you have everything to gain. All memories to the farthest place you can reach across time will galvanize incomparable knowledge, gifts, attributes, and abilities within you. Everything you have ever known since you entered this world through THE STARGATE will become activated. You will remember much more easily the things of the past and bring forth your godly powers with little effort. It is worth the risk, to be sure. If you are successful, you will be able to go forward completely on your own."

"What do you mean?"

"I mean you will no longer need me or anyone else to assist you in claiming the powers of Godson still dormant within you. Do you understand all the implications of what I am saying?"

"I understand only that I am ready. That is all."

"Good. That is enough. We will begin our exercise as we have done so many times before. But first you must make contact with the internal consciousness of your body. Once you do so, explain your intentions to allow the body to prepare for the departure of your Soul. The Soul's intelligence resides deep within at the inner core of your body's consciousness. You can rest assured that once you make contact with your body vehicle in this way, you will find returning to your body much easier. Your body vehicle will prepare for hibernation and give you more time to accomplish your task. Are you ready?"

"Yes, I am."

"Good. So, ready yourself, for a trip through THE STARGATE at the micro levels of existence!"

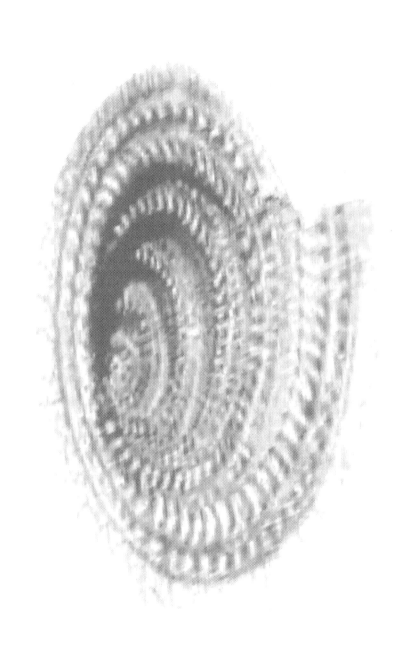

37

JOURNEY TO THE BEGINNING OF TIME

Keep following THE LIGHT and keep telling
yourself, I want to go back, all the way back,
to the beginning of time . . . to the Void itself!"

Domaine readied himself to show young Solar the way. Although he had inspired him to reach the *Void*, the beginning and the end of all things, he hoped young Solar would at least reach THE STARGATE, when he had crossed beyond its threshold and arrived in The Kingdom of Oceana. If so, young Solar would reclaim his *Divine* nature and directly link to the powers as Godson, and Domaine would be able to bypass many Initiations on his behalf. Although this was a shortcut with great risks involved, it was one worth taking. With the end times of The Final Reckoning already a reality, there was no more time to waste.

"Young Solar, I would like you to close your eyes and keep them closed until we have returned from our journey. Release all tension from your body through the breath and clear your mind of any thoughts that may run interference with you. Align yourself to your innermost center so your energy runs freely along your body without obstruction. Breathe slowly and rhythmically until you bring your entire body into alignment with your breath. As you do, set the intention to open all doorways to your cellular memory from across the whole of time. As this takes place, invite the powerful presence of everything you are and everything you have ever been to merge with your consciousness until you are glowing as pure radiant light."

Domaine tracked young Solar's transformation until his body had shifted into the glowing transparency of radiant light.

"That's it! Now, invite your Soul to open all pathways of consciousness that include the entire continuum of yourself from across the whole of time. Keep setting this intention, expanding your light, until you become like the radiant sun yourself!"

Young Solar became unified with his Soul and dissolved into pulsating radiant light beyond any form whatsoever. Shifting into pure consciousness, young Solar began witnessing the whole of his experiences from across time. A multitude of different aspects rose to his awareness in rapid succession. All he had ever been came flooding back to him, until he began witnessing the myriad forms of consciousness whirling interchangeably from infinity back to himself. The whole of creation coalesced in and out of shifting realities of light. Out of this revelry of being, Godson heard Domaine speak.

"Listen to my voice and release yourself from all else. Let my voice guide you until there is no other sound except my voice!"

Godson sustained a connection to Domaine's presence, even though he had also dematerialized into light.

"As you know, Godson, you are a doorway to everything you have ever been from across time. All memory is locked inside of you. Within each individual cell, there is a blueprint, not only of your present physical body, but also of every past life you have ever known. That blueprint is contained within the double-stranded sacred spiral of life existing within every cell of your body. Each strand represents the spiraling energies of male/female, past/present, form/formlessness within you. Together we will journey through the inner dimensional doorway existing at the center of the sacred spiral of life to go back to the beginning of time. Are you ready?"

"Yes, I am!"

"Materialize the doorway to the sacred spiral of life, so we can enter its center together. Ready?"

"Yes," Godson replied. Without a moment's delay, Godson materialized a glowing doorway and shot through it with Domaine, traveling like shooting stars at record speed through the sacred spiral of life.

"Oh, my God, Domaine, *it's a tunnel!* . . . *It's a tunnel with light at the end of it!* . . . You have never taken me this way before!

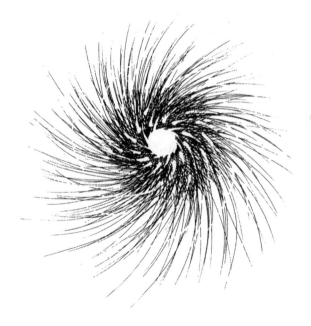

Doorway Through the Sacred Spiral of Life

"Because I have never taken you *the beginning of time* to the *Void* itself! So, keep moving! Keep following THE LIGHT and keep telling yourself, I want to go back, all the way back, to the beginning of time! I want to go back, all the way back, to the beginning of time! I want to go back, all the way back, to the beginning of time . . . to the *Void* itself!"

Domaine and Godson traveled beyond any speed imaginable, conscious of each other, yet separate from one another.

"This is another world!" Godson shot back, telepathically, confident his thoughts would reach Domaine. He then sensed rather than heard, *"Yes, it is!"*

As colors, vibrations, and sounds, echoed past the whirling vortex of time travel, Godson wondered how Domaine could keep up.

Godson sped through the whirling vortex faster than any speed he had ever gone, although THE LIGHT kept its distance regardless of how fast he traveled. Domaine's words kept reaching him, *"You want to go back, all the way back, to the beginning of time . . . to the Void itself!"*

Traveling beyond any speed imaginable, even *in consciousness,* Godson maintained his direction with intense concentration. He strained to keep up as lifetimes blurred and no time existed, and speed shifted into unbearable high-piercing frequencies. When Godson felt he would disintegrate from an implosion of blinding speed, he burst through THE LIGHT into a silence so profound that no experience matched the depth of it. Godson checked for Domaine, but he was gone. Godson looked around to see if he could see something, *anything,* but he could see nothing. He found himself suspended in a vast ocean of empty stillness, as unfathomable as infinite space within infinite time. Within the limitless womb of consciousness, there existed a peace unparalleled by any other reality he had ever known.

Godson tried repeatedly *to see something* because his mind would not accept the existence of nothing at all. But he saw nothing, as he became reduced to a point of consciousness where his body and memories disappeared into nothingness. Everything he had ever known of himself slipped away as he was met with no sound, no colors, and no visuals of any kind. Nothing existed because *there was nothing in matter!*

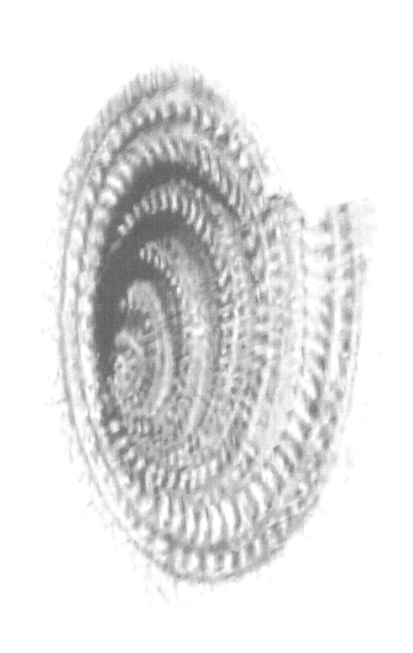

38

THE FREQUENCY OF LOVE

Throughout eternity, the FREQUENCY of LOVE
would remain the HEARTBEAT of LIVING
CONSCIOUSNESS—as the ALPHA and the
OMEGA—the BEGINNING and the END—
of DIVINE CONSCIOUSNESS!"

How long I remained in timelessness and empty space without a care, without a thought, and without a desire, I cannot say. I could have continued in that way forever. But in a lightning impulse of consciousness, I wanted TO CREATE!

DESIRE became my FLAME, LIGHT became my CRUCIBLE, and CREATION became my EXPRESSION. A spiraling vortex of escalating sound frequencies began rising higher and higher until they exploded into CONSCIOUS LIGHT giving rise to THE GREAT MOTHER GODDESS and THE GREAT FATHER GOD, simultaneously! As the TWIN FLAME OF LOVE, they mingled in full expression, as all CREATION exploded forth from the charged polarities of their union.

GALAXIES and UNIVERSES exploded into CREATION from their union. Shooting stars streaked across the Heavens giving rise to SUNS, MOONS, and PLANETS, while DIMENSIONS of Colors, Sights, and Sounds erupted into landscapes of shifting realities. A vastness so extraordinary was created that worlds were born to exist across distances of unspeakable breath as well as side-by-side one another.

DIVINE CHILDREN came forth to become CREATOR GODS, expressing the FREQUENCY of LOVE in the charged polarities of their union, giving rise to their own Universes. Having Dominion over their own Universes in expression of FREE WILL, they were given the opportunity to act out their dreams and their fantasies, their nightmares and their torments, their loves and their hates, as TIME and SPACE became a function of their expression. Given full expression without limits or restrictions of any kind, they were charged with FULL RESPONSIBILITY over ALL of their CREATIONS, for together they reflected their ONENESS of BEING.

THE DIVINE RECORDS of CONSCIOUSNESS documented the progressive acts of all GODS, so balance could be maintained throughout the WHOLE of CREATION. PROPHECIES were foretold, should any GOD stray too far from THE LIGHT without a way back home from THE DARKNESS.

THE SACRED SPIRAL of LIFE became the KEY to LIFE; the DANCE became the LIVING VORTEX of LIGHT's expression; the STARGATE became the DOORWAY to anchoring consciousness into form from the STARS.

The JOURNEY of the GODS brought all things full circle: LIGHT shedding DARKNESS; REMEMBRANCE restoring UNITY; THE FINAL RECKONING restoring WHOLENESS—to become ONE in ALL and ALL in ONE.

Throughout eternity, the FREQUENCY of LOVE would remain the HEARTBEAT of LIVING CONSCIOUSNESS–as the ALPHA and the OMEGA— the BEGINNING and the END—of DIVINE CONSCIOUSNESS!"

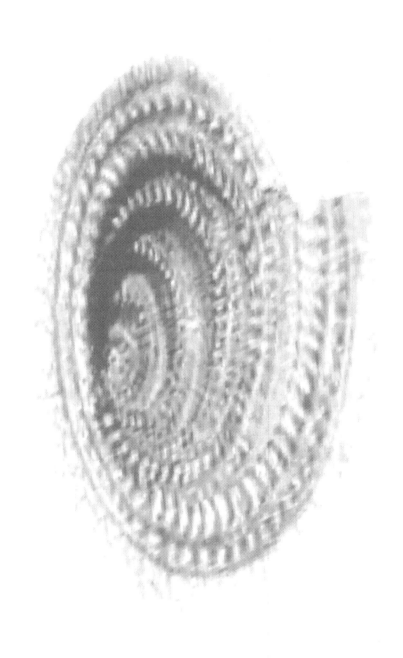

39

DIVINE METAPHORS

Regardless of how different we appear to one another,
we are all living metaphors to Divine expression.

Solar shot into his body and slammed against the wall before stopping. Domaine instantly teleported to his side and shook him firmly to bring him back.

"Solar! Solar!! Wake up! Wake up!!"

Solar groaned painfully as tremors shook his body forcefully. Domaine released a low currency of energy across his temples to help Solar align energetically with his body. The journey had been long, and his body had gone into shock from the extended absence of his Soul.

Solar's eyes started fluttering as Domaine sighed in relief.

"You had me worried, Solar," Domaine said, in a nervous whisper, knowing Solar was not yet present enough to hear him. "I was beginning to think I had lost you."

"Solar! How do you feel?"

"Where am I?"

"You are back at The Temple of Healing."

"I am back at The Temple of Healing," Solar responded, mouthing his words like parrotfish.

"Solar, can you open your eyes?"

Solar withdrew from the light that accosted his eyes. Slowly, as he became accustomed to it, he began looking around as if seeing things for the first time. Upon seeing Domaine, he jumped up and grabbed him.

"Domaine! Domaine! I did it! I did it!"

"Indeed you did!"

"It was incredible, simply incredible! It was like nothing I had ever experienced! I was in the *Void* before time! *Before time!* Can you imagine that?"

"Yes, I can."

"But how did I ever get back?"

"What makes you think you ever left?"

Solar looked at Domaine quizzically and then began chuckling.

"You mean?"

"Anything goes!"

"Hah! But I am here now, in flesh and Soul!" Solar said, grateful to see the flesh of living consciousness. Looking around, he suddenly felt a tumultuous landslide of sensations slipping into frequencies that blurred the edges of reality for a moment. Steadying himself, he stopped and refocused, as the earth beneath him grounded him once more.

"Domaine?"

"Yes, Solar."

Solar wanted to speak, but words became desperately inadequate.

"Domaine?"

"Yes?"

"I know what it's like before time."

"Can you tell me?"

"I experienced *the living consciousness of the Void*. I now understand what is meant by the *Frequency of Love*. It is an awareness that extends out in all directions into endless space. It is the proverbial all-present, all-powerful, and all-knowing consciousness. No separation exists in that unified field of consciousness as it continually pulses with pure ecstasy. When I experienced that level of ecstasy, I understood the *Divine Immortal Nature of the Universe!*"

"Did you?"

"*Yes! As the Frequency of Love!* The living consciousness of the *Void* that gave birth to the polarities of The Great Mother Goddess and The Great Father God as the Twin Flame of Love.

"Yes, Solar, that is true."

"Then why are *The Sacred Sea Scrolls* wrong?"

"What do you mean?"

"*It is written* that The Great Mother Goddess existed before God. In fact, *The Sacred Sea Scrolls* say, '*She* created *God!*'"

"*The Sacred Sea Scrolls* were written to reflect *all things metaphorically.* In fact, when you realize all realities come from the *Void* and are conscious reflections of the *Void*, then everything can be reduced to pure metaphor because at the core of our existence, we are *Divine* reflections of consciousness because we are all the same at the core, existing as pure energy. As such, we remain eternal and unchanging and are always one with everything. Regardless of how different we appear to one another, *we are all living metaphors to Divine expression.*"

"Living metaphors?"

"Yes. All things are metaphoric expressions of the *Divine*! Since we are all *Divine* at our core, that gives us access to great power. The greatest power we can exercise is in connecting to our Soul. Why? Because once we connect to our Soul, we can connect to all consciousness, including *Divine* consciousness, through Soul-to-Soul communication. At that inner core of unified power with all consciousness, the Soul transcends the limitations of time and space. We can then see ourselves playing out different realities, as pawns on a stage, in an ever-changing landscape of different worlds. In this way, our Soul sets out to experience every aspect of the *Divine*. To make sure we stretch as far as we can, we keep dying to the realities we have known, so we can reincarnate again to live within entirely new worlds. Regardless of how often we change and coalesce in and out of different personalities across time, we remain *living metaphors of the Divine* in manifest form.

Godson blinked, saying nothing, processing all Domaine was saying at lightning speed.

"The Mysteries ultimately shelter this great truth, Godson, for only in understanding this great Mystery can the veil of separation finally lift, allowing us to see that we are actually *Gods playing a fool's game of separation.*"

"I get it! I finally get it!" Solar said, releasing the built-up tension in his body by dancing around like a child, before stopping abruptly in front of Domaine, knowing his mentor was telepathically calling his attention.

"To answer your original question, Godson, "Why are *The Sacred Sea Scrolls* wrong?", know that great emphasis was placed on the importance of The Great Mother Goddess because she represents *the womb of creation*, which in turn represents the *Void* metaphorically. That is why it was said that *She existed before God and gave birth to Him* because *The Sacred Sea Scrolls* were referring to Her *metaphorically*. Actually, it was intentionally meant to be a great Mystery seeded within language, so the truth would be revealed only to those Initiates, especially Priestesses, who sought answers to deeper Mysteries *not outside of themselves but within themselves*. Priestesses, aligned with the *Divine* revelations of their own truth, would discover their womb to be an open portal to the *Void*. Having such access to the *Divine* primordial energies of creation gave Priestesses awesome powers because they could *bring forth life without having a male counterpart*. By linking directly to the *Void*, the spark of *Divine* consciousness could be ignited within their womb, making possible *Divine conception*."

"*Oh, my Goddess!*"

"That's correct! Only after Priestesses shifted from *Divine* unity, did they lose the awareness that they could spontaneously bring forth life from their womb. *It was this great Mystery, which was lost and burned within records originally known as The Book of Life, that ushered in the jealousy of the male god, who in manifest form believed in his inability to spontaneously bring forth life as well.* He then became polarized into his identity as a male, overlooking and even forgetting about his ability to shape-shift into any form within creation, including shape-shifting into his feminine counterpart. As a result, he collapsed into anger and revenge and turned with great vengeance to brutalize The Great Mother Goddess and repress Her existence, together with all Priestesses, so this great Mystery would be permanently lost to them all."

"That's *impossible!*"

"Impossible, but true. One of the great Initiations that existed in the early days secured the polarities of *Divine* consciousness within *one being of consciousness*. The Dance of the Sacred Spiral of Life is an example of all I am speaking."

"But how?"

"The Dance of the Sacred Spiral of Life metaphorically represents many things.THE STARGATE represents the doorway to all that exists in creation, including the *Void*. The Sacred Sea Dragons, as Gatekeepers of the *Void*, are the male Sentinels and female Guardians of the *Void*, capable of channeling the awesome powers of the *Void*. When sacred eels unite during the sacred dance of spring, the spark of energy ignited between male and female polarities of the flesh automatically unify them with their *Divine* aspects, if only for a moment. At the 13,000-year-mark, the *Divine* aspects of them existing as The Sacred Sea Dragons become visible. Once visible, The Sacred Sea Dragons unite even further into *one being of Divine consciousness*, creating an epiphany of light discharged through the thunderbolt of their union. By annihilating all connection to the flesh, they make possible a direct bridge of conscious *Divine* Light between Heaven and Galexia."

"So I was transformed by *Divine* Light into Solar during The Dance of the Sacred Spiral of Life."

"Yes! You were restored to your true essence. In fact, take a look at yourself in the mirror."

Puzzled, Solar moved to the mirror on the wall and noticed that he was no longer a teenager, but a fully-grown adult. His voice had changed, reflecting the deeper baritone of fully-grown males.

"By re-emerging from the *Void*, you shape-shifted into your adult self, bypassing your teenage years completely."

"Unbelievable!"

"Coming full circle to your original question, putting the Goddess before God was meant to metaphorically represent the importance of connecting to the heart *first* before the mind. Without making contact with the *Frequency of Love*, we cannot discover the intrinsic connection we automatically have with the *Divine*. Without Love, a deep and profound honoring of The Great Mother Goddess cannot be realized, nor the honoring of the sacredness of life. Without honoring the sacredness of life, there is a failure to honor the sacredness of children. Life then becomes expendable and degenerates into war, chaos, and destruction. Without God becoming a loving Sentinel to the Goddess, who in turn becomes a loving Guardian to Her Children, and all of nature, then the delicate balance existing between them all is destroyed."

"How true."

"It must be noted that the loving Sentinel who shifts and turns to conquest compromises that balance by attempting to usurp *the power of creation* belonging to The Great Mother Goddess. *The Sentinel then becomes a warmonger, grasping for power, making war inevitable, because of conflict over its own impotence and inability to bring forth life, until no life remains.* That is what took place with Nabyss, who turned into Egoson, when he experienced his own impotence to bring forth life directly from himself. He knew that without this awesome power, he had not conquered the power of the gods.

Without it, he became reduced to a mere mortal. Thus, Egoson chose to reign supreme over all living beings by overriding free will and having no regard for life."

Solar became silent as he remembered his brother, feeling pain and regret for all that had taken place between them. Yet, he dismissed his regret recognizing that his brother had chosen his path very consciously and deliberately. There was no point in dwelling on what could have been, but only on what could be in the future, as a result of the inevitable confrontation awaiting them both. Solar shifted uneasily and then continued his questions.

"Why is The Final Reckoning so critical? I had discussed this with Jason, and he said it would lead to either peace or annihilation?"

"That is true."

"He also said we have a chance of returning to The Original Ancestry of the Gods?"

"Yes, we do."

Solar and Domaine shifted into silence while the prophetic implications of all they were discussing gathered in their minds. Domaine stopped speaking, allowing Solar to process all that had been said. While they stopped, time slipped away as Solar's world moved into another Universe, for the one he had known, was never to be the same again.

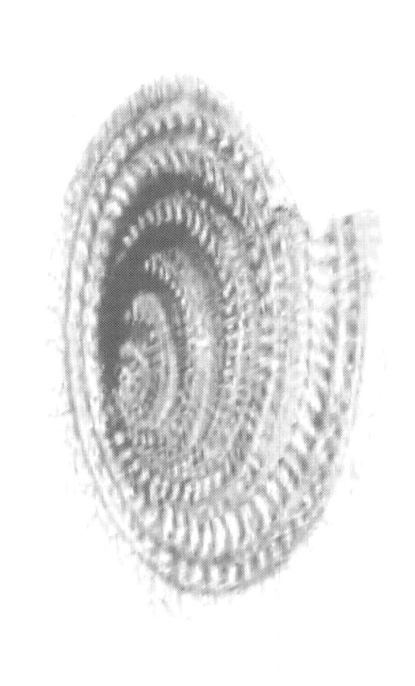

40

I AM LOVE THAT I AM

Bravo, Solar, you have rediscovered one of the
great Mysteries that offer a Key to Divine
Immortality.

Solar resisted bringing his time with Domaine to an end because his mind whirled from the revelations crowding out well-known realities, whose doors were closing, while chasing new realities, whose doorways loomed before him.

"Domaine, *The Sacred Sea Scrolls* quote another phrase, 'I AM THAT I AM', as a way of linking up to *Divine* consciousness. But the phrase is missing one very important word. It is missing the word, *LOVE.* I believe, it should say, 'I AM *LOVE* THAT I AM,' thus linking us to the *Divine* consciousness of the *Void* itself!"

"Bravo, Solar, you have rediscovered one of the great Mysteries that offer a Key to *Divine* Immortality. Nabyss had not only ripped out the last pages from *The Sacred Sea Scrolls,* he also tore out the first few pages, which preceded the story of creation. Within that page was the Key to understanding all Mysteries and the source of all power. The words were simple, yet profound. You can access those words and restore *The Sacred Sea Scrolls* as they were originally written. So, I suggest you shift into *Divine* consciousness and bring forth those missing words."

"But why, Domaine, if you already know the words. Why not simply tell me?"

"Because you must *re-learn* to do all things yourself, without relying on me or anyone else to do things for you."

"But . . ."

"No, buts. Just do it! Nothing is ever as difficult as it seems when we surrender and trust in our own intuition. We must always remember *we have the power* to reclaim all knowledge and information from across time and bring it forth into the present. Simply shift into *Divine* consciousness and bring forth the missing text. In fact, you can imagine yourself reading it directly from *The Sacred Sea Scrolls*."

Solar wanted to object again, but he realized it was no use. Having just accomplished the greatest feat of all time, this task seemed ridiculously easy by comparison. Thus, he closed his eyes and began shifting into the omnipresence of consciousness that would make his full manifestation into Godson a living reality. Once he shifted into pure radiant light, he set forth his intention to return to that time/space continuum where he once had full access to *The Sacred Sea Scrolls*.

The Doorway of Time opened before Godson, and he instantly went through it and found himself materializing in a library as large as the Great Hall of Temple grounds. He marveled at the immense proportions of this library, and the great activity taking place within it. All manner of sea creatures gathered to read about every imaginable subject. At its center, there was a book propped on a pedestal, inaccessible behind glass. It was the original text of *The Sacred Sea Scrolls* written in Luna's hand.

Godson saw himself as Solar, a merman of great power and light, standing before *The Sacred Sea Scrolls*. Godson drew near and noticed that Solar was looking through the glass and rapidly turning the pages with his mind, absorbing the contents of its pages in rapid succession. By a prompting from Godson's mind, Solar telekinetically closed the book and then gently opened to the first page within *The Sacred Sea Scrolls,* allowing Godson to read its contents with instant clarity.

THE GREAT MOTHER GODDESS wanted to know
about THE POWER and FREQUENCY OF LOVE
that bore Her, when LOVE spoke:

I AM the ALPHA and the OMEGA
the BEGINNING and the END
of all CONSCIOUSNESS!

I AM ALL THAT LOVE IS
from across the WHOLE OF TIME!

Wherever I AM, THOU ART.
Wherever THOU ART, I AM.

I AM THAT I AM
FOR I AM LOVE THAT I AM!

I AM THAT I AM
FOR I AM LOVE THAT I AM!

Godson threw back his head and bellowed, as Solar immediately leaped and turned, picking up on Godson's presence. Godson instantly disappeared, returning through *The Doorway of Time,* and closing it behind him as he re-materialized before Domaine.

"Oh, my! That was easier than I thought! Everything is becoming so effortless!"

"I see you found the information for yourself."

"Yes, Domaine, and I am grateful to you for prompting me to stretch myself beyond all previous limits."

Godson surrendered to the *Frequency of Love* returning to him from the *Void* in his moment of revelry. Domaine also shifted. Never had Domaine sought to leave his solitude and seek companionship because he had remained co-existent with the *Frequency of Love* as a reflection of his own *Divine* being.

Godson spontaneously found himself between the pulse point of two worlds–*the world of consciousness existing within the Void and the world of consciousness reflected within matter*. Although the initial journey to the *Void* had been a long and arduous one of intense concentration, he had become consciously connected to the *Void* and was now able to shift back and forth between both worlds easily.

"To think we are all struggling to reach the *Divine*," Godson said, with a touch of irony, "when the *Divine* has been within us all along. Oh, what an extraordinary adventure this is! We are journeying in the space vehicles of our bodies, within the time capsules of our lives, searching for the Mysteries to our existence, when they already exist within us! Is this the great cosmic joke you spoke of?" Godson said, finishing with a chuckle that turned immediately into laughter.

"Close enough."

"To think how seriously I have taken this world! Imagine my dilemmas and anger toward The Great Mother Goddess. Imagine my fierce sense of justice and contempt for violence and death, when it is nothing more than a . . ." Godson fell backwards, bellowing with laughter and could not stop. He began rolling on the floor, and even Domaine found his laughter contagious. Both laughed uncontrollably because of the mutual revelations crisscrossing their minds.

Godson never fathomed he would arrive at this conclusion. He now saw the world like a dream reflected in multi-dimensional realities experienced within the shifts and changes of time and space. Regardless of how things turned out in the world of matter, he remained *an Immortal Soul!* Only as a sea creature bound to flesh was everything lived as *a reaction to fear and the terror of death.* As a Soul connected to the *Divine, death did not exist!*

As a result of these revelations, Godson felt he would never again forget the truth. He felt ready to face Egoson, utilizing the immense powers of the Gods, to bring forth a peaceful end to The Final Reckoning.

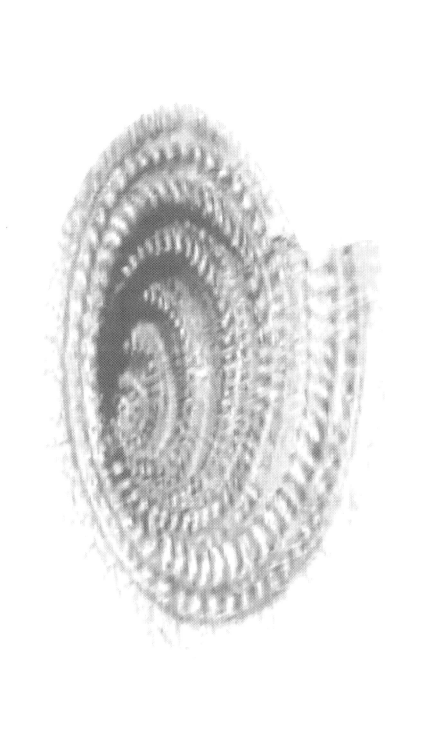

41

APPRENTICESHIP
OF THE SOUL

A text for The Divine Records of Consciousness?
There would be no physical place large enough to
house them, not even in the entire Kingdom of Oceana.

With gentle strength, Domaine spoke words that came spontaneously into his mind," *. . . and then will LIGHT stream into the world and into the hearts and minds of all creatures at The Final Reckoning. All will experience the Frequency of Love and know themselves to be full of LIGHT!"*

"Where do those words come from, Domaine?"

"From *The Sacred Sea Scrolls.*"

"How come I never saw them?"

"Because they are at the end."

"But Nabyss had destroyed the last pages of *The Sacred Sea Scrolls.*"

"He did. But I decided it was time to retrieve them."

"You did, just now?"

"Yes."

"Really, Domaine? If so, that was the fastest exit and re-entry through *The Doorway of Time* I have thought possible."

"But I did not retrieve them in that way."

"But that is how you taught me to retrieve them."

"I retrieved them instantly from *The Divine Records of Consciousness*."

"I don't understand. I thought it was necessary to access original past-life records by traveling through *The Doorway of Time*?"

"Let's take a moment, Godson, and place things into perspective so you can understand the natural progression of what you have been going through all these years. Are you interested in having an overview?"

"Of course. I am always interested in learning as much as I can. An overview would be nice."

"You have been undergoing an Apprenticeship of the Soul from the time you took your first breath in The Kingdom of Oceana. Everything you have experienced since then has been provided for your evolvement. The first official step in the Apprenticeship of the Soul took place when you awakened into knowing there was more to life than what was self evident to your eyes. You began shifting from the experience of separation from your Soul and began learning how to do things by connecting to your Soul. The first moment you experienced telepathy, for instance, you found yourself engaged in Soul to Soul communication. Remember your first experience of telepathy?"

"Yes, when I encountered the sea monster and heard its thoughts clearly."

"That's correct. You also made mention that you remembered encountering an elusive *Presence of Light* after you molted your shell for the first time. It was your Soul that picked up on this presence and made you aware of it. There was no one to tell you that presence was there, and even your eyes deceived you into thinking you were making it all up. But your Soul made contact, and in doing so, the activation of your higher intuition began. This has all to do with the first stage of the Apprenticeship of the Soul. Is that clear?"

"Yes, quite clear."

The second stage of the Apprenticeship of the Soul shifts you into the consciousness of your Soul, giving you the opportunity to witness the world from inner dimensional planes of existence. Your first contact with The Record Keeper is an example of this stage. You ordinarily could not speak to a rock. But when you shifted *inner dimensionally* and made contact from your *Soul,* you were able to speak directly with the consciousness of the rock existing as The Record Keeper. You successfully shifted from third dimensional consciousness to fourth dimensional awareness. Any questions, or shall I go on to the next step."

"You may."

"Now, the third part of the Apprenticeship of the Soul has involved shifting into the evolving consciousness of a Master, who surpasses the abilities of the ordinary citizen of The Kingdom of Oceana. Once you were able to sustain the energy and light of The Dance of the Sacred Spiral of Life, your inherent abilities as a Master began re-emerging. For instance, you can now open THE PORTAL OF LIGHT and release Souls of Darkness who have taken possession of sea creatures. You can begin the healing process simply by touch or the sweep of your vision and even *see through matter.* You have developed the clairvoyant abilities to see into a sea creature's past simply by being in their presence. You prophetically sense things to come. You have also been taught to communicate with the sacred deities in charge of the fundamental elements of earth, water, fire, and air, and shift the weather by a command alone. You have been practicing these things and have succeeded in every attempt. Any questions so far?

"No, not yet."

"The fourth part of the Apprenticeship of the Soul involves applying Universal Laws of Creation. For instance, as a self-realized Master, you can shift into *Divine* consciousness, *at will,* without using any methods previously taught to you. It is the stage where, *the Word is made flesh,* immediately upon the spoken word. You will bear witness to this stage more easily now that you have returned from the *Void.* Only at this stage are you capable of facing Egoson, having the *Divine* powers to appropriately disarm him. By doing so, you will return The Kingdom of Oceana to its original state."

"I hope so."

"Hope is not an option to exercise at this level. Hope implies the presence of doubt. Only *conviction* will grant you effortless access to the powers of the *Divine* you exercise as Godson. Is that clear?"

"Yes, very much so."

"Good. The fifth and final step catapults you beyond any Apprenticeship whatsoever. This step involves becoming inseparable from the *Divine* and experiencing *Immortality* as a way of being. *The Divine Records of Consciousness* then become fully accessible to you without your having to do anything to reach for them."

"Domaine, I hope you'll forgive me for saying this, but I must. If everything is so easy for you, then why aren't you, Godson?"

"But I Am, Godson! And so are you! Being *Divine,* I can be anyone I wish! But the story must unfold *as it was written!* So, I exist as 'The Wizard' and you exist as 'Solar of The Original Ancestry of the Gods', shifting into Godson when it is necessary to play your part," Domaine said, winking.

"Slow down, or I'll never find my way back!"

"Have you had enough for one day? Shall we stop here?"

"No, I was joking. Let's finish and then I'll retreat to meditation and prayers for I am anxious to give thanks for this day."

"Good. So, let's see. Being *Divine,* I am able to easily and effortlessly access *The Divine Records of Consciousness.* For quick and easy access, think of them as existing all around you in the omnipresence of consciousness of the *Divine* that is part of everything. Get away from relying too much on your mind. *Your mind is your greatest obstacle because it is your greatest deceiver.* Unless what you ask conforms to what exists within the parameters of your mind, you may never get to the answers you seek. So, continue to loosen up as you already have. Otherwise, things may exist right under your nose, *but you will not see them!"*

"Oh, I see . . . I mean, *I know* what you mean," Godson said, drifting off to think about all that was said.

"Is that all?" Domaine asked, ready to close the subject.

"Actually, just one more thing. Does a text exist for *The Divine Records of Consciousness?"*

Domaine looked at Godson and in the next moment, laughed without stopping. Godson wondered why he found the question so funny.

"Don't ask me any more questions," Domaine said, stopping his laughter. *"Check for yourself!"*

Godson did check and then understood why his question was ridiculous. A text for *The Divine Records of Consciousness?* There would no physical place large enough to house them, not even in the entire Kingdom of Oceana.

Godson admonished himself for being irresponsibly reckless in his thinking. But then he realized he was meaning something else and began to clarify.

"Perhaps what I am asking is not so ridiculous after all. Doesn't everything that comes into manifest form become a record of consciousness in itself?"

"Yes, that's true."

"Isn't every point of consciousness connected to every other point of consciousness?"

"Yes."

"Therefore, if everything in manifest form is a record of consciousness, and it is connected to every other point of consciousness, then isn't everything in manifest form a doorway to *The Divine Records of Consciousness?"*

"That's correct!"

"As a result, isn't a grain of sand all I need to access *The Divine Records of Consciousness*? I do not need a library as big as the universe because all the records of the universe can be found by accessing the consciousness of one grain of sand and using it as a doorway to access everything else."

"Bravo, Godson!"

"In fact, I could access everything I need to know about The Kingdom of Oceana by looking into the coded records of information within the sacred spiral of life, which is far more minute than a grain of sand."

"Bravo, Godson, bravo! You are now living up to your name!" Domaine exclaimed, firing thunderbolts from his crystal wand as they dispersed into glowing tendrils of Starlight Magic.

Godson halted, glowing with pride, and then shrugged, recognizing he had had enough for one day. He then shifted from pure radiant light back into his physical form as Solar, while Domaine shifted back as well. As silence fell between them, the omnipresence of *Divine* consciousness filled their bodies with radiant light, vibrating with higher frequencies that could actually be heard all around them. In this higher state of communion within living flesh, they continued telepathically moving back and forth from each other effortlessly, *as one being of consciousness.* Solar succumbed to exhaustion when he deliberately shifted down, abruptly collapsing into the grounded energy of his body. Although he was very tired for having processed so much in so little time, he smiled knowing he had crossed over into the Immortal consciousness of the Gods, and he would never have to return to the way he had been.

PART V

THE FINAL RECKONING

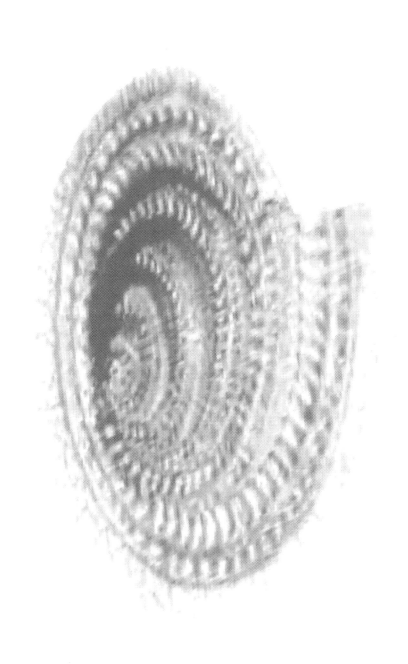

42

TRACKING DARKNESS

Seeres never let on that fear had entered her,
which could be DEADLY in tracking Darkness.

Theia moved silently into the open doorway of Solar's room, thinking she went undetected. Solar could feel her near and was always expectant of her before she entered. But this time, he chose to remain observant of her without turning to greet her.

Theia was able to get closer to him than usual and study the luminous Mantle of The Sacred Sea Dragons in the spiraling pattern that dominated his huge back. In eight months he had miraculously recovered from all his injuries–his wounds were healed, his eyesight was restored, and overnight he had shape-shifted from young Solar into an adult. She also marveled over his extraordinary leaps in consciousness, knowing it was the work of that Magician and Wizard, Domaine.

Theia had grown very fond of the old Wizard, who could shape-shift back into youthful flesh at will. But it was his example as an incomparable healer that won her admiration and respect. No one at The Temple of Healing could match his unparalleled abilities. She wondered how long it had taken the Wizard to reach such a level of knowledge. She had often tried teasing his age out of him, but she had not succeeded. Having lived in seclusion all his life, Domaine could not tell her. Without common references to daily life, he had no way to mark his time or his age. He had simply said, "Old enough."

Theia took the opportunity to remain in Solar's presence during his intense distraction. She assumed he was in deep meditation, looking across parallel worlds and dimensions, or even time traveling. Since she could no longer pick up on his thoughts, she had no idea he was bearing witness to all her thoughts, feelings, and speculations.

Once Domaine had taught Solar how to keep his thoughts blocked from others, the roles between Theia and Solar had dramatically changed. She was still recovering her pride. Although The Mantle of The Sacred Sea Dragons proved he was the reincarnation of Solar, her doubts remained. This was *not* the god she expected. How could this be Solar if he could not shape-shift back to a merman and restore himself to The Original Ancestry of the Gods? And what about Luna? Where was she? When was she going to show up? Nor did Theia imagine the Prophecies would come to be fulfilled in her lifetime. All this made her profoundly skeptical.

Theia had only recently begun to see past Solar's appearance and dwell on the radiant light and inner love that filled him with beauty. It was this inner beauty that deeply moved her, as she began to feel self conscious in his presence. Feelings stirred inside of her she could not explain. Whisperings of vague memories surfaced at the edge of her awareness. Feverish dreams of heartache and disappointment crowded her nights, as she struggled to understand why these conflicts recently emerged and persisted. Whenever she tried to pursue such memories, they vanished! Only in Solar's presence did she find tranquility in her heart, which left her feeling more baffled than before.

Theia thought of avoiding Solar because of her growing affection toward him. She had thought of him often and had begun wondering whether she should counsel with Domaine. Perhaps Domaine could teach her control over her thoughts and feelings and how to effectively block them as well.

When Theia considered calling out Solar's name, he turned as if in response to her thoughts. For a moment, she wondered whether he had been distracted at all or whether he had picked up on all of her thoughts. This made her blush before she brought her reaction under control.

"Well, hello! It is always a pleasure to see you!" Solar bellowed, to distract Theia from her reaction. "I hope there is nothing urgent that has brought you around this morning."

Solar spoke quickly so as not to betray her, nor himself, for his inner dimensional voyeurism. He had become very sensitive to her feelings and protective of his own. When he had finally looked into the eyes of the Priestess, who had been but a voice to him beyond the veil of his blindness during his recovery, he became thoroughly overwhelmed by her beauty. His heart tangibly leaped inside his chest, and he was pierced by feelings he had never known.

"It is easy to get away from my responsibilities when it means looking in on Godson himself!" Theia said, bowing.

"Please, Theia, please!"

"I was only teasing. But, actually, I did come for a very good reason. I thought you would like to know that Domaine has announced he will be leaving today."

"What? *No! He can't be!*"

"Yes, he is. He says his work is finished. Since you have regained your health, strength, and powers, he feels it is time to move on and return to his life of seclusion."

"Then I must see him!"

"Of course, you will. After he finishes teaching his last class at The School of Mysteries, we are scheduled to meet with him. I have arranged a small gathering at the Great Hall, so we can bid him farewell."

"Who else will be there?"

"Sonar, Starborn, Seeres, Mysteia, and myself. Everyone else at the Temples has already taken leave of him."

"Seeres will be there too?"

"Yes."

"How could that be? I thought she was seriously ill?"

"She was, but not any more."

"Domaine?"

"Yes, by the one and only. Seeres had caught Domaine's attention because of her piercing cries during her feverish delirium. He then personally attended to her and recovered her Soul because she had gotten stuck between worlds. I understand that is what he did with you at the beginning of your healing."

"Yes, we first met in the Realm of Lost Souls. It was an experience I will never forget," Solar said, shifting away from Theia and recalling the cord that had bound him to the Lord of Darkness. Solar remembered the eyes where hell reigned in perpetual Darkness. In his innocence, he was not frightened, but curious.

"Solar?"

"Sorry, Theia, I was recalling my first meeting with Egoson and still wonder how Nabyss could have fallen so far. Anyway, did Seeres recover completely?"

"Yes. Once Domaine recovered her Soul, his next step was to heal the growth that had swelled inside her brain adjacent to her third eye. It was because of the growing pressure of the tumor inside her head that she went delirious. Domaine miraculously healed her of this, although she will be unable to return to her duties as the High Priestess of The Temple of Prophecies and Oracles. She can no longer shift into altered states without triggering the growth of the tumor once again."

"How did Domaine heal her of the tumor?"

"Actually, Seeres was beyond any help we could give her because of the location of the tumor. But Domaine taught us healing techniques we had never employed at The Temple of Healing, which will dramatically shift the way we do healing in the future. For instance, he demonstrated how we could communicate with the consciousness of the body and dialogue with the diseased part to find the cause of the imbalance. He taught us the entire body is not only *conscious,* it is also *intelligent.* Every cell and organ is quite capable of communicating any imbalances that exist within it and then provide the information required to bring about a cure. To witness such a dialogue with the body is quite extraordinary. Once we understood how we could deal directly with the imbalance, following the method of healing prescribed by the body, we were able to dissolve her growth in a very short time. Today, she is completely healed."

"Wonderful! But I thought the High Priestess of The Temple of Prophecies and Oracles could not become ill because she maintained a direct alignment with *Divine* consciousness?"

"Yes, that is ordinarily true."

"Then how did Seeres develop the growth?"

"In one word, *fear."*

"What do you mean?"

"Because Seeres was being called upon daily to anticipate Egoson's moves, she was carrying most of the burden of tracking Darkness. She never let on that fear had entered her psyche, and that is *deadly* in tracking Darkness. The purity she possessed was her protection because without fear, nothing could penetrate her defenses. In fact, she was so good at tracking Darkness that she was able to crack the mystery of how Egoson got hold of the smaller Blue Crystal of Galexia, held in keeping at The Temple of Worship. It was quite a shock to us when we realized it was through *telepathic mind control.* At least we were relieved that it was not someone from the inside playing both sides."

"Have you found a way to guard against that in the future?"

"Yes. We have established force-fields of energy in most critical places to prevent telepathic intrusion using the sonar capabilities of dolphins to block any transmissions. But we do not have enough dolphins working round the clock to cover Temple grounds completely. We are still vulnerable in some places and at certain times. At least, we have more protection than we had before."

"Apparently, it was not enough to protect Seeres."

"Solar, no Priestess can be protected while tracking Darkness. If fear should enter, it needs to be cleared immediately. Seeres said nothing about her fear because she believed she could handle it. Otherwise, she would have been placed behind protective force-fields to recover her strength and release any negative disturbances that might have penetrated her natural barriers of protection. Since tracking Darkness creates quite a strain on anyone, Seeres nearly paid with her life. She collapsed when trying to find out what became of the two sacred eels missing from holy ground. We were trying to determine whether to send out a search party for them. We should not have pushed her so far, although she insisted on doing everything she could to find them."

"What a shame."

"Yes, it was unfortunate. Mysteia and others at The School of Mysteries have debated whether tracking Darkness should ever be given to someone of such innocence in spite of having automatic protection. Considering what atrocities she witnessed in her visions, how could she sustain her innocence?"

"Who would tract Darkness if not the High Priestess of Prophecies and Oracles?"

"Someone like me because I have a lower physical vibration that would be in less conflict with the lower energies of Darkness."

"But unless you are free from fear entirely, you, too, can get trapped by your visions as well."

"I have an understanding of Darkness no other Priestess has because I had spent the first half of my life in the outside world being exposed to all manner of Darkness. It was the Will of The Great Mother Goddess I should be born outside Temples grounds to know evil by having direct contact with it. When you are born surrounded by evil, it becomes very difficult to see beyond it. I was chosen, like you, to see if I could rise above it on my own and become an example to others. I almost died trying to see beyond evil by loving creatures who turned their hate on me with greater vengeance because they were tortured by my love instead."

"I am sorry to hear of your painful trials, Theia. How did you arrive here?"

"I was left as an offering for the dead after being subjected to torture during black mass. If it weren't for Jason, a giant sea turtle, I would not be here today. He discovered me floating near shore, barely alive, and carried me on his back to The Temple of Healing."

"Oh, my! I had no idea!"

"Jason saved my life, and I shall always be grateful to him. We all face difficult trials, and I was no exception. Through those trials I was taught about the forces of Darkness, and how far they go in submitting sea creatures to relentless torture until they finally die. If it were not for those painful experiences, I would not understand why it is so difficult to live in the world beyond holy ground, and how easy it is to succumb to anger, hatred and revenge in reaction to evil."

"I have heard that Mysteia teaches about the challenges of evil at The School of Mysteries."

"Yes, she does. She has alternated her lifetimes between living on holy ground and the world outside to bring her experiences into the classroom, providing actual encounters with evil from her many lifetimes. Mysteia has become an expert on evil. For instance, during a lesson, she said:

> 'Without claiming the Keys to understanding evil, sea creatures
> are lost in a world they do not understand. Corrupted by forces
> of Darkness, they are eaten alive by predators living in the
> underworld of their minds without their knowing. It is one thing

*to face a predator that threatens your life physically; it is another
to face a predator that exists in contact with your mind! Such
invisible predators claim your mind slowly until you become
like the walking dead yourself. Without conscious intervention,
the underworld of the mind gives rise to these insidious
manipulations by Souls of Darkness, who simultaneously rob you
of life force. If not removed, they become increasingly threatening
to your health. Invisible predators will also trigger your fears
and then feed on the energy of your reaction. Like sharks feed on
blood, they will continue to do so until they have devoured you.'"*

"Mysteia is quite blunt in her teachings, isn't she?"

"Yes, she is."

"Domaine made a point of providing many lessons on evil to help me understand how Egoson malevolently gained access to the collective underworld of our minds. Egoson increased fear so dramatically that he is now able to manipulate sea creatures by the thousands."

"Solar, you will inevitably need access to all of your resources, knowledge, and power when you finally confront Egoson."

"I know."

Solar wanted to know more about Theia's trials, but he would not trespass into her deeper memories. Flashes of distressing memories came spontaneously into his mind from her past, but he shifted away from them because he found it unbearable to think of her as a victim of evil. He hoped that Theia would someday share her more personal experiences with him as a way of inviting him into her life as a friend.

"I will bring Seeres by the Great Hall about the middle of the afternoon. Will you be there?"

"Of course."

"Is there any chance Seeres might return to The Temple of Prophecies and Oracles again?"

"Solar, once a Priestess leaves the womb of that existence, if only for a short time, she can never go back. Another Priestess is already in training, undergoing the Initiations necessary to become the High Priestess of The Temple of Prophecies and Oracles."

"I see."

"For the time being, Seeres has been placed on a special diet to lower the vibrational field of her body, so she can be exposed to sea creatures of lower energies without getting nauseous and sick because of her heightened purity and sensitivity. At least, she will no longer live a life of isolation. In many ways, Seeres is experiencing all of this as a blessing. She has wanted to come into personal contact with others, but she would never have asked to be relieved of her duties, as long as The Great Mother Goddess was in need of her services. Her extreme loyalty to The Great Mother Goddess ultimately set her free."

Solar studied Theia as she spoke, noting every nuance of her expressions, while all other things faded around her. At times, he heard no words. She stood before him as the glowing embers of a fire that ignited the first moment he saw her and continued to burn without pause ever since. Solar allowed his energy to expand toward her in loving affection, so he could express his feelings beyond the imprisonment of his shell. Outwardly, he gave her but a weak smile.

"What if I bring Seeres a little early to meet you before the others arrive?"

Theia waited for an answer, but Solar did not reply.

"Solar?"

"That sounds like a good idea," Solar instantly replied, snapping back to reality. "I am looking forward to it. It will be a wonderful celebration!"

"One word of caution, though."

"What's that?"

"This will be the first time Seeres comes in contact with others in a social context. She is quite sensitive and very, very shy, so be mindful of her."

"Would I be anything else?"

Theia smiled, while Solar felt the rippling effects of that smile reduce him to a child in love.

Theia shifted uneasily and decided to change the subject.

"By the way, Solar, have you gotten any guidance on what is going on?"

"What do you mean?"

"Egoson, of course."

"Oh, yes. Egoson is stepping up his reign of terror, and the results have been devastating. It may be time to stop him before things get any worse."

"Do you think you are up to it?"

"Apparently, or Domaine would not be leaving."

"No matter where he goes," Theia said, thoughtfully. "Domaine will *never* be far from us again."

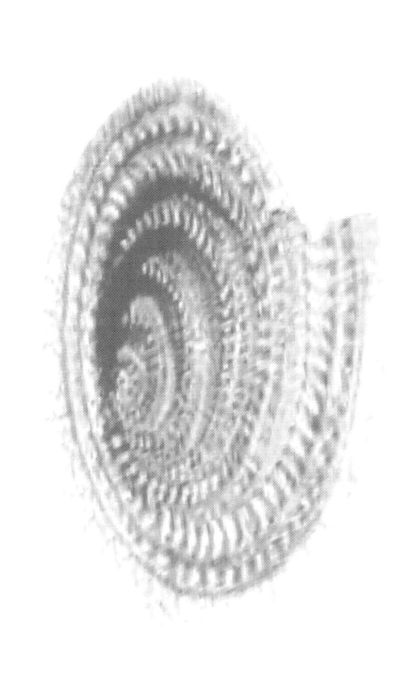

43

SOVEREIGNTY OF
FREE WILL

Any attempt to heal him becomes a trespass
violating the Sovereignty of his Free Will . . .

Solar entered the Great Hall feeling heavy hearted. Although he was looking forward to seeing his friends again, he was saddened that his mentor was leaving. Never did he believe Domaine would leave The Temples of the Goddess of the Sea knowing the threat Egoson posed to The Kingdom of Oceana. No one was safe any longer except on holy ground. He had assumed Domaine would continue to guide Temple Priests and Priestesses in developing their healing abilities and even seek protection for himself.

Solar began reviewing his memories of Domaine with nostalgic affection. He lingered on two, in particular, where Domaine had changed one of the most fundamental doctrines of healing that had been in existence at The Temple of Healing since its inception. His thorough assessment of a situation on multidimensional levels poignantly reminded Initiates that traditional healing methods were not always the most effective way of healing, when one considered the will of the Soul. Although controversial,

Domaine's wisdom remained uncontested and thus set a new precedent within the healing community for the caring of those sea creatures, especially those *without a will to live.*

* * * * *

"There is no more we can do for this sea creature," Domaine concluded, after examining a sea horse taken ill. "All we can do is make him comfortable until he transitions."

"But we have seen this kind of illness before," Sonar interjected impulsively, "and we have been able to cure it."

Sonar spoke up among the Initiates of Temple Priests and Priestesses, who were studying healing methods at The Temple of Healing under Domaine's guidance.

No one but Sonar questioned Domaine's authority and healing methods, especially after witnessing miraculous healings performed by him that were previously thought impossible.

"That is correct," Domaine said, looking over at Sonar with loving patience. "I am well aware of what can be done. Perhaps you can tell me what is different in this case?"

Sonar said nothing. He had spoken up too soon without considering the deeper reasons for Domaine's diagnosis. Rather than coming up with shallow reasons to cover his pride, he withdrew rather than defend his ignorance.

"I don't know," Sonar said. "I realize there must be more than is apparent to the eye."

"That is correct. The *more* involves looking into the inner dimensional realms of consciousness where we make contact with a sea creature's Soul. If a sea creature's Soul is not in alignment with healing, you will attempt all manner of healing methods to save him, but it will be for nothing. You would only be postponing the inevitable, and perhaps, even increase his suffering.

It is always appropriate to scan a sea creature's internal consciousness, make contact with his Soul, and then ask if healing is possible. If it is, then continue to do everything you can. If it is not, then do everything you can to make the sea creature comfortable, but do nothing to rescue it from its own fate."

Uneasy feelings stirred among the Initiates. This idea was new to them and ran contrary to their oath to heal all sea creatures, regardless of circumstances, whether they served Darkness or Light.

"I understand your concern and your oath," Domaine responded, without anyone speaking up. "Allow me to give you an example of what I am saying. This sea horse lost his mate to the gangs of Egoson, when a group of his friends and his mate were surrounded and killed. He was the only one who survived because he was left for dead. By tapping into this memory, you can see this sea horse has *no will to live!* Because sea horses mate for life, his only desire is to surrender his life so he can be reunited with his beloved. Any attempt to heal him becomes a trespass violating *the sovereignty of his free will* that would only prolong his suffering. Under these circumstances, I doubt anything you do can save this sea horse from himself."

The Initiates became silent, including Sonar. I, together with other Initiates opened up our consciousness to communicate directly with the Soul of the sea horse, and it was then we felt overwhelming sadness and grief emanating from his energy field. It permeated his entire being, and with greater awareness among us all, it permeated the entire room. Some Priestesses started to cry in response to the terrible tragedy that instantly came to mind when we communicated with his Soul. We then understood why this sea horse had succumbed to incurable grief that had translated into incurable illness. Without the companionship of his friends and the love of his twin flame, there was no reason to live.

Sonar withdrew energetically from the room, embarrassed that his question had brought such a poignant answer affecting us all very deeply. He was unaware how grateful we all felt toward him, for his question revealed an answer about the power of free will we may not have learned if not for him.

* * * * *

The most recent healing Solar had witnessed in Domaine's presence had to do with The Sentinels of the Sun.

The Sentinels of the Sun had been on extended watch for three days. They were working round the clock. Two and sometimes three or four sets of The Sentinels of the Sun were acting as Guardians at the entrance to The Temples of the Goddess of the Sea. The sudden flood of sea creatures moving across the borders of holy ground fleeing from Egoson and his gangs made it necessary for them to double up. The dramatic increase in possession by Souls of Darkness forced them to work like never before. Exhaustion had been setting in and several Sentinels of the Sun were taken to The Temple of Healing to restore their energy levels with the help of Initiate Priests. One in particular came to Domaine's attention.

Domaine and Solar went immediately to the Sentinel of the Sun because death was feared. Long hours of work and persistent nightmares had not permitted this particular Sentinel of the Sun to recuperate his life force sufficiently to carry on. Infusions of energy from Temple Priest and Priestesses were not creating a sufficient shift to recapture his energy and strength. Without appropriate intervention, this Sentinel of the Sun was doomed to die.

Domaine invited Solar to join him. He invited Solar to shift into the faculties of his *Divine* Spirit so they may together dialogue with the Sentinel's Soul and determine the healing to be done. Ever since the healing session with the sea horse, Godson's first priority was now to dialogue with the Soul to make certain that the Sovereignty of Free Will would take precedence over any action that would be deemed appropriate.

Godson stood on one side of The Sentinel of the Sun, and Domaine stood on the other side of him. With a nod from Domaine, they both shifted inner dimensionally and created an inner Sacred Sanctuary of Light around them where the Soul might be called in, and a dialogue could proceed between them all.

"We now invite Firelight's Soul to come through the doorway of the Sacred Sanctuary of Light so we may dialogue with him," Domaine said, with solemn intention. By holding Firelight's name in their minds, the Soul stirred from its place of refuge and appeared before a doorway that materialized within the Sacred Sanctuary of Light. With a little telepathic prodding from Domaine, Firelight's Soul entered.

"I am Domaine, Divine Emissary of The Great Mother Goddess and Master Gatekeeper between Worlds, and this is Godson, Divine Spirit of the Sun God. We have called you forth so you may dialogue with us and tell us how we may serve you."

Firelight's Soul burst into flames and the Sacred Deity of Fire spoke in his place.

> *"It was for the purpose of making contact with you, Domaine*
> *and Godson, that this Sentinel of the Sun known as Firelight*
> *was taken ill. It must be brought to your attention that Nabyss*
> *is plotting a major assault against The Temples of the Goddess*
> *of the Sea. His relentless persecution of sea creations has turned*
> *into wanton cruelty and mass murder. The general morale of*
> *the population is collapsing, making it easier for Nabyss and*
> *his Souls of Darkness to possess sea creatures. As a result, he is*
> *creating a formidable army likened in flesh to the Realm of Lost*
> *Souls, but of the walking dead! He is a Master Strategist whose*
> *powers grow with every day. So, BEWARE, for he, too, seeks*
> *your death!"*

The presence of the Sacred Deity of Fire instantly vanished, and Firelight's Soul was left hovering in its place.

"Thank you, Firelight, for becoming the Messenger of the Sacred Diety of Fire that you are. We express our deep gratitude to you," Domaine said, bowing simultaneously with Godson. *"Now, do we have your permission to do everything we can to restore you to the healing grace and oneness of being with The Great Mother Goddess?"*

"You have."

"Then we release you through the doorway of the Sacred Sanctuary of Light, so you may return to your body and assist us in restoring you to wholeness."

"Very well," Firelight said, bowing, before turning and exiting through the doorway. Domaine and Godson instantly materialized in the room, fleshing out their bodies in full consciousness. Domaine then signaled towards Godson to shift opposite him, as Domaine took his position at the head and began channeling energy through the temples. Godson channeled energy up through the body so that a circle of healing light would encompass Firelight and restore him energetically to wholeness.

Firelight stirred into full consciousness and color returned to his cheeks. The mask of Death that had begun to overshadow his face disappeared. He returned back to life to join the living in the energyzing presence of Domaine and Godson.

Just then another Sentinel of the Sun burst into the room before Domaine and Godson had completed their healing work and drew near. It stood in silence while the healing work continued, although it was apparent to Domaine and Solar that its distress filled the room from the moment of its entry. It was one of the reasons why healing rooms were locked so such interference could not take place.

In the omnipresence of consciousness, both Domaine and Godson continued their work, and also extended their life-force energy to the other Sentinel of the Sun. It too was in need of rejuvenation. Noting Firelight was stirring and coming to full wakefulness, a heavy sigh escaped into the room from this Sentinel of the Sun, who bore great love to the one whose life was almost eclipsed by death.

"Firelight!" The Sentinel of the Sun burst forth, without waiting for Firelight to become fully conscious. "Firelight!" he said once more. Firelight's eyes fluttered open at the mention of his name. With greater restorative energy from Domaine and Godson, he sat up to address his companion by name. Solar noted that Firelight's extraordinary recovery would not have been possible if his condition had not been deliberately created by his Soul. Once the reason for his condition was fulfilled by his Soul, recovery became effortless with Domaine's and Solar's help.

"Blaze, aren't you supposed to be on duty?"

"This is where my duty lies. Here beside you."

"You are always one to speak your mind and act out your own will," Firelight said, with taunting affection.

"Only when such service abides in the Name of The Great Mother Goddess!"

"My dear friend, you always have a *blazing* answer for everything! I wish I were as articulate!"

"On the contrary, you are more articulate than I!" Blaze said, turning to Domaine and Godson, who were witnessing this exchange without a word. Blaze then began the formalities of introduction by way of telepathy.

"Domaine, permit me to introduce myself, for I have heard of your extraordinary magic and evidence shows me all I have heard of you is true. I am Blaze, and you must be Godson. It is a pleasure to meet you both."

"And for me, it is a pleasure beyond words," Firelight cut in.

There was a mutual exchange of loving affection, natural and spontaneous between them all. Godson shifted his energy and so did Domaine, so they could all speak in the lower vibrational atmosphere of their physical presence.

It was the first time Solar had noted that while these Sentinels of the Sun were both male, Blaze had a female Soul, and Firelight had a masculine

Soul. Their love and attraction to each other became apparent in spite of their masculine form. Regardless, they deeply cared for one another with an abiding love. Solar noted that they too had become trapped by the physicality of their bodies and avoided any direct physical expression of their love. Yet, their male comradery allowed for physical affection, but only appropriate to the protocols of friendship.

Solar returned from his thoughts feeling nostalgia for the impending loss of Domaine's presence. He was deeply grateful for the healing protocols Domaine had taught him. It allowed him to be make contact with the Soul and follow the Sovereignty of Free Will, which always made possible the appropriate methods of healing. In Firelight's case, the healing was easy and immediate once Firelight had fulfilled the imperative of his Soul to deliver its message.

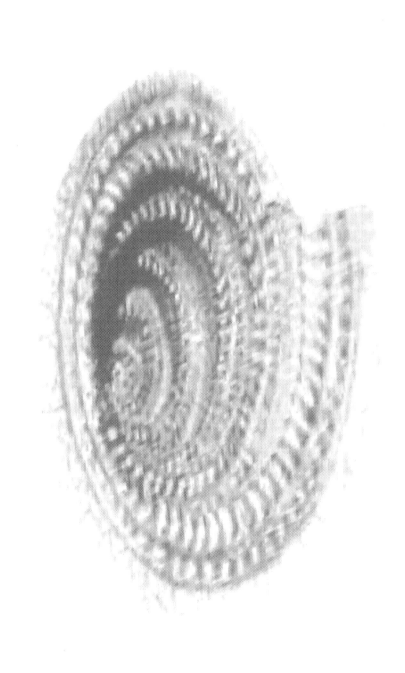

44

MYSTEIA, HIGH PRIESTESS OF THE MYSTERIES

Mysteia discovered that the Soul had an ingenious
way of transplanting the time capsules of unresolved
issues from past lives into the present-day consciousness
of the body.

The main teaching classroom at The School of Mysteries burst into radiant light. Shimmering colors coalesced into form from radiant light, as Mysteia fully materialized in the room. She had been time traveling, picking certain junctures in time and looking in on scenes from the past like an invisible ghost. She had been seeking answers to questions from past-life events and examining details overlooked when she had lived during those times. She had narrowed her focus to examining critical turning points in those lives that had dramatically shifted her life course into a direction of greater illness, pain, and suffering. She sought very specific, emotionally charged situations and reviewed them. She looked for clues that might help her understand the dynamics of her behavior over time, and how those events had shaped her future lives and impacted her health.

Mysteia felt she was becoming old, insofar as she had already lived three hundred years consecutively. While she prided herself in being one of the oldest living creatures in The Kingdom of Oceana, she felt three hundred years was nothing compared to the Immortality of the Soul. Although she was the High Priestess of the Mysteries, Mysteia failed to extend life in a body beyond two or three hundred years. Although she was praised for maintaining herself in excellent health and vitality by using the knowledge gained from the Mysteries in her keeping, she felt like a failure. She had not yet answered the most important question of her lives, which forced her to continue to drop her aged bodies in order to reincarnate into youthful flesh.

What has kept me from immortalizing
my flesh, so I would never have to grow old?

Mysteia's time travels were geared toward understanding the reasons for her failure, and why she was unable to sustain youth without triggering the aging process. In her research into the Mysteries, Mysteia had come to learn many things that made possible her extended life. As a result, she followed her own practices that guaranteed longevity within youthful flesh. Her methods were simple.

The first imperative was to enter into deep and profound meditation, until she became fully conscious with her Soul. Once she aligned with her Soul, she would shift the energy of her Soul into every living cell within her body. She achieved this by breathing the power of awakening consciousness into every cell of her body. She continued these breathing exercises until every cell became fully awakened and activated by light. Once she achieved this unified state of total consciousness, bridging the consciousness of the Soul with the consciousness of the body, she went on to the next step.

In the second step Mysteia then expressed gratitude to every part of her body: every atom and molecule, every cell and fiber, every bone and limb, every muscle and ligament; every organ and system, until she had reached every part of her *without exception*. Since the body was alive with its own consciousness, the expression of gratitude made possible a loving connection to the entire body. This created a unified, cohesive, working relationship between all consciousness within the body. Once the body became doused with the life-giving waters of gratitude expressed from self love, imbalances in the body became virtually impossible. The cells achieved optimal health and vitality as they achieved joyful cooperation with one another.

The third step was to invite an open dialogue with any part of her body that needed to unload any emotional tension within it. Whenever emotions became stuck in the body, they created tension, and then conflict, and then interferences until they blocked the natural flow of energy. Once energies became blocked, illness and aging became triggered.

Mysteia took notice where the emotional tensions emerged in the body. She discovered that their placement in the body would signal what kind of emotion she would discover there. For instance, the kidneys had to do with repressed fear; the liver with unexpressed anger; the stomach with self esteem issues or a lack of will or courage; the lungs with unexpressed sadness or grief, and the heart became a storehouse for emotions having to do with relationships, in addition to emotions such as remorse, regret, rejection, abandonment, isolation, loneliness, and so on. Each organ became a haven to emotionally specific, unexpressed or repressed emotions.

The fourth step followed the open dialogue with the body, once the negatively-charged emotions, which created disharmony and tension in the body, became known. Clearing away the emotional debris demanded a precision for detail and personal honesty to understand the underlying reasons for disharmony, so deceit would not be added to the list of emotions needing to be cleared. Only with the eyes of a seer committed to truth could the negative emotional currents of energy in the body come to light to be cleared.

The fifth step, once the body was cleared, was life-altering. It had to do with forgiveness. Any person, situation or circumstance that triggered a grievance where forgiveness was withheld of oneself or another person became a time capsule of pain that would inevitably progress into illness. Unforgiveness was like dropping burning embers into the emotional field of the body and expecting it to go out by itself. Over time denial of inherent goodness would take the place of unforgiveness and destroy the natural harmony of the body from the inside/out. Pure love and acceptance of oneself and others was an essential condition to eternal youth. Without it, aging was inevitable.

The sixth step was another important step. It required making contact with the consciousness of the Master Architect residing within *the sacred spiral of life*. It was this Master Architect working in cooperation with the Soul who triggered the aging process in all sea creatures. Aging was naturally triggered over time. Yet, by making contact with the Master Architect *telepathically*, Mysteia altered the aging process *by slowing it down*. Although this was considered a phenomenon reserved only for the High Priestess of the Mysteries, there was nothing mysterious about the way Mysteia proceeded to communicate with the sacred spiral of life.

Once Mysteia had shifted into the consciousness of her Soul, she called forth the Master Architect responsible for triggering all processes within her body, particularly aging. A radiant presence came looming before her, like a deity whose presence commands authority, knowledge, and wisdom. After expressing her gratitude and appreciation for all this deity does for her, she then set forth her intentions, impressing the image of the body she chose to keep.

Once her wishes were dispensed with the authority of a goddess who expresses dominion over herself, Mysteia received a response in the affirmative. The deity in charge of her sacred temple would dutifully carry out her directives. She then expressed gratitude without doubting all would be carried out, for it was a matter of *free will* expressed *without contention!*

The seventh step was also critical in slowing down aging, and the one that eluded her the most. That step had to do with past lives. It was the reason why she became compelled to time travel across lifetimes to dissolve the unresolved issues from previous lifetimes that still intruded upon her in the present lifetime.

Mysteia discovered that repressed memories, especially of unpleasant experiences, didn't go away. All memories got filed away and became imbedded in the deeper memory banks of her psyche and the energetic matrix of her Soul. Unless those memories surfaced and emotional issues became resolved, the unhealed issues of the past became the unhealed demonstrations of illness in the present.

Mysteia had recognized that all illness, without exception, could be tracked to painful emotions that never got properly processed or expressed. This became self evident after performing thousands and thousands of healings over the many years of her lives. Since emotions became currents of energy traversing the body, negatively-charged emotions had devastating consequences on the body, deteriorating its harmony over time, until serious illness became the result. Thus, illness accelerated aging, until death became inevitable.

Understanding this overall scenario, Mysteia came to understand that past lives contributed to present-day health in a similar fashion. Since the Soul contained all memories from previous incarnations, unresolved issues from past lives intruded upon and even compounded present-life situations. In fact, they often became the root cause that triggered present-day emotional conflicts.

Mysteia discovered that the Soul had an ingenious way of transplanting the time capsules of unresolved issues from past lives into the present-day consciousness of the body. Since the template of the Soul carries within it *all past-life memories,* the Soul transplanted the unresolved issues of past lives *energetically into the body at the time of reincarnation and birth.*

Although Mysteia was born into a pristine body at birth, the Soul triggered unresolved past-life issues during critical, parallel junctures and turning points in the present lifetime, reminiscent of previous lifetimes, so they might finally be resolved and released from the Soul's energy field. Once corrective healing measures were taken, unhealed issues and traumatic memories dissolved from the energy template of the Soul, never to be repeated again.

Without taking into account the subtle and sometimes blatant unresolved issues of past lives, health would inevitably suffer and aging would result because the repressed energy of denial kept things trapped and hidden in the body's energy field. Whenever Mysteia cleared an issue from her body, her Soul quickly pointed toward the next priority that came from lifetimes before.

Throughout Mysteia's many lifetimes, the greatest unhealed issue that remained constant was the loss of her greatest love, the wise sage, Metis. She repeatedly journeyed across time for the pure pleasure of connecting to the lifetimes of The Original Ancestry of the Gods, where she and Metis had shared their lives and founded The School of Mysteries together. Those sojourns into the past triggered present-day, ever—recurring emotions of sadness and grief, which made the present times stark and oppressive.

Certain memories of Metis remained as vivid as yesterday's experiences. Mysteia had only to close her eyes, and she would find herself in that time and place where she and Metis had shared their lives together. In her dreams and during her time travels, she often went to experience Metis in the fullness of love that existed between them. Yet, the memory became a double-edged sword when she returned because *the reality of the past became an illusion in the present.*

Mysteia remembered the day when her life changed forever and the Immortality of the flesh passed into history. The horizon to the east had cast colorful threads of a rising Sun God, orchestrating a symphony of musical tones Mysteia could perceive with the senses of her Soul. The music of the spheres of Heaven was most evident during the rising and setting of the Sun God and the rising and setting of the Moon Goddess.

Mysteia closed her eyes and instantly teleported herself to that time. She and Metis moved hand in hand ready to enter the Sacred Sanctuary of The School of Mysteries together. It existed in the uppermost room of The School of Mysteries. At this apex, the structure was totally replaced by glass except for the stone floor.

The Blue Crystal of Galexia stood in the middle of this immense room. It had been shaped into a conch shell, standing 7 feet high and 7 feet wide, reflecting the *Divine* insignia of The Great Mother Goddess in a carved representation of the sacred spiral of life. A small fragment carved in the same image of The Blue Crystal of Galexia had been kept on the altar in The Temple of Worship.

During the day, these windows reflected the rays of the Sun God from every direction. The light penetrating the glass would make contact with The Blue Crystal of Galexia, which would vibrate and cast forth *Divine* light. Together with sunlight, this *Divine* light would extend for countless leagues in all directions, making possible the name of origin for *The City of Light*.

Mysteia saw herself and Metis walk into the Sacred Sanctuary together, shifting into the solemnness and mindfulness of the *Divine*, although their hearts were filled with the playful flushed sensuality of their evening of love. They approached their morning prayers with sacred reverence, filled with joy in their hearts and a cheerful readiness to celebrate their lives in joyful reunion with the *Divine* Mother and Father of existence. They experienced the omnipresence of the *Divine* as an expression of themselves inclusive of the entire Universe.

This room was a Tabernacle for the Holiest of Holies–*the Blue Crystal of Galexia*—and therefore, was a place forbidden. The Blue Crystal of Galexia made possible direct access to *The Divine Records of Consciousness*, sometimes referred to as *The Book of Life*.

Mysteia, as the High Priestess, and Metis, as the High Priest of the Mysteries, held the Key to this room, and it was a Key coded within the sacred spiral of life within their being. Only during the Spring and Winter Equinoxes or the Summer and Winter Solstices did the other members of The Original Ancestry of the Gods come to this room to perform the sacred ceremonies that gave them access to The Blue Crystal of Galexia, which perpetuated their Immortality. Luna and Solar were the exception. They could come to this Sacred Sanctuary and access the *Divine* crystal whenever they chose. Nabyss was the other exception. Once he developed jealousy for his brother, Solar, he was no longer able to enter the Sacred Sanctuary under any circumstances.

The doorway into this room could not be trespassed, except by those who had undergone the highest Initiations into the *Divine*. The presence of the *Divine* crystal made certain of that. No one could be in the presence of the *Divine* crystal without succumbing to piercing frequencies that burst blood vessels in the brain and caused instant death.

That morning everything was the same. Mysteia and Metis had completed their prayers, and they reached for each other in a passionate kiss and a loving embrace which they held onto, knowing a full day would pass before their time would be their own once again. When Metis turned to leave, his flipper caught the edge of the *Divine* crystal, which cut him. Metis flinched.

"Metis, what is it?" Mysteia asked. Before he could answer, blood was already spilling from his wound.

"Metis! Your bleeding!"

"Darling, why be alarmed? It's probably a scratch, nothing more."

"I think it's more. Let me look at it."

Mysteia checked the wound. The gash was deep. Applying pressure would not be enough to stop the bleeding.

"I do not like the looks of this," Mysteia said, becoming serious. "You will have to stop by The Temple of Healing and perhaps get a spidercrab to stitch up this wound."

"Come here, my darling. Your passion rises even now. Why not hold me and let us seal the wound together with our love?"

Mysteia stood back for a moment and then relaxed into the arms that were already enfolding her. Metis always reminded her of the presence of *Divine* Love that he easily expressed towards her at all times. He adored her and worshiped her as a Representative of the Goddess, and when he made love to her, the gates of Heaven would open and ecstasy in every moment they shared together became the result.

As Metis kissed her, releasing her into the swoon of his love, they became as one flowing consciousness. Their bodies, kindled by the fire of their love, burst into radiant light as the frequencies of their escalating emotions carried them higher and higher until they became united with the *Frequency of Love.*

Mysteia and Metis remained suspended beyond mortal flesh, relishing the ecstasy of their union in *Divine* Love. Only at that level of consciousness did their Love transcend the pleasures of the flesh for a respite in Heaven and other worlds of exalted consciousness. United with the Stars, they experienced their Divinity in the omnipresence of consciousness. In that instant, the *Divine* crystal began to hum and then burst into radiant light, sending forth light in all directions. Only the Sun God could get this response from the *Divine* crystal when it reached the summit where it made contact with it.

Mysteia and Metis abruptly shifted back into their bodies, noting this phenomenon, which had never before taken place. As they did, *Divine* light from the crystal also became subdued and then quieted, until it returned to normal. They looked at each other and burst into joyous laughter because their love had ignited the *Divine* crystal into the full expression of its power, which had only been achieved by the Sun God.

"Oh, my Goddess!" Mysteia exclaimed, still wondrous. "Do you think we could incur the jealousy of the Sun God?"

"Only if the Sun God believes our love could compete with his light," Metis said, thoughtfully.

"Another answer would be better, my dear Metis, especially in this holy place. Let us say that we, as *Divine* children, liken the light of our love to that of the Sun God, who blesses us with the remembrance of our Divinity, every day that it graces us with its light."

"Indeed! Well said, High Priestess of the Mysteries! May those words be placed on *The Divine Records of Consciousness* so we remain ever one with the sacredness of all life, recognizing ourselves as part of everything. In the expression of sacred reverence, there is no place for competition of any kind. Everyone and everything has its place, and as long as we honor ourselves, we honor creation in all its expressions."

"Oh, I could stay in this holy place forever," Mysteia said, still swooning in the ecstasy of reunion.

"It is time we should be going, nevertheless" Metis said, taking Mysteia's hand and moving toward the door. We are going to be late for the teaching of our classes."

"Oh, Metis! What of your wound?"

"You need not look for it. *In the inviolable reality of love, I am healed of all things.*"

Mysteia flushed, recognizing that Metis did not doubt for a moment he would be healed. How often did she speak of *"the Word made flesh"* in classes with High Initiates, and it was Metis who constantly demonstrated to her the reality of those words because of his attunement with the *Divine*. In his presence, Mysteia felt she stretched beyond the reality of the mind into the reality of the heart.

Mysteia shifted back into the present moment mournful that it was the last time she would share the Sacred Sanctuary side by side with Metis. Although they had both dismissed the seemingly inadvertent cut by the

Divine crystal, it presaged a passing from the *Divine* into the mortality of the flesh. On that day Nabyss cursed his brothers and sisters of The Original Ancestry of the Gods and pledged his allegiance to no one but himself. By his words alone, he rent asunder the *Divine* matrix existing between them all, and from one day to the next, they became mortals as the beginning of the War of Chaos began. From that day forward, the Sacred Sanctuary remained a universe apart because no one was able to enter beyond its doorway once the *Divine* matrix was shattered.

Mysteia had often wondered about the experience she had had with Metis in that holy Tabernacle, and whether they had in fact angered the Sun God. The immediacy with which Metis had been "cut" by The Blue Crystal of Galexia upon their return from Heaven seemed an omen too obvious to overlook. Her words in that holy place were also better left unsaid. The power of manifestation at that level of *Divine* communion was always immediate, and in a place of holy power, instantaneous! Could it be they had gotten cursed that day, which finally explained why she had become separated from Metis by thousands of years?

Mysteia brushed off these thoughts impossible to fathom because she could not understand how their exalted love could ever be subject to such an unimaginable backlash. Perhaps there was, after all, an inevitability about the rise and fall of gods, from Heaven to Galexia, and back again. Did not the Ancient Ones of the Stars say, in *The Book of Life*, that during the cycle of the Great Year, consisting of approximately 26,000 years, there would be upheavals in the 13,000-year, crossover points of time, leading from the Golden Age of the Gods to the Iron Age of Mortals? Would not the Golden Age of Gods then inevitably return? If this was true, then Mysteia and Metis, even as Gods, were pawns within a greater stage of the Universe playing within the alternating cycles of the Great Year. Having completed a half cycle of the Great Year since the world had descended into chaos, then the Return of the Gods became inevitable and grace would be restored to one and all once again.

Mysteia shook her head trying to dispel such thoughts. At times they were too much to bear. A good day for her was when her mind would be distracted by the common occurrences of everyday life, and she would not think of such things. She often desired the life of an ordinary citizen because a life of simplicity would be a welcome relief after carrying the yoke of so much knowledge and information within her for so long. Because her clairvoyance never faltered in accessing *The Divine Records of Consciousness*, she was repeatedly pulled back into the unfathomable depths of such knowledge. Yet, as a High Priestess of the Mysteries, it was her Soul's mission to contemplate the Mysteries in her keeping. If not, her history with Metis and the life she had known with him would never have taken place.

Although Mysteia loved her work and service to The Great Mother Goddess, the absence of Metis took its toll on her, and no amount of service given open-heartedly could compensate for the absence of her one and only true love. Without Metis, she was cast adrift, alone in life. Although she had mentored many sea creatures undergoing exciting Apprenticeships, her reward in teaching was never enough to sustain her emotionally over the long run.

Part of Mysteia's passion for teaching was fueled by her search to find Metis, although she admitted this to no one. By looking through the windows of many Souls, she hoped to find his Soul living in another body, waiting to be awakened by her into full consciousness. Her desire for staying young was also because of Metis. She had promised him a long time ago that when they would meet again, she would look the same as when he last saw her.

Mysteia drew strength from her travels to the days of The Original Ancestry of the Gods, as she observed the effortless way she did everything. She never struggled with hesitation or doubt. She did not banter with indecision or worry about trifles. She did everything flawlessly. Her mind was a moving currency of energy with lightning impulses able to spontaneously ignite the primordial energies of the *Void* and manifest anything her mind and heart desired.

Mysteia shifted fully into the present, bringing her thought processes to an end. Weighted by a feeling of sadness and resignation, the glow of youthful vitality was inevitably drifting into aging, despite her vigilance to halt the process. Immortality eluded her as long as she remained incomplete without her true love. Her heart could not be satisfied with the promise of things to come, when the present-day reality left a stark void in her heart.

Mysteia looked in the mirror and brightened into a broad smile. When she looked deeply into her eyes and connected with her Soul, she shape-shifted into a more youthful image of herself. She ran her hands down her limps to awaken her passionate sensuality. Reflecting greater luster and vitality, she straightened up, contacting every cell of her body with the imperative to shift into radiant splendor. As the fullness of her presence became fully manifest, the Goddess Representative emerged, worthy of claiming herself as High Priestess of the Mysteries. The transformation was effortless knowing she was about to meet the incarnated aspect of Solar of The Original Ancestry of the Gods. Solar's appearance meant The Final Reckoning was near, and the time of her beloved's appearance, nearer as well. Her heart leaped ahead, leaving behind her sadness, as she headed toward the Great Hall with a lighter heart.

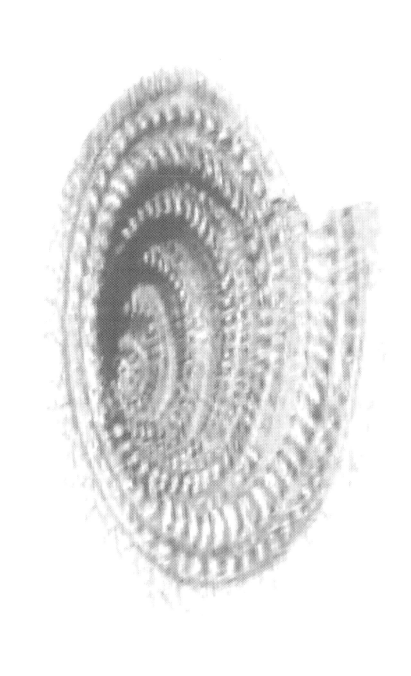

45

THE PROPHETESS

With his mind's eye, Solar saw no High Priestess next to
Theia, but a radiant light glowing in an oval form that was
undoubtedly Seeres. Solar smiled knowing the rare
novelty of meeting the High Priestess of The Temple
of Prophecies and Oracles.

Solar shifted back into the present moment after reviewing his recent times with Domaine. He looked down the length of the Great Hall and noticed the longest table he had ever seen. Marble columns framed the Great Hall on either side, supporting a cathedral ceiling of extraordinary breath and design. Stained glass windows cast beautiful peach-colored light throughout the entire hall, which magnified the sacredness and harmony of holy ground.

Solar looked for the altar to be found in every room on Temple grounds, which was a reminder of the omnipresence of The Great Mother Goddess. He took time to kneel and pray before the altar to express gratitude for his life. He celebrated the miracles he had witnessed, the mysteries he had come to know, and the friends that now filled his life. Though happy, an ominous feeling returned. Assuming it was because Domaine was leaving, he dismissed it, accepting he would be completely on his own again. Remembering the warning given by the Sacred Deity of Fire, he shuddered. Though his confrontation with Egoson was inevitable, at least today, he could forget about all of it and enjoy his time with his friends.

Solar asked for guidance because he knew his confrontation with Egoson was near, and he wanted to be prepared for that inevitable moment. As he waited for the answers to materialize in his mind, Theia approached before he had completed his prayers.

Using his mind's eye, Solar saw no High Priestess next to Theia, but a radiant light glowing in an oval form that was undoubtedly Seeres. Solar smiled knowing the rare novelty of meeting the High Priestess of The Temple of Prophecies and Oracles. How extraordinary that such a High Priestess had spent her entire life in isolation, so she could remain in perfect communion with The Great Mother Goddess.

Solar felt a tremor move across Seeres's energy the moment she caught sight of him. He saw her dim a little, as she began to study the luminous Mantle of The Sacred Sea Dragons on his back. He got up slowly and turned because he suspected she would know the significance of it, if given enough time to penetrate its secrets.

"Seeres, I want you to meet a very dear friend. His name is Solar. He has been working with Domaine at The Temple of Healing."

Solar turned to Seeres and looked down, as a show of respect for meeting a Goddess Emissary, before looking up again and into her face without focusing on her eyes. He thus avoided becoming too personal. She also did not look at him directly, but nodded her head ever so slightly to acknowledge him. Solar smiled, as he brought up his light with enough intensity to match the same luminous light coming from her, so no conflict of energy would exist between them.

Though subtle, Solar's shift in energy became apparent to Seeres. She then turned more fully toward him, acknowledging in her way what had transpired between them. Such a subtlety would have been lost on anyone else. But Seeres was so sensitive that her gifts of perception made everyone transparent to her. She immediately felt this stranger was no stranger at all, although she could not explain why. She was surprised to discover she could not get a reading on him, although she was quite mesmerized by the image on his back. It was a haunting, and yet, chilling image. Seeres knew it had great significance, but she did not study it long enough to get a full impression. Instead, she waited patiently for the mystery of it to unfold within the recesses of her prophetic mind.

Meanwhile, Solar noticed the stunning beauty of the High Priestess, whose skin shone like alabaster and whose energy bathed the entire area like moonlight.

"Solar, now that Domaine is leaving, how long will you stay with us," Theia asked, realizing he may be following in Domaine's footsteps.

"I cannot say. I will seek counsel with *The One Who Knows* to see about my next priority."

"I see."

"An answer you will have before the day is through," Seeres answered, telepathically.

Both Theia and Solar looked at Seeres in a state of query, but she did not say anything more.

"May I take the liberty of addressing you directly, Seeres?"

"Yes," responded Seeres, again telepathically. She was not accustomed to speaking with words.

Solar opened his mind to carry on a conversation without speaking.

"How does it feel to be out in the world, Seeres? Is it the way you imagined it would be?"

Seeres thought of her response before answering.

"Flesh, born of projection, does not know itself. I see only Soul, and creatures see only flesh."

"A good way to put it!" Solar said, nodding.

"Seeres's clairvoyant abilities will be a great asset to us at The Temple of Healing," Theia said. "She will be able to communicate Soul to Soul to get a diagnosis and detect the cause of any illness simply by the sweep of her vision."

"Fascinating! May I ask you another question, Seeres?"

Seeres nodded.

"Are you disappointed most sea creatures are not in alignment with their Soul?"

"I accept what is. What is not, I do not judge."

"I see."

"Having spent a lifetime speaking in oracles and nothing else," Theia explained, "it will take Seeres some time to master the spoken language. She has already come a long way. She has been practicing with Mysteia at the School of Mysteries."

"Good."

"Now . . . may I ask you . . . a question . . . as well?" Seeres queried, looking in Solar's direction.

"But, of course."

"The image? What is it?"

"What image?"

"The image on your back?"

"Oh!" Solar exclaimed, flashing onto The Dance of the Sacred Spiral of Light, as The Sacred Sea Dragons rose and explosively united in an epiphany of light that seared the image onto his back for life.

Seeres gasped and reeled backwards.

"See what happens when you let down your guard?" Theia said, teasing Solar.

But Seeres was not taking it lightly. She knew the significance of what she had seen. Because of her penetrating vision, Solar instantly shifted into Godson, whose brilliant light became drawn into full presence. He then opened his heart and beamed an invisible light toward Seeres to ease her alarm. The light enveloped her and brought her under its power. She was able to relax, but not before she brought her hands to her eyes and began to cry from the overwhelming shock of realizing her most secret desire—*to meet Godson in the flesh!* The Great Mother Goddess always grants a dream that has not been forsaken.

Theia went over to Seeres and put her arms around her to ease her uncontrollable reaction.

"It's all right, Seeres, it's all right. You have seen the truth for yourself. It was not meant to shock you. But you were fated, nevertheless, to know this moment."

"Forgive me. I have . . . never cried before. Even this . . . a blessing . . . from The Great Mother Goddess. So many gifts . . . all at once. I feel . . . so blessed!"

"Yes, you are, my dear sister," Theia said.

With a powerful yet gentle voice, Godson spoke on behalf of The Great Mother Goddess: *"Never again will you have to prove yourself to The Great Mother Goddess. Your purity of heart and fervent commitment to Her Will has won you favor with Her. Nothing will be denied you because of your faith and love for The Great Mother Goddess."*

A new wave of tears shook Seeres as she cried in reaction to The Great Mother Goddess speaking *through* him as the words penetrated her heart with a piercing glow. She became like a child again. A new life had begun, and she was never to be the same again.

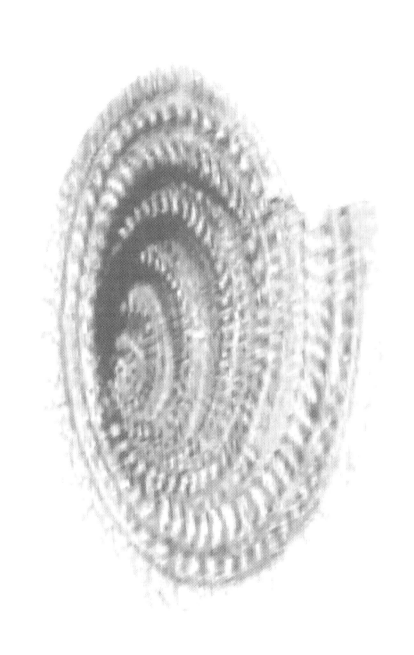

46

A GATHERING OF FRIENDS

Sonar smiled back and relaxed knowing he was
in a gathering of friends.

Theia sat holding the High Priestess who had never felt anyone's affection as flowing energy enveloping her with radiant warmth. Her life of isolation never permitted such physical contact since she was five years old. Even then, affection had been minimally expressed to her. She gratefully submitted like a child to the energy of love, which she did not know she craved until then.

"Well, Seeres, I thought I had already brought you out of your feverish delirium," Domaine said warmly, as he approached with Mysteia, having read the entire situation and responded to it in a light-hearted way. He charged his words with gentle meaning to make her feel at ease and allow her to accept herself with openness and freedom.

Seeres turned to Domaine and lowered her head in acknowledgment of her veneration for the Wizard. He bowed in return, as she turned to Mysteia and telepathically acknowledged her as well.

Domaine acknowledged Theia and then bowed toward Godson, lowering himself even further at the waist saying: *"My Lord, Godson!"*

Laughing, Godson resumed the more earthly manifestation of himself as Solar, so all could relax in the lower vibrational atmosphere of his physical form.

"It is always such a pleasure to see you, Domaine," Solar said, as he tapped Domaine affectionately on the shoulder.

"No, no, it is *mine,* especially when I am in such beautiful company!" Domaine said, with eyes beaming toward Theia, Seeres, and Mysteia.

"Solar, I believe you are the only one who did not meet Mysteia, the High Priestess of The School of Mysteries."

"It is a pleasure to meet you finally," Solar said, extending a warm smile. "I have heard much about you. Whenever I visited The School of Mysteries, you were impossible to find," Solar said, alluding to Mysteia's ability to shift into a place of invisibility, which was not lost on Solar.

"It is an honor to meet you also, Solar," Mysteia said, her eyes sparkling, extending her webbed hand before she retracted it as she looked down at his claws.

"No, no, the pleasure is all mine!" Sonar interjected, as he cut directly in front of the beautiful Seeres before stopping before her. Starborn followed closely behind.

"My name is Sonar, a Temple Initiate," Sonar said, bowing. I do not believe we have met."

Seeres reeled backwards from Sonar's intense energetic response before Theia managed to get between them and shelter her from his energy.

"Sonar, I did not get a chance to tell you about Seeres!" Theia said, in a tense, restraining manner, simultaneously blasting Sonar's mind with enough information about Seeres, so he could act appropriately toward her. Sonar was shaken to the core at the realization that Seeres had only recently left the holy sanctuary of The Temple of Prophecies and Oracles. Without need for further clarification, Sonar became subdued.

"Seeres, it is an honor to meet you," Sonar said, turning to Starborn immediately. "This is my friend, Starborn. Starborn, this is Seeres," he said, looking toward Starborn, so everyone's attention might be redirected at him.

"How do you do?" Starborn said, awkwardly.

Seeres bowed her head in either of their direction.

"Greetings to you, also, Mysteia, and to you all," Starborn said.

"Oh, Mysteia, yes, how are you?" Sonar shot back.

"Ah, youth," Domaine said, chuckling, "it makes me feel so young and alive. I can hardly believe I have spent a lifetime in seclusion living entirely *out of my mind,* when this could have been the alternative."

Laughter erupted, dissipating the awkward tension as everyone noticeably relaxed. Seeres was the only one who witnessed the phenomenon of laughter without responding.

"To be sure, real experiences are filled with many more unexpected surprises," Domaine continued, as laughter swelled again.

"Yes, the mysteries of life are never ending," Starborn acknowledged, raising his star-shaped face into a smile.

"But where did the time go? I cannot tell you. It all seems like a dream now," Domaine mused, looking over at Solar and winking.

"Why don't you stay with us living on Temple grounds?" Theia asked, unable to keep from trying to change the Wizard's mind.

"Think of it. I have spent a lifetime in seclusion, and it has become a way of life for me. While I am very grateful for the adventures I have experienced here, it is time for me to leave and return to the silence of my own being. When I am needed again, I will be called out of refuge and return once more to The Temples of the Goddess of the Sea."

"I will miss our chats," Starborn said, already feeling the loss.

"There wasn't enough time!" Sonar cried out, dejectedly, as he became distracted from feeling self conscious around the beautiful Seeres.

"I had looked forward to our lessons, Domaine. There are still so many questions! Even those at The Temple of Healing will feel your loss."

"Remember one of the first things I had taught you, Sonar. By using the medium of your Soul, you can communicate with anyone—past or present, living or dead, far or near, creature or God! That means there are no limitations, whatsoever! Let Starborn explain many things to you ordinarily believed to be impossible, but automatically understood by his Star race. His innate ability to change form or regenerate a limb, for instance, by simply changing his thoughts, is a perfect example of what I am saying. Thought is the creative force capable of shaping the primordial energies of creation directly into manifestation. It would be wise, then, Sonar, for you to start accessing things in this way. You can delve into the deepest reaches of your being and bring out the unexpressed potential that lies at the very core of your restlessness."

Sonar retreated energetically in response to Domaine's words, hoping Domaine would not continue to speak about him too personally. But Domaine returned to the company of High Priestesses beaming with joy and shifted the subject.

Solar patted Sonar on the back as a way of reassuring him. Sonar looked into Solar's smiling eyes and felt the deep love and appreciation expressed towards him, and it calmed him. Solar reassured him telepathically that he always made a significant contribution to every situation. He was never to doubt it.

Sonar smiled back and relaxed knowing he was in a gathering of friends.

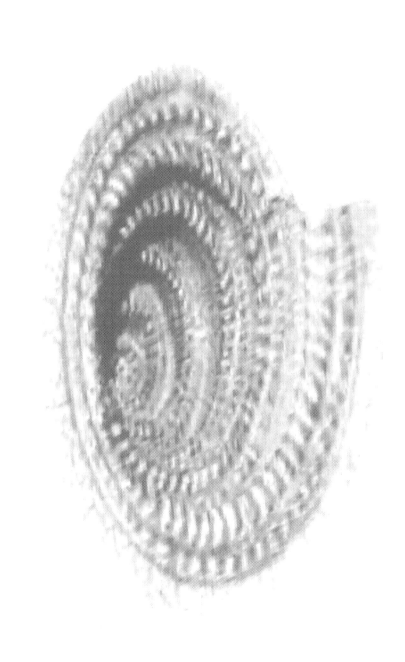

47

DEATH OF A WIZARD

Godson looked down into the impenetrable darkness
of the abyss and lost hope. Beside it was Domaine's
staff and crystal wand still glowing with radiant but
unchanneled power.

A scream shattered the empty pause and filled the Great Hall as a lightning impulse brought everyone to attention. Seeres screamed again as she brought her hands to her temples, while her face contorted with pain, and an ugly grimace took over her face. Another scream brought Domaine and Solar instantly to her side. Dropping to the floor, Seeres began to fight and kick as if struggling with an invisible demon. Domaine began channeling energy to either side of her temples to neutralize any negative forces attacking Seeres.

"Stop! Stop! Please stop!" Seeres screamed.

Domaine and Solar immediately withdrew, looking confused because the change in Seeres' energy, voice, and flow of words had changed dramatically.

Seeres went limp as she shifted into a fetal position. Her eyes remained open and unseeing. Domaine and Solar drew near again, but she waved them away as her body jerked forward. Undergoing a seizure, her body trembled violently. Again, she stopped, as the glow of moonlight around her body darkened dramatically. It was clear Seeres was no longer present. Something was taking over her body, revolting all of them from the sight of it. Seeres uncoiled from her fetal position and rose slowly and deliberately, as her eyes darted around the room from one to the other.

"Let me handle this," Domaine said, looking at Solar who was about to take action. Solar backed away in deference to his mentor. Domaine took hold of his crystal wand and stamped it to the ground and then brought it up to the sky as a lightning bolt moved through the length of it from Heaven to Earth. In the flashing brilliance of thunderlight, Domaine spoke ancient words as his physical form disappeared from sight. Only light remained in his place. Thundering words then echoed throughout the Great Hall, *"Who dares trespass the sanctity of my holy domain!"*

"Sonar! Theia exclaimed, unable to contain her surprise. That's *The One Who Knows!"*

"No way! That's Domaine!" Sonar insisted.

"No, it isn't."

"Yes, it is!" Sonar exclaimed!

"Who dares, but I . . . *EGOSON himself!"*

Sounding as hard gravel against stone, the booming voice spoke through Seeres, as Darkness intensified all around her. To everyone's shock and dismay, an abominable image materialized in place of Seeres. Her eyes turned into blackened pits of spitting flames. A flickering tongue reached up and covered her, as she disappeared into the blackened midst.

"We can't just stand here! Let's do something!" Sonar screamed, as he lunged forward to try and redeem Seeres from the Darkness that possessed her.

"Wait!" Solar said, throwing out his claw and grabbing Sonar by the tail. "Domaine will take care of this!"

"That's not Domaine!" Theia cried. "It's *The One Who Knows* who has taken his place to confront this monstrous creature!"

"But Theia. *The One Who Knows* would *never* materialize to fight in Domaine's place, unless . . ."

"Unless, what?"

"Unless, he is one and the same!" Godson thundered.

"Finally, we meet again! But this time, you will not be able to reverse my power and use it as a weapon against me. Now that I've found your physical counterpart in this world, you cannot attack me without attacking one of your own!"

"We shall see!" thundered *The One Who Knows*. A crackling currency of energy was discharged from Domaine's crystal wand toward Seeres, as Darkness dissipated around her instantly, and her limp form could be seen materializing below the disappearing mist. Seeres screamed as Darkness lifted, and her body was jolted off the floor from the magnitude of energy piercing her body. *The One Who Knows* checked the flow of energy, as Darkness returned in full potency."

"See what I mean?" the voice hissed, bringing with it a stench so fowl that everyone began to cough with sickening nausea, including Solar, who was helplessly bearing witness but was unable to act. Bound by honor, he could not interfere. Solar knew *The One Who Knows* had struck Egoson with the full potency of his power and wounded him through the inter-dimensional doorway. He sensed the stench was due to oozing membranes on the surface of Egoson's joints. Only *The One Who Knows* could reach Egoson on the other side of the dimensional doorway.

"Domaine, it's now my turn to send you to back to the Void!"

"You have no power over me, Egoson! Not with all the powers of Darkness at your command!"

"We shall see! I have powers at my command that not even you can overcome!"

Egoson thundered incantations in ancient words that brought tremors to the earth below and billowing waves moving in all directions as chaos erupted. Screams emerged from panicked sea creatures confused by the shifting earth and stormy currents that instantly materialized without warning.

Godson, Starborn, Theia, and Mysteia spontaneously shifted into unified consciousness, creating a force-field of energy powerful enough to spread in all directions, so all manifestations of chaos would cease. Sonar, although taught to shift in such a manner, was unable to release his rage, leaving him helplessly scrambling apart from them.

Together, they shifted into a powerful force gathering momentum, until the earth beneath them split apart as two spiraling forms of radiant light rose from the yawning chasm of the earth, rising higher and higher, until they reached the outer limits of the Great Hall. In the midst of blinding light, the unified force of consciousness faltered. Returning to normal consciousness, Solar, Starborn, Theia, and Mysteia emerged in time to witness The Sacred Sea Dragons poised to discharge their venomous powers.

"Sacred Sea Dragons, Gatekeepers of the *Void*, I command you to send *The One Who Knows* back to the *Void* from whence he came, *NOW!*" Egoson thundered.

Flames of iridescent lightning immediately discharged from the blazing mouths of The Sacred Sea Dragons directly onto the invisible force-field protecting Domaine's body. All sea creatures bolted as Solar, Starborn, Theia, and Mysteia emerged in breathless horror to witness thunderbolts of lightning ricochet upon impact with the invisible force-field.

The ground shook violently, shattering the stained glass windows along the length of the Great Hall, as shards of glass rained in all directions. Marble columns swayed from their foundations, toppling the cathedral ceiling in a thunderous pandemonium of unparalleled destruction.

"Take cover!" Solar shouted, as he grabbed Mysteia and Theia to protect them from the glass shards dangerously raining all around them. Never before had Temple grounds been shaken with such violent force that everything reeled in response. Thunderbolts of energy shot from the Great Hall killing everyone in its path and pulverizing them upon contact. All sea creatures panicked throughout The Temples of the Goddess of the Sea by what was undoubtedly The Final Reckoning taking them by surprise.

"Domaine! Domaine! Fight back! Fight back!" Solar screamed. *"Seeres cannot be saved no matter what you do! Save yourself then! Take charge of The Sacred Sea Dragons and destroy Egoson!*

No answer came from *The One Who Knows.* Instead, the apocalypse of The Final Reckoning was leveling the Great Hall in sections. When it seemed all would collapse in lieu of the impenetrable force-field sustaining the body vehicle of Domaine, an explosion rocked the Great Hall and everyone and everything was thrown back in all directions.

Muted silence engulfed everything as Solar raised his head in slow motion, wildly keen on bringing this nightmare to a dramatic end. Senseless, he had but one thought. *Domaine!* Moving invisibly amidst the raining debris, Solar shifted into a silence impossible to imagine, except in the *Void,* as everything stopped. His Immortal Soul had shifted into a parallel world where he was able to witness the chaos suspended outside of time.

Solar shot to the place he had last seen Domaine. As he came near, he looked down into the impenetrable darkness of the abyss and lost hope. Beside it was Domaine's staff and crystal wand still glowing with radiant but unchanneled power.

Solar snapped back into his body as the thunder crack of a column falling under crushing weight plummeted toward him in plain sight. Taking hold of Mysteia and Theia, he shot out of the way in time to avoid the shattering of marble against stone. Unharmed but shocked, Solar released the High Priestesses under the cover of a fallen roof, then dashed toward the place where he had last seen Seeres and Domaine.

Arriving at the place in his vision, Solar dropped to his knees alongside the still humming radiant crystal wand poised alongside the abyss. A cry of lamentation exploded from his war-torn heart that reached every corner of The Kingdom of Oceana with a message that the venerable Wizard was gone for good. The pall that fell upon sea creatures cannot be described for everyone had heard of this remarkable Wizard. Solar's lamentation was taken up by every sea creature at The Temples of the Goddess of the Sea until even The Great Mother Goddess became oppressed by it.

Solar got up abruptly as he thought of Seeres and made one more sweeping search to see if he could locate her body in the mountain of rubble before him. He dug madly through glass shards, wooden beams, and toppled marble columns in a feverish search for her. Finally, he lifted a beam and saw her bloodied, mutilated body lying in a heap. Though crushed, she was still glowing like moonlight in the shifting dust. Solar rent the ocean with a cry that thundered once more throughout The Kingdom of Oceana.

Solar could no longer bear the formidable pain of this reality, the shocking terror of it, nor the horrible violence that characterized it. Although he understood by the sheer power of Domaine's guidance that it was but a dream suspended in the world of matter, he longed for *Divine* unity and the reality of Heaven. He wanted to escape the wrenching avalanche of pain burying him into a pit of Darkness just then.

Solar recognized he could no longer vacillate nor doubt what he came to do. Egoson had to be stopped and stopped for good. No one else could stop him, and no one else could conquer him . . . except himself!

* * * * *

When Egoson came to, he was lying on his back against the wall adjacent to his altar. Yellow-green pus was oozing from his mouth and leaking from his joints, creating little running pools of festering maggots. He licked the pus from his mouth and joints with his flickering tongue and then swallowed hard because everything in his body was steeped in pain. He became angry because his body felt like it had become severed at the joints. Still, he had only to think of his magnificent triumph—destroying the physical counterpart of *The One Who Knows*—and his paralysis became reduced to incidental discomfort.

Egoson decided to savor his triumph by taking time for rest and relaxation, for recovery and healing, and for extended playful recreation. He wanted to have the final showdown with Godson when he was cocked to peak performance. By extending his foreplay of Godson's anger, fear, and rage, he would inevitably seize the ecstatic moment when he would destroy Godson. Egoson did not doubt Godson's weaknesses would become his strengths, now that Domaine was destroyed and his *Divine* counterpart, *The One Who Knows,* was released from The Kingdom of Oceana forever. Godson was already his prisoner, and he had only to put him into the chains of his own emotional reactions to destroy him.

Egoson commanded the Abominable Hags of Anger, Hate, Guilt & Shame, together with their Abominable offsprings, Lust, Blame, and Regret to appear before him. As soon as they came into view, they unleashed their venomous powers, so thick was their hatred for him. It instantly gave him the energy he needed to move freely. He sighed as their formidable energy made his joints and muscles swell enough to release him from paralysis. He then utilized their energy to make pawns of them under his will. Moving upon them one by one, Egoson hissed uncontrollably, unable to contain his pride from releasing all of his venomous passion into their despicable wombs in celebration of his most magnificent triumph to date!

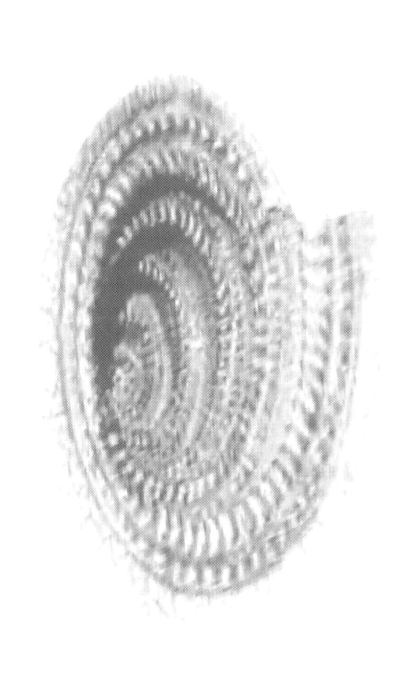

48

EDUCATION IN DEATH

What began as a celebration of life
became an education in death.

Solar needed time to sort things out by himself with the help of The Great
Mother Goddess. The loss of his mentor, friend, and guide, left him in a
blind state of grief, while the loss of Seeres, left him in a profound state of
bewilderment.

Mysteia had snapped from shock and was under heavy sedation at
The Temple of Healing. Theia had few injuries, but was seething with anger
from the violent trespass of Egoson's monumental cruelty and unparalleled
abuse of power. Starborn had suffered the loss of three limbs, and Sonar had
nearly lost an eye. Many sea creatures on holy ground had died struck by the
Thunderlight charges of The Sacred Sea Dragons power, or become impaled
by glass shards, or had been crushed by wooden beams and heavy marble.
What began as a celebration of life became an education in death.

Solar knew Egoson had penetrated to the very core of his being. He
had instantly reverted back to his old self when he reacted without trying
to understand what was happening with the help of his Soul rather than

the logic of his flesh. How could logic explain what happened when it did not make sense on any level?

Solar reeled from the tragedy based on what *appeared* to happen. By allowing the insanity of it to pierce his heart, he unavoidably reacted in pain, anger, and a readiness for vengeance. Solar knew he had dangerously come close to forsaking himself and his destiny. By allowing the full expression of his feelings without the tempering of wisdom, he had risked everything. A slip like that in the future would have devastating consequences. It would inevitably give Egoson the edge he needed to destroy him.

The reverberating pain of a reality steeped in madness persisted. Egoson had finally committed the most heinous crime imaginable on holy ground that could easily justify Solar's response in retaliating with all the powers of creation to destroy him. Since Solar could not kill Egoson, he needed to return him to the *Void* rather than plunge him into a pit of Darkness that had become for him a place of unparalleled power.

If Solar became tempted to destroy Egoson's body, it would be an empty victory because Egoson's Soul would rise to power in another body *possessed* by him. Only by assisting in his transformation back to his original consciousness as Nabyss could The Original Ancestry of the Gods be restored to *Divine* unity working in alignment with The Great Mother Goddess and The Great Father God once again.

During his lessons, Domaine repeatedly reminded Solar that Egoson, however deranged he was, remained his brother, Nabyss, who had succumbed to the insanity of power achieved at whatever means necessary. Nabyss set a precedent for evil when he chose to set himself apart from the natural laws of spiritual harmony to create a state of separation founded in fear, terror, and even death.

The One Who Knows had always turned Egoson's power against him, so Egoson remained at the direct effect of his own actions. But *The One Who Knows* had made an exception this time and counter-attacked Egoson, hoping to get him to withdraw from Seeres long enough to get her to safety.

His tactics only succeeded in creating a precedent for destruction never before seen within the holy sanctuary of The Temples of the Goddess of the Sea.

What Egoson did in destroying the body vehicle for *The One Who Knows* could not be underestimated. The Great Mother Goddess directed the evolutionary development of The Kingdom of Oceana through *The One Who Knows,* who in turn assisted Temple Priests and Priestesses with their Initiations into higher consciousness. Without that anchor of light in The Kingdom of Oceana over the past 26,000 years, The Kingdom of Oceana would have succumbed to self-destruction a long time ago. Now, it was Solar's turn to confront his brother Nabyss in the form of Egoson, but without making the same mistakes of the past. If Godson did not succeed, The Final Reckoning would inevitably bring on total annihilation, and the full cycle of re-genesis would begin again.

Solar had learned much during Egoson's tragic confrontation with Domaine. Egoson had destroyed the body vehicle of *The One Who Knows* by turning the primordial energies of the *Void* against him. Until that moment, Solar did not understand the full significance of The Mantle of The Sacred Sea Dragons, The Dance of the Sacred Spiral of Light, and the powers he reclaimed as a result of assimilating that awesome energy. He could equally invoke The Sacred Sea Dragons and return Egoson back to the *Void,* although Solar was perturbed by several inexplicable facts. How could *The One Who Knows* not have known ahead of time what was going to happen, since *Divine* Spirit was capable of knowing past, present, and future events? Also, did Domaine, as his physical counterpart, have any idea what was going to happen to him? Or was Domaine deliberately sheltered from that awareness by his own *Divine* Spirit?

Solar needed to break the fall of his pain before he fell any further. He needed to reach for the highest perspective to fully understand the events that took place without taking it all to heart and then reacting with pain and vindictiveness. Solar especially needed to know what to do next. Only by bringing himself into full communion with The Great Mother Goddess would he know how to fulfill his destiny and the prophecies of old.

When Solar entered The Temple of Worship holding Domaine's staff and crystal wand, a silence permeated the Temple that had never before existed. The presence of *The One Who Knows* had filled this holy sanctuary for 26,000 years giving guidance and counseling on behalf of The Great Mother Goddess to all sea creatures that came seeking guidance. During that time, no one ever suspected *The One Who Knows* had a physical counterpart in another part of the world, and therefore, could be subject to death like other sea creatures. But what is the significance of death if one could live thousands of years?

Solar placed Domaine's staff and crystal wand upon the altar of The Great Mother Goddess and quieted his mind, until his breathing had synchronized his entire body into one flowing consciousness. He then said the ancient words that would allow the full powerful presence of *Divine* consciousness to become fully accessible to him.

Once *Divine* communion was invoked, Solar shifted into Godson and was instantly released from his pain and anguish, as he transformed into magnificent light. Godson then shifted inter-dimensionally, disappearing from sight, taking leave of The Temple of Worship and seeking the doorway that would give him access to a parallel universe existing beyond time.

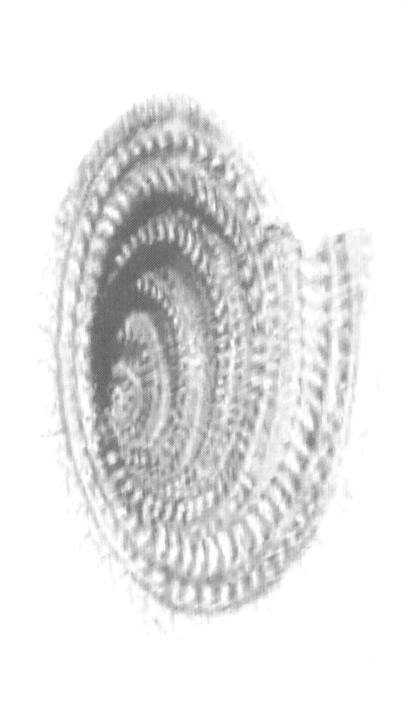

49

STARLIGHT MAGIC

For every Initiate, a conscious Initiation with
Death was inevitable to transition in full consciousness
into the everlasting life of the Immortal Soul.

Godson set the intention to travel into a parallel universe he often visited with Domaine, who taught him how to access Starlight Magic in order to gain answers to any questions he had. He could bear witness to the past in animated events and gain answers that would assist him in resolving any dilemma.

Godson materialized a doorway to a wormhole tunnel capable of accessing the parallel universe he sought. Once the doorway appeared, he shot through it, traveling through the wormhole at lightning speed, leaving the reality of his world behind. A loud thunderclap signaled his entrance into the parallel universe he sought, as he drifted into space. Finding himself under a night sky where stars twinkled like jewels, he lingered and found relief and forgot for a while, why he had come.

* * * * *

Godson marveled at the extraordinary miracle of consciousness to deliver and manifest *anything by intention.* As he looked up at the stars glowing in the night sky in another reality beyond time, he shifted into sacred reverence. In his practices under Domaine's guidance, he had often come to this place where Starlight Magic could answer any questions in incredible detail. Each star symbolically represented a doorway into an infinite number of parallel realities. He simply had to hold a question in his mind and close his eyes for a moment. Upon opening his eyes, one star would become more radiant than any other. It was then he would journey faster than the speed of thought and burst through the doorway of Starlight Magic and gain the answers he was seeking to his questions.

As he brought his first question to mind—whether *The One Who Knows* knew of Egoson's planned attack—Godson closed his eyes and asked his question and released it into infinite space. Upon opening his eyes, he searched the night sky for the most prominent star knowing it had become a lighted doorway into *The Divine Records of Consciousness.* Locating it, Godson shot toward the star and exploded through the doorway to the other side of reality. He found himself hovering above an empty Temple of Worship, and thought for a moment, he had not succeeded in penetrating the secret of Starlight Magic. He was about to try again, when the side doors of The Temple of Worship swung open, and two sacred eels made their way to the center of the altar. As they approached, a light began to glow until the altar disappeared and only light remained.

"Invoke the full power and presence of the *Divine* within you so we can communicate," said *The One Who Knows,* piercing the silence with a booming charge.

The sacred eels burst into two spiraling flames of light that pushed back the ocean waters and filled The Temple of Worship with radiant light. The final transformation of flesh into light revealed The Sacred Sea Dragons hovering in their place.

"I have summoned you about a critical matter," *The One Who Knows* said, thunderously. "Egoson will be taking his campaign of terror to yet another level of wanton cruelty, as he plans to abduct two sacred eels from Temple grounds to sacrifice them and take charge of their Souls. He will then attempt to use them as a channel to penetrate secrets about me. He will then discover he can target my own body vehicle and return me back to the *Void.*"

The Sacred Sea Dragons, straining in power, spoke in unison. "Body vehicle? Are you not *Divine* Spirit without flesh?"

"To you will be revealed one of the greatest secrets of all time, for not even my own flesh is conscious of its direct communion with me. I charge you then with the Will of The Great Mother Goddess, and thus reveal the secret that once passed onto you will earmark your flesh in its lowly form to become the sacrifices necessary to bring on The Final Reckoning. Do you choose by the Universal Law of Free Will to serve The Great Mother Goddess in this way?"

"Yes, we do," The Sacred Sea Dragons said, in unison, without hesitation.

"Then charged to your *Divine* Spirit, the name of Domaine is inscribed, which is the name of the body vehicle of a hermit crab existing in direct communion with me. I have already called Domaine into service, although the nature of that service is yet unclear to him. He is already near. Under my guidance, he is the only one capable of healing the wounded Solar and bringing him into alignment with *Divine* consciousness as *Godson.* I charge your *Divine* Spirit with this most sacred and important mission, although your body vehicles will be unaware of their fate. To insure you will become the weakest links, your Souls will separate from your body vehicles, enough to lower your vibration, so Darkness will target you specifically. *Darkness can only strike among those weakly aligned with their Souls.* You will feel lost and confused and thus be perceived as a perfect haven for Darkness. Be assured that The Final Reckoning will restore your natural state of *Divine* communion. Do you both agree to become the sacrifices necessary to bring on The Final Reckoning for The Great Mother Goddess?"

"Yes, we both agree, and charge the Will of The Great Mother Goddess to our *Divine* Spirit."

"*So be it!* I now command, by the Authority granted to me in the Name of The Great Mother Goddess, that your Souls now separate from your body vehicles sufficient to lower your vibration, but without death. Once you complete your transformation into lowly consciousness, you will have no further contact with Me."

The Sacred Sea Dragons immediately shape-shifted back into their body vehicles and went into seizures. When their seizures stopped, their body vehicles had aged and their light had considerably diminished. They crawled along, haltingly slow, inching their way from The Temple of Worship, as the presence of *The One Who Knows* disappeared from sight.

Godson instantly teleported back underneath the star-filled sky, processing the vision he had just seen. *The One Who Knows* had obviously known of the plot against him and had even assisted Egoson in discovering a way to destroy his body vehicle. For what *Divine* purpose would he have allowed such a thing to happen? Did Domaine also come to know his destiny before he was executed?

Godson felt he needed more answers about Domaine. He closed his eyes, set forth his intention, and then looked up and located the next bright star. He went zooming into Starlight Magic in the next breath and found himself back in the Great Hall with Domaine speaking.

"But where did the time go? I cannot tell you. It all seems like a dream now," Domaine said, looking over at Solar and winking. Godson then flashed onto him saying," . . . it is time for me to leave and return to the silence of my own being. When I am needed again, I will be called out of refuge and return once more to The Temples of the Goddess of the Sea."

The vision disappeared and Godson was back again under the star-filled sky, processing the full implications of his vision. He needed to take a little time to examine it before moving on to his next question.

Nothing was apparent in Domaine's words that revealed any awareness that he knew what was going to happen, although his words were filled with meaning. Could his words "return to the silence" imply he was returning to the *Void* as a result of transitioning? What about his words, "When I am needed, I will return to The Temples of the Goddess of the Sea." Could Domaine have meant he would be returning from the *Void* to The Temples of the Goddess of the Sea at some future time? Did this also imply he was going to die and someday return? Did his words, "Where did the time go? I cannot tell you. It all seems like a dream now," sound like someone reminiscing about a dream coming to an end?

Godson concluded Domaine must have known his destiny was coming to an end. Did he not wink at him and reveal there was more to what he was saying than the words he was speaking?

Godson realized Domaine was at peace with his destiny, whether he knew the exact details of his fate or not. Since Domaine had always been utterly guided by his Immortal Soul and *Divine* Spirit, he always lived in a state of grace and a willful acceptance and resignation to his destiny, regardless of how his path evolved. He never held onto life too tightly, because he never lived imprisoned by the fear of death. He was always quick to remind Solar death did not exist. Perhaps Domaine sustained his Immortality of the flesh because he held onto this truth with a level of conviction that made death impossible. Without fear, complete communion with the *Divine* was not only possible, but inevitable.

Godson relaxed into a profound sense of relief for the events that took place. He then thought about Seeres and the feeling of bewilderment returned. Could he say the same about her?

Seeres had spent her entire life in complete conscious service to The Great Mother Goddess and was given the opportunity to start a new life outside the seclusion of The Temple of Prophecies and Oracles. Why was she cut down at such a juncture in her life after working so hard and sacrificing so much of herself to The Great Mother Goddess? Why was she made to believe she was being rewarded by The Great Mother Goddess to serve in another way? Godson himself had channeled the message and assured her of this. Surely, Seeres did not know she was being set up anymore than Domaine. Is this how The Great Mother Goddess rewards her own?

Godson decided to take another journey to answer these haunting questions, so he could be released from the grief and bewilderment of her death. Godson closed his eyes, set forth his question, and then opened his eyes and then soared instantly through the center of the largest star, so he could pierce the mysteries of the questions at hand.

On the other side of the doorway, Godson found himself in a stark room where Seeres was lying in bed. A small night table was next to her bed with an alabaster image of The Great Mother Goddess. Seeres was just getting out of bed, steadying herself, while holding her head. She reached into the drawer of the night table and got out a closed vial containing a deep red liquid filled three-quarters of the way. She then disappeared into the bathroom, after glancing at herself in the mirror.

A few moments later, Seeres returned holding the vial, which was now filled, and placed it near the edge of the table. Godson telepathically understood it was menstrual blood. Godson also understood that Seeres was completely capable of controlling her bodily functions to such perfection that she could collect her menstrual blood at intervals until she had recovered the whole of it without wasting a drop.

Seeres went into a small closet and pulled out a small golden chalice and placed it on the altar before the alabaster image of The Great Mother Goddess. When she grabbed the vial filled with menstrual blood, she slipped and accidentally dropped the vial on the floor. It shattered upon impact and her blood splattered everywhere.

"Oh, my Goddess!" Seeres cried, engaging her larynx in raspy gasps of air. She bent over, frantically trying to collect the blood with her night robe before it became diffused throughout the room. She squeezed what blood she could into the golden chalice, until she stopped in painful and bitter resignation. Although she tried desperately to recover as much blood as she could to make an offering of it to The Great Mother Goddess, it was to no avail. The blood was defiled. She would be unable to use it as a final offering, and a final offering was necessary to close out this phase of her life in service to The Great Mother Goddess.

Seeres turned and looked into the mirror and caught sight of an unforgettable image that cast a prophetic vision in her mind. She gasped from the shock of it. Her face, hands, and robe were covered in blood. The terrible vision pierced her heart, as she wailed in recognition that the final offering was to be made after all.

As Seeres moved away from the mirror, tears fell from her eyes, and Godson heard her whisper to herself: *"Let Thy Will be done, dear Mother. Let Thy Will be done!"*

Godson closed his eyes to halt the rush of tears before returning to the vision, but it was already gone. He had gotten his answer and was standing again under the star-filled sky.

Godson allowed his tears to flow without restraint to release his unexpressed grief. The poignancy of that moment pierced his heart deeply. He cried aloud until he had emptied the charge of his emotions that had gathered inside of him since the apocalyptic drama at the Great Hall. Once he did, he lightened, but yet remained heavy-hearted and questioning. Would he also be willing to give his life so easily and effortlessly for The Great Mother Goddess?

Without hesitation, Godson knew the answer. He would willingly surrender the illusory dream for the conscious everlasting life of communion with the *Divine*. Only love could inspire faith strong enough to release the dream and dispel the hardship of a life dominated by imprisoning illusions.

Godson realized that if he feared Death, he would be destroyed by the greatest illusion that existed in The Kingdom of Oceana. *For every Initiate, a conscious Initiation with Death was inevitable to transition in full consciousness into the everlasting life of the Immortal Soul.* Perhaps this was the Initiation that Domain and Seeres had fearlessly faced?

Godson pondered this for a long time before realizing he had no more questions. He left the parallel world of Starlight Magic and returned through the wormhole back to The Temple of Worship. After shifting back into Solar, he continued processing the information until a shift had taken place inside of him energetically. At that moment he knew what he had to do next.

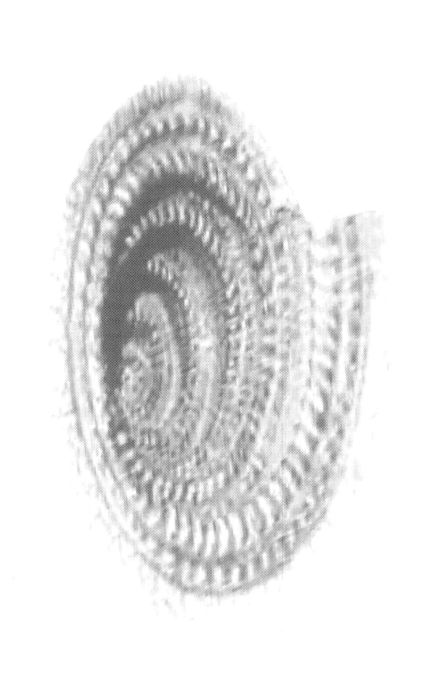

50

SCEPTER OF
DIVINE POWER

Guard The Scepter of Divine Power well,
my Son, and take back what is truly yours."

"But Domaine," Solar said, speaking aloud from his aching heart and the loss of his dear friend, "You said I could always reach you across all worlds by calling upon your *Divine* Spirit. How can I reach you now?"

Solar claimed the reality of all he had learned with Domaine and began calling upon him to appear. He kept affirming that anything is possible *once you believe!* Solar was prepared to remain all night holding steadfast to the intention of making contact with Domaine. Not an hour had passed, when Solar heard Domaine speak, *"It is easy to reach me across any distance, when you speak to me from the deepest reaches of your heart."*

Solar closed his eyes and shifted more deeply into trance and into the realm of his heart. He invited Domaine to manifest directly in front of him. He desperately wanted proof of his ability to reach him *not only in consciousness* but also *in physical presence!* He wanted to speak with him as he had witnessed Domaine speaking directly to other Souls who had manifested directly in front of him in response to his invocations. When Solar felt Domaine's presence materializing, he opened his eyes and found himself before Domaine's magnificent light, radiating indescribable love.

"Domaine, is that you?"

"Yes, my Son."

Solar kneeled in breathless wonder and let his tortured heart fill him with light.

"So, it is you, Domaine, who was *The One Who Knows* all along?"

"Yes."

"Domaine? Why did you sacrifice yourself to Egoson's tactics of terror and allow him to destroy your body vehicle?"

"Did I?"

"Did you not?"

"Solar, you must ask yourself, was I destroyed or did it *appear* as if I was destroyed?"

"Of course! Of course! What am I thinking? You are here with me now!"

"Yes, *I AM!* And you must *never forget* that Egoson is the Master of Illusions, while you, on the other hand, are a Master, who must come into full remembrance of all that you are. This also means asking yourself, who is the *real* you? To forget your true identity before Egoson will surely mean death. After all, did he not become *Death* when he chose to separate from *Divine* consciousness, thus setting a precedent for us all?"

Godson nodded, nervously.

"Yes, he became *Death*, the Gatekeeper to the Realm of Lost Souls, which became his Empire of Darkness. He created a parallel world of existence made possible by triggering fear and terror as a way of getting sea creatures to separate from the *Divine*, thus making death real. It was his longing to express sole power in creation, exacting upon sea creatures the most depraved hideous reflections of death and dying, that he inevitably claimed a power unimaginable in the world of Light."

"So true, so true," Godson said to himself in a whisper, feeling the poignancy of that truth dispel darkness still lingering within the depths of his Soul.

"It is why Egoson created rituals exploiting the desecration of the flesh to perpetuate the terror of death. The most far reaching of these rituals where the greatest number of sea creatures are marshaled together to desecrate the sacredness of life is in the advent of war. Initiating war divides sea creatures against each other. War spurs sea creatures to act brutally toward one another, justifying a desecration of the sacred within living flesh on a massive scale. Egoson has even succeeded in reducing the greatest of Masters who were once part of The Original Ancestry of the Gods into slaves and the most sublime expressions of innocence into victims of unspeakable horror."

"When will this come to an end?"

"Only when one who is connected to all in consciousness is able to see to the truth."

"What do you mean?"

"The answer lies within you and *you must find it!* Otherwise, you will do this again and again until you get it right!"

"No! I do not want to do this again!"

"So be it! You have been initiated into the Mysteries for the purpose of creating Heaven in Galexia as the only reality upholding everlasting life. It is for this reason I held back the tide of Darkness until your coming. The Scepter of *Divine* Power is now in your keeping," Domaine said, materializing his staff and crystal wand directly from The Temple of Worship and placed it directly into Solar's keeping, who reverently took hold of it. "Guard The Scepter of *Divine* Power well, my Son, and take back what is truly yours."

"You mean from Egoson?"

"I mean, *you must heal the separation you are in!*"

"Oh, my Goddess!"

"Now look before you, and you will see the vision of your future. Be willing to surrender to it completely in alignment with the Will of The Great Mother Goddess."

As Solar bore witness to his fate, he did not resist or deny it. He surrendered to it completely prepared to play out his destiny *as it was written at the beginning of time!*

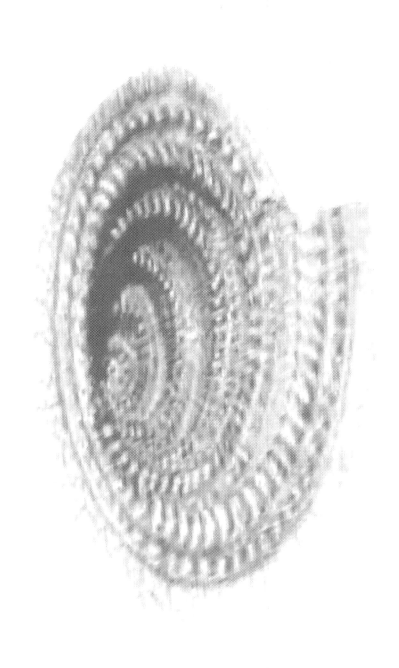

51

A MASTER'S INVOCATION

The whole of Temple grounds would soon be
buzzing from the news of this extraordinary
spectacle.

After several days of retreat, Solar left The Temple of Worship. His first priority was to see how Theia was faring, in addition to looking in on his other friends. Mysteia had been given the room previously occupied by Seeres and was still under sedation. Sonar had been undergoing healing sessions with Temple priests for his injured eye, and Starborn was still regenerating his lost limbs.

When Godson came into his room, Theia was waiting for him, looking out on Temple grounds. Theia immediately turned to face him, although he had moved with such stealth that not even The Sentinels of the Sun would have been alerted to his presence.

Theia looked into Solar's face and studied it, because it was there she was going to find any clue as to what he was thinking. Instead of finding anger and rage, grief and sorrow, she found a warm smile reflecting inner tranquility and love. She did not smile in return but looked away when she realized he had found peace.

"I can see you have been to The Temple of Worship and found your answers. I hope I will be as fortunate and find peace as well," Theia said, facing the plaza below.

"You will undoubtedly find peace as I have done."

"How can you be so sure?"

"Because I felt exactly as you do."

"How can you possibly know how I feel?"

"Because I was also ready to seek revenge as well. Having *Divine* powers at my disposal, do you think I could unleash that kind of power in anger and ever believe, I would be reconciled to my pain as a result of the destruction I could cause?"

Theia turned to face Solar, ready to object, but was stopped by the emotional poignancy of his eyes reflecting his deep and abiding love for her. Instead, she said nothing.

"Your pain, Theia, comes from a lack of awareness, as mine did, and nothing more. If you shift into a higher perspective and gain knowledge of the truth, you will come to understand the reasons for the abominable acts of Egoson and begin to forgive him."

"How can you be so sure, after all that has happened!" Theia snapped. "How could you let Egoson get away with all this and even forgive him? Why didn't you do something when you had the chance? Instead, you let Egoson make a mockery of you," Theia said, snarling.

"Because it was not my time to act. It would have been devastating to us all if I had simply *reacted* instead. As far as forgiving what's happened, no one can forgive a wrong if it is perceived as a wrong truly done. Most sea creatures believe they can forgive a wrong and then forget. But no one ever forgets. One always remembers the pain of a wrong until it is corrected, not by forgiveness, per se, but by seeing the perceived wrong from a higher perspective. From that vantage point, the truth is exposed, and erases the wrong from a deeper level of awareness and knowledge. Thus, only *truth* can correct a wrong. When one sees to the ignorance that prevails in acts of separation, then it is possible to forgive completely."

"But forgiveness is the key to all healing. That is what we are taught at The School of Mysteries."

"Yes. But there's more to be said. Forgiveness becomes a temporary bandage to allow the healing process to begin. Forgiveness allows the mind to relax in spite of the pain it feels. Forgiveness allows wounds to heal so they will fester no further. But forgiveness alone cannot lift scars. Only *truth* can. Acknowledging a greater truth than what is self-evident means demonstrating our humility before acts we cannot understand. Unless we take into account the overall complexity of all things that have happened across time, we cannot shift from forgiveness to the discernment of truth. The exercise of forgiveness allows us to take a leap of faith and leave justice in the hands of The Great Mother Goddess where it belongs. Only *She* can tract a Soul across time and know the reasons behind its actions. Only *She* can know why a Soul must fulfill its fate in a certain way so destiny can be fully realized in the wholeness of time."

"Fine! All that theory is wonderful, but none of it releases me from my pain! I saw two lovely creatures of magnificent light utterly destroyed by Egoson—that ugly, stinking, hateful bastard! And *that* is what I cannot release. My hate and my pain!"

Solar raised to full height as lightning impulses began streaming into the room from the radiant energy of his body shifting into the higher vibrational presence of Godson. Instantly, Theia grabbed her stomach and contorted in pain from the impact of radiant light.

"I now invoke the DIVINE of ALL THAT I AM by the POWER and FREQUENCY OF LOVE. In full alignment of the DIVINE within me, I COMMAND the Souls of Darkness, seeking hatred and revenge within Theia, to be released from her Sacred Temple, NOW!"

A black formless mass discharged from Theia's solar plexus and filled the room with screaming Souls of Darkness as Theia fell to the floor. The screams prompted volunteer crayfish orderlies to come rushing into the room, as Godson held them back with the light of his presence.

"In the Name of THE GREAT MOTHER GODDESS, I COMMAND the opening of THE PORTAL OF LIGHT so these Souls of Darkness may be discharged through it and returned to the DIVINE Source! Now, BE GONE!!!"

The doorway to THE PORTAL OF LIGHT opened as the black formless mass of screaming Souls of Darkness were sucked through the doorway and were gone in the next instant.

"May the doorway to THE PORTAL OF LIGHT now CLOSE!" Godson commanded, as THE PORTAL OF LIGHT closed. The light softened and a warm radiant glow filled the room. Theia's energy immediately returned to normal and color returned to her cheeks.

Godson shifted back into Solar and released the crayfish orderlies from their shock.

"You may go now. I will take care of Theia myself," Solar said to them.

The crayfish orderlies backed away and left, swept into a frenzy of excitement. The whole of Temple grounds would soon be buzzing from the news of this extraordinary spectacle. At least the doom and gloom that had descended upon Temple grounds would dissipate a little and give renewed hope to sea creatures battered from Egoson's tactics of terror.

"Theia," Solar said gently, as he reached out and turned Theia to face him. Just then, a two-legged Starborn leaped into the room, ready to attack, looking peculiar from the growth of three stumps making their appearance above his star-shaped face.

"Is she all right?" Starborn shouted.

"Yes, she is. Just dazed from her experience."

"I was afraid Egoson had done it again."

"No. The Temple of Healing is completely protected by force-fields. Egoson could never reach her here."

"Then how did the Souls of Darkness get into Theia?"

"When Theia was still in shock at the Great Hall after the force-fields collapsed, and her normal defenses were down completely. Her extreme reaction to the devastating tragedy cracked an opening in the energy field surrounding her body. As a result, Souls of Darkness entered, drawn to her distorted energy, resulting in greater pain. But Theia has been exorcized of all that had taken possession of her. She will recover now," Solar said.

Returning his gaze toward Theia, Solar extended loving energy toward Theia, so she might quickly recover from the extremes of energy. He picked her up from the floor and gently caressed her face experiencing *grace* for having the opportunity to be this close to the one he loved.

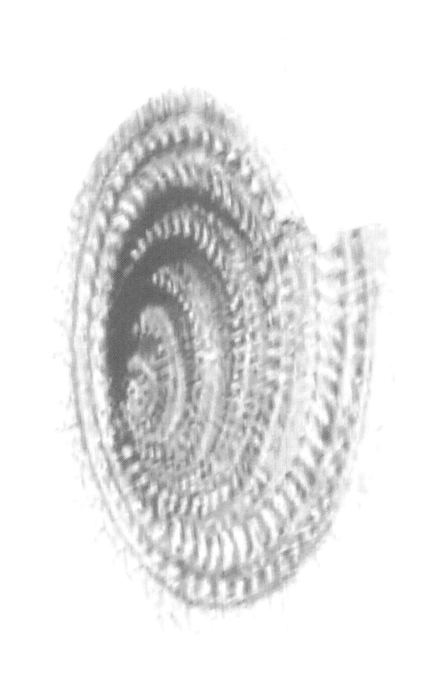

52

CRUEL LOVE

As Starborn looked on, he saw the love that
existed between Solar and Theia, and he became
sad a moment. It was a doomed love because the
overwhelming depth of it would force regret on
them both . . . . They would realize a great love, yet
know the frustration of its unrequited passions.

Theia came to as Solar gently rocked her body to awaken her into full consciousness. Theia began focusing as she held her raw throat.

"Solar? Solar?" Without another word, Theia flung her arms around Solar and held him as she cried sorrowfully for the first time. The poignant loss of Domaine and Seeres spilled from her without anger, pain, or regret. She felt only the piercing grief of her sorrow. She understood that Domaine and Seeres were actually the lucky ones for having been released from a reality of pain.

Theia immediately found comfort in knowing she could always access their Souls through prayers and send them love from this side of the veil. She had forgotten these truths because of Darkness, and she had paid dearly for that loss of awareness. She realized The Final Reckoning had not yet come to pass and smiled knowing Solar was proof that there was still hope.

Solar welcomed the opportunity to hold Theia without having to withdraw. She had flung herself against him and for the first time, he deeply regretted being born a crab and not a merman. While he had always considered himself fortunate to be given an armor of protection that almost no predator could pierce, it was an impenetrable shield that now separated him from Theia in the cruelest way possible. Even so, at least they shared an indestructible bond that not even death could sever.

Starborn looked on, seeing the love that existed between them, and he became sad a moment. It was a doomed love because the overwhelming depth of it would force regret on them both. Looking at their own reflection, they would always be reminded of their stark differences in spite of their common feelings. They would realize a great love, yet know the frustration of its unrequited passions.

Starborn began easing himself out of the room because he did not want to disrupt their intimacy by reminding Solar he was not alone with Theia. Solar had cast him into the role of a reluctant voyeur, and he was anxious to remove himself. He was nearly out the door when Solar called him back.

"Starborn, *please,* come back!"

Starborn stopped and turned. Both Solar and Theia were looking in his direction. Meanwhile, he was tiptoeing out the door looking quite ridiculous for the effort. Solar and Theia began laughing, and even Starborn had to laugh at himself.

"Starborn, if I didn't know you were growing back your limbs," Theia said, with affection, "I would be quite concerned." How are you feeling? Are you all right?"

"I am very, very tired, actually. The energy it takes to regenerate three limbs at the same time would not be believed. Otherwise, I am doing quite well, thank you."

"Have you looked in on Sonar?"

"You mean the one-eyed jack?"

"Is he still wearing the patch over his eye?"

"Yes, and he's milking that handicap to perfection with the ladies. I suspect he would have taken the patch off if it did not serve him so well. I believe his eye has fully healed."

"I'm glad to hear it," Theia said.

"Things have become quite impossible these past few days," Starborn said, shifting his energy and becoming quite serious. There is a strained tension among us all, as though a storm is about to break. The Sons of Egoson have subdued their terrorist tactics for the time being, which has led me to believe that Domaine must have done some serious damage to Egoson across the veil between worlds. Still, there is no telling how long this will last. Are you going to wait until he makes a move, or are you going to go after him yourself?"

Solar was startled by the unusual bluntness of Starborn's question. It was not like him to be so direct. Yet, Starborn was not alone in his change of attitude and posturing. Everyone on Temple grounds had shifted and many were ready for aggressive measures. An edged tension, which had never before existed on holy ground, sparked a growing sense of urgency. Apparently, the loss of *The One Who Knows* was already being felt. There was a looming threat of something so unpredictable, that everyone was withdrawing into a mute suspension of feeling. It was apparent that The Final Reckoning was drawing near, and everyone could feel it, like the stressed calm before the storm.

Solar considered Starborn's question. He would never expose anyone to personal risk from Egoson's mind-control penetration by letting anyone in on his vision. Such information might subject someone to kidnaping and even death. The thought of it made Solar shudder.

"Starborn, for the safety of everyone involved, I cannot speak of the Will of The Great Mother Goddess. All I can say is that Her Will has filled me with purpose, and when the time comes, I will see The Final Reckoning to the very end."

"Is it finally upon us?" Starborn asked.

"Everyone can feel it," Theia said, looking around her and picking up on the energy of the present mood on Temple grounds and throughout The Kingdom of Oceana. The force-field of light that had permeated Temples grounds since its inception had collapsed with Domaine's demise and the release of *The One Who Knows.* In its place, crystals anchored in the ground around the perimeter of the Temples were still pulsating with the distinct power of *Divine* light held in place for thousands of years. Yet, it was quite evident to them all that the crystals could only sustain that level of power with re-activations. Without the presence of *The One Who Knows* maintaining that level of *Divine* power, holy ground would eventually equalize to the energy of The Kingdom of Oceana, until no sacred ground remained.

With the awareness of these thoughts shared by them all, a new level of urgency gripped them. The Final Reckoning now loomed, quite possibly, as a foreshadowing of the forces of Darkness *overunning* them, rather than a foreshadowing of the forces of Light *upholding Divine power.*

"There is one thing I must ask of you, Theia," Solar said, shutting out any more thoughts. You must, *under no circumstances,* leave The Temple of Healing for the next few days."

"That will not be difficult, Godson, since I am feeling so weak."

"Good."

An alarm sounded throughout The Temples of the Goddess of the Sea, as crayfish orderlies came crashing into the room without knocking.

"Godson, come quick! There are several families rushing onto Temple grounds. They say they are the last surviving relatives of several hundred families in the northern territory that have been tortured and beaten and even murdered by the Sons of Egoson. They are begging for assistance to retrieve their children from the Sons of Egoson taken just a few hundred yards beyond Temple grounds. Can you help?"

"Of course!" Solar said, immediately shifting back into full radiant power as Godson. Excusing himself from Theia and Starborn, he turned and abruptly left.

"I think The Final Reckoning has just begun!" Starborn exclaimed, alerted to the change in energy.

"Impossible!"

"Take a moment and open your mind, and you will feel Egoson close at hand. Godson will not only meet the Sons of Egoson outside of Temple grounds, *but Egoson himself!*"

"It cannot be!"

"Check for yourself!"

"If that's true, *I'm going too!*"

"No, you can't! You just gave your word!"

"No, I didn't! I said I would follow his request because I was feeling so weak. I had no idea that Egoson was close at hand. What if Godson needs my help?"

"Godson already has all the help he needs."

"But I must also help! I cannot stay locked inside of Temple grounds without *doing something!*"

"Theia, *think* of what you risk by acting out your own will! Don't you see? You are setting yourself up for disaster and Godson too!"

"But I must be near him!"

"If you *love* him, Theia, *please* let him do this thing alone!"

Theia gasped, shuttering. Starborn's words pierced her heart and tremors shook her body. She turned away from Starborn's penetrating eye and sought to find a reason for her trembling response.

Theia had never admitted to herself that love had already taken charge of her heart and bypassed her mind. She never wanted to admit to something too painful and cruel to bear, especially considering her past trauma with the Dark side. Yet, to be awakened to true love was something that nothing had prepared her for—not the wisest sages at The School of

Mysteries nor all the Mysteries combined. Although she had experienced unparalleled ecstasy when she came into communion with The Great Mother Goddess during her Initiations, this new feeling left her helplessly vulnerable to passions she had never felt before. The ecstatic union of mind, flesh and Soul, while in love, was as mysterious as it was bewildering. It was like a sweeping, ravaging storm—annihilating all reason, purging her of all boundaries, and leaving her naked to tremble in its wake.

Theia shuddered uncontrollably for her psyche was not prepared to receive this truth so bluntly. She instantly recalled a lesson taught to her at The School of Mysteries: *"Nothing can teach you more about life than true love."*

Theia had believed she understood the meaning of true love, but she knew *nothing* about true love til now. Only true love could teach her about herself and reveal how far she would go for love. Only true love made possible a rite of passage into the deepest part of her being. Only true love could give her back a part of herself she could not reclaim from books or teachings, from inspirations or visions. She immediately recognized she could never feel complete without the experience of true love. It did not matter that she could never know the total reaches of ecstatic union with Solar. Love exchanged in mutually acknowledged feelings and spiritual communion could compensate for love expressed in the flesh. Now that a part of her Soul had returned in shocking clarity to the fullness of love, nothing could rob her of this awareness. The mystery of it had finally dawned in her heart, and she was not prepared to deny it, not even facing death!

"I would rather die at Solar's side," Theia said, screaming with emphasis, *"as Seeres died by Domaine's side, rather than remain here never knowing of Godson's fate until it was too late!"*

Theia rushed to the door without looking back. Starborn cut in front of her and cried out in anguish.

"Stop, Theia, stop! Remember what Godson said to you! Please, do not martyr yourself to love! That is not love! It is treason!"

Theia stopped, as the pain of Starborn's words pierced her heart and flesh all at once and left her crying in utter helplessness. Her resolve to go, in spite of all feelings to the contrary, collapsed into resignation. She looked up at Starborn, and for one brief moment, she acquiesced.

"Theia! Theia! We need your help!" cried a crayfish orderly, as he burst into the room. "Many are near death! Everyone is being called into service! Legions of Egoson's army are nearing The Temples of the Goddess of the Sea at this very moment! Panic has many creatures falling into delirium near the border! Everyone is needed to assist in pulling as many as we can onto holy ground before they succumb to death!"

Jolted back to reality, Thea cried, *"The Goddess has spoken!"*

Turning to Starborn, Theia answered firmly, but gently, "Go with me, Starborn, for I must go and face Egoson's army as well. I cannot stay here no matter what Godson has asked of me. You cannot ask me to do nothing as well. If it is death we face by standing up to Egoson, then *death it is, remembering it is only death in the flesh!* Let's die with honor, if we must, Starborn, and preserve the dignity of our faith and truth, as we act from love in The Final Reckoning."

Starborn paused, considering Theia's words, before dropping energetically to resignation.

"So it is," Starborn answered, in utter disgust. "If you will not heed the warning of Godson's wisdom, then I can only suggest we at least invoke all the protection we can. Once you leave the safety of force-fields surrounding The Temple of Healing, there is no telling what Egoson will do. If he scans you for only a moment, he will know the secrets of your heart, and he will undoubtedly use you as a weapon against Godson. Are you sure you won't reconsider?"

"No! I surrender myself to The Great Mother Goddess and, as always, I will serve in Her Name."

"May The Great Mother Goddess protect you!"

"And you as well!"

"Let's go!" Theia said, as she burst out of the room with Starborn limping behind.

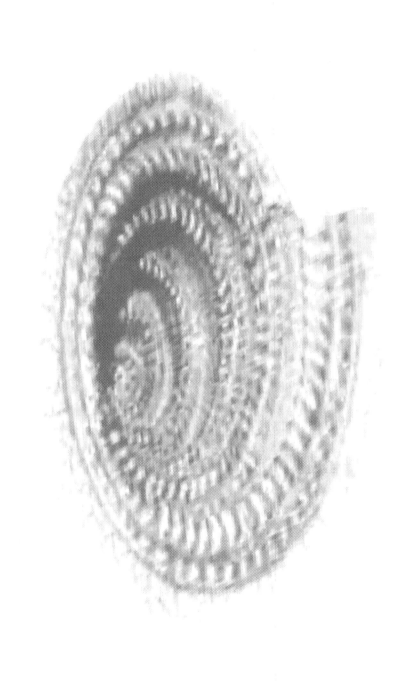

53

THE FINAL RECKONING

The Final Reckoning was unraveling in the exact
way Godson had witnessed, and there was nothing
he could do to stop it.

Egoson was riding on the back of the Great Black looking toward The Temples of The Goddess of the Sea from the high pass where Godson took cover during The Dance of the Sacred Spiral of Life. From this vantage point, Egoson watched the Sons of Darkness torture and butcher sea creatures fleeing in droves toward Temple grounds for refuge and safety.

In every direction, sharks bloodied the ocean with dismembered sea creatures, sting rays paralyzed prey to be eaten alive, squids and octopus sprayed black ink to create chaos. All manner of scavengers fed on the flesh of mutilated sea creatures scattered on the ocean floor. Even the Abominable Hags of Anger, Hate, Guilt & Shame, together with their offspring Rage, Blame, and Regret, polluted the ocean waters with venomous emotional currents that made sea creatures turn on their offspring to defile and attack them and even kill them.

From another direction, leagues of jellyfish discharged poisonous fluids from their many tentacles into the surrounding waters, paralyzing sea creatures into helpless prey to be eaten alive by others. Legions of lamprey eels attached themselves to all manner of sea creatures, large and small, as they gorged themselves of blood, making sea creatures too weak to fight. Sea lice were so thick in places that it was difficult to see beyond them. Sea creatures caught in their midst became covered with white acid that burned them alive. Piranhas traveling in schools attacked the largest of sea creatures, including whales, dolphins, and sea lions, which became reduced to bare bones without flesh.

Egoson shrilled with sardonic laughter as fear and terror bled into his energy field from the senseless slaughter. No black mass, not even the High Black Mass of Hallows Eve, compared to the ecstasy of living torture so rampant in this moment. Finally, the vengeance that was buried deep in his frozen heart thawed into a reality beyond imagining. For nearly 13,000 years, Egoson existed in blind darkness, a consciousness without flesh, festering in brutal agony because of the hatred that consumed him. Setting a precedent for hell where none existed, he brought on the fires of hell within a parallel world and dimension that became a pit for lost Souls.

Egoson's consciousness proved to be more powerful than flesh. Without having direct incarnation in The Kingdom of Oceana, Egoson managed to gain access to sea creatures by the sheer power of his indomitable will. By force of intention, he pierced the veil between worlds and found himself looking in on The Kingdom of Oceana through the eyes of others. Once he made contact with sea creatures in this way, he began manipulating them, forcing them to act out his will. In the last thousand years, he had gained influence over sea creatures by becoming increasingly aggressive and territorial until predator eating prey became the result.

Holy ground, once omnipresent throughout The Kingdom of Oceana, became isolated to one small area made holy by Seeres, the High Priestess of the Prophecies and Oracles, who sustained a *Divine* connection to The Great Mother Goddess in the flesh, and *The One Who Knows,* who served as a Goddess Emissary in the invisible. It was now left to Godson and Mysteia, along with the Initiate Priests and Priestesses, to defend holy ground.

As Egoson's cursed exile drew to an end, the tide of peace existing in The Kingdom of Oceana had finally erupted into perpetual war and chaos. Egoson had turned into a war monger, who diligently worked as a Master Strategist to reduce sea creatures, who were once free, to become slaves as a result of his insidious manipulations and control tactics. Sea creatures had become increasingly accustomed to an unnatural way of life that became normal.

Egoson shifted his attention to Temple grounds where black fallen stars gathered in great clusters near its borders. They discharged their pointed needles like missiles and killed sea creatures trying to get across the borders onto holy ground. The Sentinels of the Sun disintegrated most missiles using their laser-like eyes, while sea turtles used their shells as shields to deflect many more. Yet, spears were getting passed them killing Temple and sea creatures alike.

In every direction, there was a cacophony of piercing, shrieking cries of terror unlike The Kingdom of Oceana had witnessed since the end days of The Original Ancestry of the Gods. Adding to this mayhem were Souls of Darkness engaged in a feeding frenzy, intoxicated by a bloodbath without equal.

Egoson summoned greater hysteria into the minds, hearts, and Souls of sea creatures with his shrieking incantations until the entire scene looked like the bowels of hell had been discharged into The Kingdom of Oceana. There was no end to the wailing cries of brutal misery.

Egoson stood at the highest vantage point waiting to flush out Godson, who might take the lofty initiative to defend The Temples of The Goddess of the Sea from the siege of terror attacking its borders from every direction. Egoson remained ever watchful and attentive to all Temple guardians whether Priest or Priestess, angelfish or catfish, sacred eel or Sentinel of the Sun. He was telepathically scanning each one as they came into view to see if he could get anything on Godson that might betray any weaknesses he could use to advantage.

Egoson caught sight of a Temple Priest with a patch over its eye carrying wounded sea creatures across the borders onto holy ground. In scanning its mind, Egoson picked up on Godson's circle of friends and smiled to himself. It was just another piece of information Egoson could use against him.

Egoson noticed the extraordinary difference between sea creatures moving onto holy ground and those just outside of its borders. He noted the terrorized look of sheer panic written on the faces of sea creatures fleeing from his army just before entering holy ground. Once inside its borders, he could see a distinct black mass rise from them as The Sentinels of the Sun focused their laser-light energy upon them. Souls of Darkness were instantly discharged, taking with them all the confusion, conflict, and terror they caused. Once sea creatures moved onto holy ground and were released from the malevolent Souls that possessed them, they fell into an ecstatic swoon of revelry. Blissful, they shifted into trance and had to be dragged out of the way by Temple Guardians frantically working to keep the borders clear so others could get in. It was a curious sight! No Soul of Darkness was able to cross onto holy ground and remain in possession of their victim without being ejected by either The Sentinels of the Sun or the energy of holy ground because light burned them as painfully as the fires of hell.

Egoson waited patiently knowing The Kingdom of Oceana would soon fall under his paralyzing seize. Sea creatures loyal to The Great Mother Goddess would succumb to utter despair, for terror stalked them with every moment that passed. The supreme power of all Darkness was descending upon The Temples of The Goddess of the Sea, which threatened to alter the holy place into a graveyard for lost Souls.

Egoson broke out into raspy laughter when he sighted the two-legged Starborn striding by Theia's side. Starborn looked ridiculously funny running on two legs with the stumps of his three legs extending out from the top of his star-shaped face. Egoson made a routine scan of their minds and stopped to open up the frequencies of his thoughts to include the details of a scene still being played out in Theia's mind, as she looked around searching for someone in the crowd. A wry smile crossed Egoson's face when he found what he was looking for. If nothing had flushed Godson out of hiding, perhaps Theia would!

"Let's go!" Egoson shouted, releasing the reins that allowed the Great Black to pull out like a bullet in the direction where Theia was standing.

Instantly, Theia felt a tinkling sensation run up and down her spine. The closer she came to the boundaries of holy ground, the greater the danger she felt. As she withdrew cautiously from the border, she caught sight of a female dolphin carrying one of her wounded children in her mouth, while she was pushing another along the ground with her tail. It was difficult to tell whether the one rolling on the ground was still alive, but the mother's high-pitched sonar screams made it impossible to ignore her plea for help.

Theia blindly dismissed her instincts, as she crossed beyond the border of holy ground and headed toward the female dolphin. Sonar was also moving toward her at top speed in response to her wails, just as a black marlin speared her from the side. She instantly dropped the wounded child from her mouth as shock set in. Her eyes glazed over just as a screaming Sonar rammed the black marlin. As Theia reached the wounded dolphin, she unmistakably heard Godson break into her consciousness, but she could not respond quickly enough. Even Sonar heard Godson's warning and turned to look, as the black marlin poised to attack. Sonar shifted and avoided the cutting edge of its spear as Godson cut the water with a bolt of lightning, which stunned the black marlin and forced him to withdraw. Sonar felt the lightning bolt burn because of its nearness and intensity. But for Theia, it was too late. The moment she stepped outside of holy ground, she became enveloped by total Darkness and passed out.

"Get the children back to safety, Sonar, and *I will take care of Theia!*" Godson commanded.

It was there, outside of Temple grounds, that Godson saw the unfolding images shift into slow motion, as he prepared to face his destiny and surrender to his fate. Although he tried to change the course of his visions by admonishing Theia to stay behind the safety of force-fields, her love had betrayed him. The Final Reckoning was unraveling in the exact way Godson had witnessed, and there was nothing he could do to stop it.

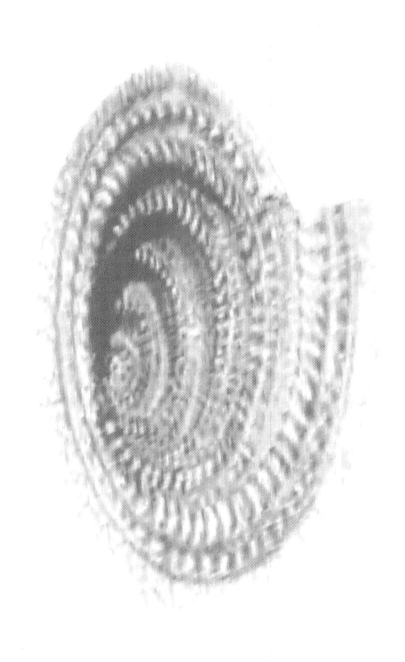

54

INCOMPARABLE LOSS

As Theia succumbed to cries of pain and lamentation,
lightning flashes of memory began bleeding into her
mind from a long time ago, when a loss as great and
terrible as this had pierced her heart with unbearable
sorrow.

As Godson moved toward Theia, all Sons of Egoson fled in all directions in response to the radiation of his light, while all sea creatures loyal to The Great Mother Goddess marveled at the awesome splendor of radiant light. Nothing could pierce that formidable barrier of light, including the hurled missiles from the cursed black fallen stars. All knew Godson's appearance before Egoson to defend The Temples of the Goddess of the Sea in its darkest hour marked the defining moment of The Final Reckoning. No one knew the final outcome of that last battle. It remained a Mystery even in Godson's mind whether they would be faced with mass destruction or liberation from the forces of Darkness. The Universal Law of Free Will made it otherwise impossible to know what the outcome would be.

As Godson's light reached the edges of Theia's body, her energy darkened, and her body went completely into seizure.

"NO!" Godson thundered, as he began channeling light into Theia's body so she could resist possession by Egoson. When Theia screamed, Godson stopped because the conflict of energy between the forces of Darkness and the forces of Light might kill her.

Godson pulled his energy and stood by Theia, watching helplessly as Egoson defiled her energy once again. Egoson's horrible grimace materialized in the Darkness surrounding Theia, as he bellowed his sardonic laughter of madness until Godson could not keep from striking back in rage.

Lightning bolts stilled Egoson's laughter, while dissipating the hovering Darkness surrounding Theia. The doorway between worlds was thrown open, and the energy made contact with Egoson's body. Egoson released Theia, as a rising stench came through the doorway between worlds, and Godson knew he had wounded him. Godson continued channeling energy into Theia's vulnerable body, but her screams tempered his response. He withdrew his energy realizing she could not manage such extremes without placing her under risk of seizures. Egoson instantly returned, defiling Theia's body, and Godson knew he could do but one thing.

"Egoson! Withdraw from her! And I will surrender to you!"

Dark mist rose instantly from Theia's body as her color returned, and she moaned from the raw pain of having channeled so much conflicting energy. Godson noticed blood trickling from her nose and mouth and began channeling healing energy on both sides of her temples to cauterize the wounds causing the internal bleeding. As he brought the bleeding under control, Godson looked up in time to see a giant row of razor sharp teeth materialize out of the dark mist in front of him. As he jumped back ready to strike, Egoson dismounted the Great Black.

"I accept your surrender, Godson. Theia is set free, and luckily for me, she is still alive."

"I said, *if you let her go . . . completely!"* Godson threatened, clarifying his conditions because he did not like the implications of Egoson's words.

"I *did* let her go. I will never force my will upon her again as I previously did at black mass."

Godson glared at Egoson in shock.

"Oh, didn't she tell you? Yes, we had quite a time with her. And I was not the only one. She lasted longer than the rest of them. She was the last to be defiled by all of us because there was still breath in her. But you never know, Godson. She might come around willingly after you are gone."

"No matter what took place in the past, Egoson, *it will never happen again.*"

"Oh, I'm sure of that! She was not the same yesterday, as she is not the same today, nor will she be the same tomorrow. Who is to say what tomorrow shall bring? Nevertheless, I vow to you my best intentions."

"You expect me to believe you?"

"Of course! You have *my word* given in the name of *Universal Law* that I will not trespass her boundaries ever again without her willingness. Do you doubt I would transgress Universal Law and risk banishment to the *Void*? Not at all. I understand that your vow to me seals my vow to you. But who is to say after you are gone, whether she will come looking for me on her own?"

"I doubt that very much," Godson answered, dryly.

"Well, you will not be around to find out, will you?"

"You cannot destroy me, Egoson! No matter how much you try!"

"Yes, I can! I can destroy you as I destroyed *The One Who Knows!* Once I annihilate your body from existence, we will see who will reign—me from The Temples of The Goddess of the Sea or you from the empty pit of the *Void!*

Egoson struck with thunderbolts aimed toward the formidable force-field surrounding Godson's body. They dispersed in a multitude of directions. Panic ignited among sea creatures suddenly fleeing for their lives. Even sea creatures loyal to The Great Mother Goddess lost hope when they saw Egoson attacking a helpless Godson.

Egoson attacked Godson with venomous force as Godson maneuvered to prevent the bolts of energy from hitting sea creatures or The Temples of The Goddess of the Sea. Madness ruled outside of holy ground while resignation ruled inside of holy ground. All Temple Guardians and sea creatures watched the desecration of their beliefs erupt in painful, nauseating waves.

"*Godson, fight back! Fight back!* Theia screamed, unable to contain the pain wrenching inside of her, as she realized the magnitude of what she had done by disobeying him.

"Please, Godson, *I am not worth it!* Take back *your word* and let me go for the love of The Great Mother Goddess and all sea creatures. *Please, don't let him do this to you!*"

"Egoson, your powers are useless against me!" Godson retaliated, as he backed Egoson against the borders of holy ground."

"Yes, I know. But I was just toying with you, Godson. I wanted your loyal subjects to realize the mistake they had made by putting their trust in you and The Great Mother Goddess."

Opening the frequencies of all minds, Egoson spoke the poisonous words that would demoralize even the staunchest supporters of Godson.

"*Look at you, Godson. You flustering coward! You humiliating piece of waste!*"

Instantly, a wave of nausea and despair materialized in all sea creatures as hope died within them. The black shroud of Death fell upon them, as terror paralyzed them into recognizing the inevitability of their doom.

"Godson, *DO something! Don't allow him to use you as a plaything of Darkness!*"

"Oh, how touching, Godson! Show her how much you love her. Get on your knees for her, Godson. Get on your knees for The Great Mother Goddess while you're at it, and don't forget to get on your knees for Domaine and Seeres too!"

With those words, Godson shifted and turned his body to face Egoson as the tension in his body was gone and his resolve ignited. Alarmed by Godson's shift, Egoson made ready to direct the primordial energies of the *Void* at his command.

"Godson, I, too, claimed the Key to all the powers of the Universe, but, unlike you, I am under no sacred covenant forbidding me *to kill*. Therefore, I will destroy you just as I destroyed *The One Who Knows*. Then we shall see who will reign forever and ever."

"May the Will of The Great Mother Goddess be done!" Godson thundered.

"Hah! The Great Mother Goddess can't save you now! *By all the POWERS given to me at THE DANCE OF THE SACRED SPIRAL OF LIFE, I, INVOKE, THE SACRED SEA DRAGONS, GATEKEEPERS OF THE VOID, to channel the primordial energies here and now, so the body vehicle of GODSON may be destroyed and his DIVINE SPIRIT returned to the VOID forever!"*

Deep rumblings shook the earth as a massive earthquake split open a widening chasm, bringing forth two spiraling forms of energy ascending in fiery thunderbolts of lighting until The Sacred Sea Dragons materialized out of blinding light. Immediately, they began discharging their venemous powers toward Godson's body. In willfull resignation to his fate, Godson began moving toward Egoson under the full onslaught of energy so powerful, it would have instantly annihilated any other living creature. Mountainous radiant light glowed around Godson, making Egoson shudder. A transfixed Godson approached, holding The Scepter of *Divine* Power. He drew nearer with the obsessive determination of a madman.

"Stop! Stop! You vowed to surrender!"

"I vowed to surrender, *but I did not vow to do nothing!"*

"Godson, *STOP! You cannot destroy me! I am Death itself!* Sacred Sea Dragons *kill him!"*

Blinding light exploded more terrible than before from The Sacred Sea Dragons as everyone fled for their lives. Forces of Darkness scattered in all directions fleeing from the agony of burning light, while many inadvertently trespassed onto holy ground only to drop dead in their tracks from the extreme shift of Darkness to Light. Sea creatures loyal to The Great Mother Goddess continued to storm The Temples of the Goddess of the Sea for safety, while others became paralyzed where they stood in utter helplessness and shock.

Godson, raising The Scepter of *Divine* Power, invoked with a booming charge:

"By ALL the POWERS of HEAVEN and GALEXIA, I now invoke THE DIVINE IMMORTAL THAT I AM, making possible a ONENESS of BEING with THE POWER and FREQUENCY of LOVE of the VOID. With this OMNIPOTENT POWER, I now open THE BOOK of LIFE existing as part of The Divine Records of Consciousness upon which the SOUL NAME of SOLAR is inscribed, thus bringing into unity EVERY ASPECT of MYSELF that had ever become separated in TIME, including NABYSS!"

Egoson could not speak or move as his terrified eyes shaded into shock. The invocation of Solar's name from *The Book of Life* paralyzed him, as a great door opened filled with radiant light. Through THE PORTAL OF LIGHT his Soul returned from Death's domain as great Darkness was unleashed from him, and simultaneously, from all sea creatures filled with Darkness. A raging storm of unparalleled fury followed, as day blackened into night, and sea creatures screamed in unmitigated terror as Darkness blazed from them. Godson shape-shifted into towering light as The Scepter of *Divine* Power reached high above The Temples of the Goddess of the Sea dispersing *DIVINE* LIGHT in all directions, activating The Blue Crystal of Galexia, so everyone could awaken in the final exhale of The Final Reckoning. Opening the frequencies of consciousness so everyone could hear, Godson spoke the words that would bring The Final Reckoning to an end.

"What I do now, my brother, NABYSS, I do out of LOVE for you, and LOVE for me, and LOVE for THE KINGDOM of OCEANA, for we together as ONE AND THE SAME can release the world from all her pain and suffering. I,

therefore, surrender myself to the POWER and FREQUENCY of LOVE, the true source of DIVINE CONSCIOUSNESS, releasing you as I have vowed, MY EGO of DARKNESS, a GUARDIAN you have been of all my pain throughout my lifetimes before. But this time I WILL NOT DENY YOU as I have in the past and increase the PAIN of our SEPARATION that has made CHAOS an ever-present reality in THE KINGDOM of OCEANA. I will not JUDGE you with HATRED nor become your VICTIM of REVENGE, but FORGIVE myself for creating DARKNESS out of LIGHT. I now claim THE SACRED COVENANT given to us all at the BEGINNING OF TIME: FROM DIVINE LOVE WE CAME, TO DIVINE LOVE WE SHALL RETURN! And so I AM!"

A powerful circular beam of light originating from The Scepter of *Divine* Power instantly neutralized the primordial energies of The Sacred Sea Dragons of the *Void.* With luminously glowing claws, Godson picked up a transfixed and paralyzed Egoson and ushered him onto holy ground.

In the next moment the spiraling energies of The Sacred Sea Dragons collided with Godson and Egoson, as all became engulfed by an epiphany of blinding light. The explosive thunderbolt of their union rocked Heaven and Galexia, as a huge tidal wave of light discharged in all directions, engulfing The Kingdom of Oceana in a revolution of consciousness that lifted all Darkness in its wake. All sea creatures succumbed to *an experience of essence* brought on by the shattering of the spellbinding dream of separation forever!

Everywhere, angelfish burst into song as holy ground returned to The Kingdom of Oceana from one end to the other. A cry rose as sea creatures awakened from the dream of separation. For the first time in eons, *the Power and Frequency of Love* filled them with awe, celebration, and thanksgiving. All fear and killing instincts dissolved, transforming The Kingdom of Oceana into a world suddenly charged by radiant love.

Theia was the first to shift from the ecstatic revelry of her celebration to look for Godson in the now empty space where she had last seen him. She swam toward the empty space looking to see if there was any trace of him.

Instead, she noticed the ground was scorched with an enormous pattern unmistakable even at close range. As she moved away to get a better look at The Mantle of The Sacred Sea Dragons, she threw herself into the pit of scorched earth in response. She cried desperately from the pain seering her heart and the loss of her love. Theia descended deeper and deeper into her loss. She scratched desperately at the charred earth, brought ashes to her face, and rocked herself gently back and forth, as she continued her cries of lamentation for the now gone Godson. Starborn and Sonar, both fully roused from their experience of essence and revelry of love, came over to Theia and put their arms around her, so they could grieve their loss together.

As Theia succumbed to cries of pain and lamentation, lightning flashes of memories began bleeding into her mind from a long time ago, when a loss as great and terrible as this, had pierced her heart with unbearable sorrow. Remembrance was so painful that Theia blacked out.

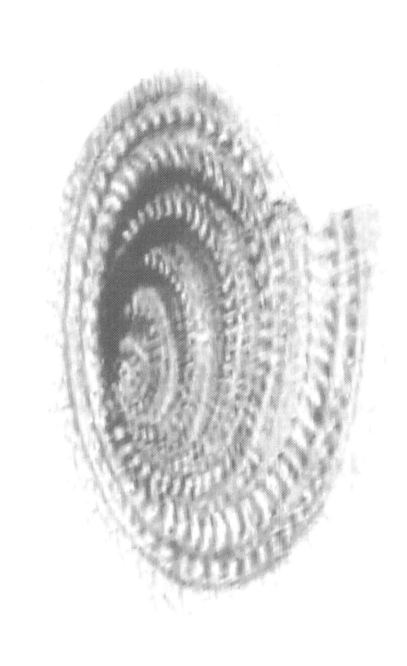

55

RETURN OF THE GODS

If there is no more time, then the illusion of separation
from the Divine is over. We return to the Frequency
of Love, where we can feel the eternal truth of love in
every moment.

In a parallel reality outside of time, Theia awakened, only to become pierced by the pain of her aching heart once again.

"Oh, Godson, dear Godson! Please forgive me!"

Theia became inconsolable as her wailing cries reverberated all around her. She succumbed to regret as the Taskmaster of her pain punished her inexorably with blind grief. When she could no longer sustain the tragic loss of her love and finally surrendered her helplessness in the Name of The Great Mother Goddess, a light emerged and began to coalesce before her. Noting this, Theia hushed her cries and waited as shifting colors began to take form.

"Godson, is that you?" Theia asked, sensing Godson's presence. After a few moments, an answer came.

"Yes, Theia, I AM!"

"Godson, oh, Godson!" Theia cried desperately. Is this how you saw it all in your visions? Is this how The Final Reckoning ends, with your sacrifice and my betrayal?"

"Theia . . . Theia! How can your love ever bring on betrayal? It was your loyalty to love that made possible the inevitability of events that brought The Final Reckoning to conclusion. The Great Mother Goddess knew your heart and its capacity for unconditional love that would always abide within you. She knew you would always serve the highest truth."

"But Godson, why did you have to pay with your life?"

"Theia . . . *Theia!* If time has ended, and there is no more time, as *The Sacred Sea Scrolls* predicted, what does The Final Reckoning really mean? After all, I AM speaking to you from across all worlds of consciousness. Am I dead or am I alive?"

"Of course! If there is no more time, then the illusion of separation from the *Divine* is over. We return to love, where we can feel the eternal truth of love in every moment.

"That's right!"

"But Godson, if you are now *Divine* Spirit acting from the Fifth Dimension of pure consciousness, you are no longer anchored to The Kingdom of Oceana in the flesh."

"But Theia, what does it mean, *Love Is All There Is?"*

"According to *The Sacred Sea Scrolls*, it means you are one with everything."

"Yes, but *The Sacred Sea Scrolls* also stated, *'Once unity with Divine Love is achieved, all things are possible.'"*

"Does that mean . . . ?"

"Yes! By experiencing the perfection of *Divine* consciousness, I have transcended the words, 'I AM THAT I AM' to realize an even higher level of consciousness, which is, I AM *LOVE* THAT I AM! This is the ultimate truth! We can again channel the primordial energy of the *Void* as we did long ago and be as Gods once again."

As Godson spoke, his form continued coalescing into radiant light, while Theia took up the sacred words and said them to herself in an ancient tongue, reminiscent of The Original Ancestry of the Gods.

"I AM *LOVE* THAT I AM," Theia said to herself, humming the words like a prayer, as radiant love burst forth inside of her. I AM *LOVE* THAT I AM," she whispered again, as love cleansed, purified, and released her from everything that ever divided her. "I AM *LOVE* THAT I AM," she said sweetly to herself, as doorways of wisdom, knowledge, and information were ignited within her, and lifetimes of memories instantly flooded her awareness, reclaiming all she had forgotten.

"Can you remember who I was, Theia, before I started to judge and criticize myself for the smallest of things and separated from the truth of my Soul? Can you remember when I became a Soul incarnating in and out of time, from one lifetime to another, losing myself more with every act of ignorance that plunged me deeper into separation? How many lifetimes of pain and suffering did I force upon myself and others until balance was restored? How often was I plagued by critical self doubt until I lost all self respect and became a lowly crab, crawling along the bottom of the ocean, eating dirt for nourishment, because I had completely forgotten who I AM?"

"But, Godson, you *know* who you are!" Theia exclaimed, as she became moved by a strange excitement as Godson's flesh continued materializing before her.

"You have only to search your heart and look to see me as I AM to see beyond the illusion of the crab you once saw."

Theia gently closed her eyes and opened her trembling heart to the deepest love she had ever known, revealing a yearning of her most secret desire. As love charged her with a longing too poignant to bear, she opened her eyes to see The Mantle of The Sacred Sea Dragons taking shape before her, while a face began to materialize out of golden mists. As Theia reached for the vision, Sonar's high-pitched sounds abruptly awakened her into full consciousness.

"Theia! Are you all right?" Sonar cried.

Theia looked from one to the other, as Sonar, Starborn, Mysteia, and a host of sea creatures from The Temples of the Goddess of the Sea crowded around. Theia straightened, slowly remembering who she was and all that had happened. Looking into the faces of her friends, she smiled as images flooded her mind and each face connected her to *The Divine Records of Consciousness* from previous lifetimes.

As the light of the Moon Goddess fell upon Theia's face and anointed her, Theia's eyes shifted into trance. Instantly, her body began transmuting into rippling energies of vibrational frequencies. The crowd stepped back, including her friends, awed and simultaneously confused by the changes taking place in her energy field.

While the crowd was focused on one reality, Theia was focused on another as visions crowded out the present reality. Theia saw herself seated among The Original Ancestry of the Gods, looking down the rows of High Priests and High Priestesses from that time. She was being crowned as the Moon Goddess, while Solar was being crowned as the Sun God. The scene faded as she went further back to the beginning of time, when she walked through THE STARGATE together with Solar by her side. At that time there was no separation between herself and The Great Mother Goddess, as she became her flesh long ago, and no separation existed between Solar and The Great Father God as well.

As Theia swooned in the piercing consciousness of The Great Mother Goddess restoring this ancient truth to her, her energy began to stabilize and the piercing frequencies stopped. As she returned to the flesh of her body, Theia knew what she had to do.

"Theia, are you all right?" Sonar asked, drawing near again and gently caressing her face.

"Yes, Sonar, I AM. Can you help me up?"

"Of course," Sonar said, gently lifting her up with Starborn's help.

"Now, would you give me some space?"

"What do you mean?"

"I need more space around me," Theia replied, moving away from the crowd.

"Of course, Theia. Everyone get back!" Sonar signaled, with high-pitched sounds, ushering everyone back. "Theia is all right!"

Theia moved farther away before raising her hands aloft. She began speaking in the ancient vibrational language of the Gods. The frequencies of her voice rose higher and higher, until everything began pulsating with greater intensity until the earth trembled and billowing waves rose in the wake of gathering power all around her.

Sea creatures shifted nervously, except Sonar, Starborn, and Mysteia, who became flooded with memories of an ancient past, heralded by the language of the Gods.

Two spiraling luminous forms emerged from the splitting earth, as desperate cries of bewilderment rose from the masses, and panic ignited chaos once again. In spite of the fear that spiked from all sea creatures, everyone became frozen in a trance-like state of disbelief. The formidable powers gathering momentum weren't threatening in any way, for it was Light charged by the *Frequency of Love* that stilled them in response.

As The Sacred Sea Dragons emerged and took form on opposite sides of each other, THE STARGATE materialized between them, simultaneously flooding Theia's body with primordial light. Initiating a transmutation of consciousness on all levels of being, Theia threw back her head, trembling in response. The lifeless forms of the Abominable Hags of Anger, Hate, Guilt & Shame, and their offspring Rage, Blame, and Regret suddenly lifted from the graveyard, where the dead littered the ocean floor in all directions. Dematerializing into a bolt of light, that light shot into Theia's convulsing body, as she continued her transformation into a luminous Being of Light.

"Starborn, did you see that?!" Sonar exclaimed, unable to contain his surprise. "Why did Theia assimilate the Abominable Hags and their offspring into her energy field?"

Starborn waited before answering, as the knowledge of an ancient truth rose to his awareness with impeccable clarity.

"Sonar, just as Godson recognized Egoson as a lost Soul fragment of himself, so did Theia recognize the Abominable Hags as fragments of her splintered Soul. In order to come into wholeness, she needed to reclaim them once again into her energy field. In the world of duality, we all have, *without exception,* split off into Soul fragments of Darkness and Light."

"Oh, my Goddess!"

Theia's features and countenance glowed as she shifted into an ethereal presence, and there appeared a crown on her head of jeweled stars. Within its center, a sacred spiral of light luminously glowed. Everyone hushed in wondrous awe, as Theia completed her transformation into radiant light.

Starborn was the first to bow before the holy presence of Luna, with profound sacred reverence, as the holy representative of The Great Mother Goddess taken flesh. His lifetimes of passionate inquiry to understand the Mysteries and *The Sacred Sea Scrolls* had finally come to an end. He considered himself fortunate for having recognized that the knowledge revealed in the sacred texts exposed different levels of knowledge and information. But the deeper Mysteries remained hidden within allegorical and metaphorical stories, which too often had been taken literally, even by Initiates. Although the sacred texts had been preserved as impeccably as possible, too many changes had occurred across years that altered facts to reflect differences in understanding, which sometimes brought new meaning to entire passages and a distortion of the truth.

"Sonar," Starborn said, as he bagan to share his thoughts aloud to his friend, "The Great Mother Goddess had not been an inaccessible Co-Creator and Overseer of the Universe, but a presence of consciousness to be recognized as part of all sea creatures. As an Omnipotent Being, She had the power to witness and be a Witness to all lives through the Windows of Her Soul, expressed in an infinite number of individual lives, as unique as every point of view that ever existed. Yet, She remained patiently waiting for sea creatures to remember their oneness with Her and The Great Father God *in full consciousness!* Only then could *Divine* unity be experienced by everyone as an ever-present reality within them all. For me, this profound revelation of truth has become the crowning achievement of all time, a solemn occasion where words have no meaning, and only feelings could preserve the sanctity of this spiritual revelation in everlasting detail."

Transformed by the *Frequency of Love*, Luna solemnly bowed, acknowledging her unity with all sea creatures. Yet, there was incompleteness without Solar, and the others who had crossed over.

Turning once again to face THE STARGATE, Luna raised her arms aloft, emitting high frequency sounds that did not originate from her throat, but from the vibrational field of consciousness inclusive of her entire being. Everyone vibrated with the power of these sounds. Towering doors materialized out of golden light etched with the insignia of The Mantle of the Sacred Sea Dragons. Luna emitted another series of high frequencies, opening the huge doors as silence abounded among all sea creatures. Materializing out of golden mist, a face appeared, like in her dream, before seeing a fully fleshed merman come into sight, bearing the insignia of The Mantle of The Sacred Sea Dragons across his chest.

Awesome splendor filled all witnessing sea creatures as cries of tears, laughter, and joy emerged. Mysteia, Starborn, and Sonar were the only ones silenced by the power of unspeakable *Love* re-emerging within them. Temple Priests and Priestesses gathered around, flanked by The Sentinels of the Sun, angelfish, sacred eels, sea horses, and all sea creatures large and small.

"Solar, The Great Merman of the Sea, I presume?" Sonar said, in his vibrational tongue, breaking the muted silence of overwhelming feelings.

Laughter erupted from all sea creatures released by the sheer tension of Solar's appearance as a merman, and all gathered around to extend warm embraces. Luna stood still, waiting in hushed silence for Solar to emerge from the crowd that had gathered around him. Momentarily, the crowd parted in response to the telepathic intention set by them both. The poignancy of heart-rending feelings flooded Luna, as she finally set eyes upon Solar. He stood before her, the beauty of his form shocking her body into immediate response. She instantly felt the magnificent glory of The Great Father God showering her with unconditional *Love,* incomprehensible to her until now. She closed her eyes allowing the weight of all time and memories dissolve into the eternal present. Savoring the reality and celebration of this exquisite moment, she experienced the poignancy of sweet sorrow, which had dominated her heart for lifetimes on end.

Solar came near and stretched forth his hand toward Luna, while flashes of energy coursed through her body before she touched Solar's hand. Solar took her hand and pulled her toward him. She weakened in his embrace and sighed deeply, as the tension of anticipation finally released from her body. When they kissed, Love ignited their bodies into flames and then back into flesh, restoring the only reality they had ever known together.

Cheers burst forth from all sea creatures celebrating the return of The Original Ancestry of the Gods. Looking into each other's eyes, Luna and Solar smiled to each other, remembering when they had originally emerged from THE STARGATE in full expression of the *Frequency of Love.* Restored by grace, harmony reigned, felt by one and all.

Luna and Solar turned and rejoined the celebrations, remembering all to be done. Turning toward THE STARGATE, they simultaneously sounded the ancient vibrational language of creation until two radiant forms began to coalesce in the doorway, as everyone hushed in anticipation. Before either form had completely materialized, Sonar shrieked, *"Seeres!"*

Seeres materialized looking directly into the deep pool of Sonar's eyes and said, *"Hello, Resonance."*

Sonar threw back his head and went immediately into seizure. Pure radiant light shot into his body from THE STARGATE, as well as light from lost Soul fragments lying in the open field, until all had to turn away from the blinding transformation of light into flesh. Moments later, another merman stood in Sonar's place.

"Resonance, how lovely to see you once again aligned with the vibrational template of your Soul," Seeres said, completing her transformation into flesh as well.

Resonance smiled and bowed respectfully before the beautiful Seeres before extending a warm embrace. He then turned to Magus, and acknowledged, "So, it is you, Magus, who was Domaine all this time. It has been a long time since we served on THE COUNCIL together. It is so wonderful to experience our return to this reality of *Love* once again.

"Yes, it is!"

"I see why you and Seeres, or rather, Ourania, the Heavenly One, came under agreement to bring on The Final Reckoning. *You played your parts so well!* It is good to see you, most beloved to each other, standing side by side."

"Yes, but where is your beloved, Frequency?"

Resonance looked around and then at Luna with an inquiring helpless look. He opened up his consciousness on all levels. He sent forth frequencies of great power and magnitude, enabling him to connect with all consciousness to the very ends of The Kingdom of Oceana. Still, he could not pick up on Frequency.

"Where is Frequency, Luna? I do not believe I know where she is. Can you help me?"

"Let us link up together to *The Divine Records of Consciousness*," Luna said. "We will get our answer then."

Luna shifted with Resonance to telepathically search *The Divine Records of Consciousness*. Once in trance, they witnessed the scene of Sonar's mother desperately trying to reach The Temples of the Goddess of the Sea. In spite of pain and weakness caused by internal bleeding, she managed to arrive on holy ground. She had just enough strength to bring Sonar into the world before she died in Theia's arms.

Resonance threw back his head as he released a terrible cry of grief, so painful was the memory of that dream world of separation. It was his beloved, Frequency, who had given birth to him as his mother and brought him into this incarnation, before taking leave of him.

Luna telepathically signaled to everyone to invoke the name of Frequency in their minds, as they looked toward THE STARGATE in anticipation. Moments later, the radiant form of Frequency emerged smiling from the doorway. With arms wide open, she called softly to her beloved Resonance.

Resonance whirled in his excitement, splashing everyone in turn, before racing to embrace Frequency, knowing death would never separate them again.

Magus spoke, as everyone was feeling the exhilaration of reunion. "There are still others amongst us who need to come into full consciousness as well."

Everyone instinctively turned to Starborn, who smiled and knew the truth in that moment. Before anyone could speak, Starborn acknowledged his true Soul Name in the language of the Gods. Instantly, light beamed into his flesh from THE STARGATE, along with many lights that burst forth from the open field of lost soul fragments of black fallen stars, thus completing his transformation into flesh.

"Asterion!" Luna shouted, unable to contain her joy. "Asterion! How I've missed you! It is good to have you back!"

Asterion completed his transformation into flesh and did not wait for Luna or Solar to invoke the presence of his dearly beloved. He raised his arms aloft and spoke in the ancient language of the Gods that had originated from the Stars from whence he came. When he spoke the Soul Name of Astrial, a clap of thunder sounded, as thunderlight fell into the open field. It connected with a black fallen star that was lifeless and quickened its body into glowing radiant light until another member of The Original Ancestry of the Gods fully materialized.

"Astrial! How long did I wait for this moment to invoke your full presence in The Kingdom of Oceana!"

"It seems like it was only yesterday," Astrial said, winking as stars do in the sea-sky world, as she ran her hands along her newly formed flesh. It is good to be back," she said, as she embraced Asterion without letting go.

Solar looked toward Astrial and remembered his encounter with the black fallen star and its curse. He knew it was the Dark side of Astrial, who had planted that prophetic oracle upon his mind, at a time when he could only respond in fear.

"So, we meet again, Astrial, on the *Divine* side of life," Solar said, as Astrial turned. They both looked at each other and laughed, as each remembered their dream encounter and their return to reality.

Everyone joined in laughter as Luna and Solar looked around in celebration of The Original Ancestry of the Gods coming into full consciousness. Suddenly, Solar remembered his friend, Jason, who he had not seen for a long time.

"What of Jason? Where is he?"

No response came as Solar scanned the area surrounding The Temples of the Goddess of the Sea and beyond. Solar could not reach Jason's mind across The Kingdom of Oceana. When he sought an answer for this from *The Divine Records of Consciousness*, a vision rose to his mind. He saw Jason come upon a school of piranhas that circled and engulfed him and ate him alive. He had screamed until there was nothing left of him except his naked shell, which fell to the bottom of the ocean. Solar flinched at the vision, and then filled with purpose, he turned to THE STARGATE.

"Dear Jason, my dear mentor and friend of this lifetime, who placed me on the path of spiritual awareness, it is now your time to come through THE STARGATE. Acting together with all the Gods, I invoke the Wise Sage, Metis, of the Original Ancestry of the Gods, to come through THE STARGATE *now!*"

In the hushed silence of everyone's anticipation, nothing happened. Bewilderment spread across them all. Momentarily, Luna and Solar felt the pull of consciousness from behind them and turned to Mysteia, whose eyes were gathering tears. Within the deep pools of her eyes, Luna and Solar witnessed the long history of her patient waiting and suffering for her beloved, Metis. Lifetimes of pain, loneliness, and sadness became transparent in her eyes, and it was clear she could not wait another moment for his return without feeling the threat of annihilation. Yet, Metis failed to materialize in spite of the Gods acting collectively.

Mysteia finally succumbed to the poignancy of a loss so great that it took her breath away. She became poised between all worlds of consciousness, hovering between life and death. At once Mysteia understood that she had lived in the absence of love, allowing the intellect of the mind to take its place, until no Mystery could provide the answers to her emptiness. Without love, she had not been able to immortalize her flesh. Without love, she could not vanquish death. Without love, she had been forced to incarnate repeatedly with the unfinished business of the past intruding upon her in the present. Continually, she had pined the loss of a great love, feeling the desperate clutch of her loss until it completely gripped her heart and stopped its beating.

Mysteia stood motionless, breathless, as her heart gave out, and she understood the dilemma of her existence. Looking for love outside of herself, *she was doomed never to find it!* She had lived like a phantom in her lifetimes, feeling incomplete, because love had forsaken her. The living poignancy of her loss finally became complete. Fearing annihilation from existence, annihilation became the only reality left for her to experience.

In astonishment, Luna, Solar and the other Gods witnessed Mysteia's disappearance from existence. Her body faded into nothingness while her eyes lingered, reflecting her terror, until there was nothing left of her. Gone from The Kingdom of Oceana, she re-materialized *into the consciousness of the Void*. There, she instantaneously experienced all she had denied of herself. Collapsing into her own emptiness, annihilation became total. Only then did she come to peace in the ocean of consciousness resulting in nothingness. Only then was the living consciousness of the *Void* able to fill her with the *Frequency of Love* as the living reality of the *Divine*. Only then, was she able to claim the Immortality of her Soul and *Divine* Spirit.

As Mysteia embraced the ecstasy and inviolable reality of the *Frequency of Love*, she simultaneously experienced the co-existence of all states of consciousness, including the *Divine* Feminine and *Divine* Masculine with herself. In hushed stillness, she came into wholeness. It was this wholeness that allowed her to understand the intrinsic unity made possible by the polarity of consciousness. It was this unity that brought her into oneness until no separation of consciousness existed on any level.

As Mysteia swooned in the ecstasy of these revelations, she re-materialized into The Kingdom of Oceana, reflecting the Immortality of *Divine* consciousness within living flesh. Claiming the greatest Mystery of her existence, Mysteia was able to take her rightful place among The Original Ancestry of the Gods, who stood by ready to welcome her with unconditional love.

The Gods gathered around her, embracing her return with loving affection. Mysteia saw herself mirrored in the myriad reflections of The Original Ancestry of the Gods. She was one and all of them at once. She felt complete because her unquelled torment for Metis was gone. She had been made whole by *Divine* Love.

As Mysteia relaxed in the profound peace filling her heart, she was suddenly pulled by the presence of another consciousness, as powerful as another God waiting to make contact with her heart and mind. Mysteia abruptly turned toward THE STARGATE to claim the vision of her heart.

"*Metis!*" Mysteia screamed, as she shot like a bullet toward her beloved. "*Metis!*" she shouted, as she put her arms around him and began to cry without restraint, tears streaking her face for the first time in lifetimes.

"Metis, oh, Metis!" Mysteia cried, oh *Metis!*"

"I am here, my dearest Mysteia, I am finally here beside you."

Mysteia and Metis both cried as they held each other tightly. The ordeal of their separation had finally come to an end.

"Oh, Metis, so many lifetimes I had tried to find you, hoping to discover your Soul existing in another form. To think! You had incarnated in this lifetime as Jason! Yet, your size made it impossible for you to visit The School of Mysteries. Had you come, there would have been instant recognition between us, and you would have remembered your true Soul Name! But The Great Mother Goddess knew of that and made it impossible for us to meet with you as a giant sea turtle!"

"I knew all my life I would unlock a great mystery if I had been allowed into The School of Mysteries. That is why I stood outside the Temple walls, time and again, praying for the mystery to dawn upon my mind. It also explains why I never took a mate, though I had no idea I was looking for you! It's so good to be back!"

Mysteia marveled that she could experience herself as *Divine* and complete in one moment, and in the next, shift into the polarity of her Twin Flame, as Metis. It was a joyous delight!

Metis felt a touch upon his shoulder and turned. Solar was putting his arm around him, acknowledging his mentor and friend.

"You'll forgive me if I call you, Jason," Solar said, hugging his friend, "until I get accustomed to calling you by your true Soul name."

"Likewise, Little Sol. It is a pleasure to be back in The Kingdom of Oceana, celebrating our return as Gods once again."

"But we are not yet complete in our reunion," Luna said, looking across holy ground in the direction of The Sentinels of the Sun. Two Sentinels of the Sun remained alive, both bleeding on Temple steps, where black needles protruded from their bodies. One lay unconscious on the ground, while the other stood as guardian. Luna made contact with the one acting as guardian and asked him to approach with the other Sentinel of the Sun, so healing could be administered to them both. The Sentinel of the Sun wasted no time in showing up with his dying friend.

As the unconscious Sentinel of the Sun was placed in the circle of the Gods, Luna telepathically understood that the one mortally wounded called Firelight had used his body to shield his friend, Blaze, from death.

Luna looked around to the rest of the Gods and communicated her understanding telepathically, so they could all act in unison. Raising her arms aloft with Solar, Luna spoke the words that would bring healing back to The Sentinels of the Sun.

Flooded by the energy of the Gods, the body of the dying Sentinel of the Sun shook violently and burst into flames, as only the legendary Phoenix could underwater. The other Sentinel of the Sun threw back his head and simultaneously began shape-shifting into luminous fire. Shortly thereafter, two Gods completely materialized from radiant firelight.

"Phoenix, what a pleasure to celebrate your return!" Asterion said, extending his hand to assist Phoenix off the ground. "And you, Lumina, it is wonderful to see you again. We can see that Phoenix continued to protect you even in the material reality of the flesh."

"Yes, he did and always has. We reincarnated as Sentinels of the Sun to serve side by side one another. Still, we could not recognize each other beyond the veil of the flesh, especially since we came in as two males! It now explains why we felt so profoundly bonded to one another and loved each other deeply. In fact, we became inseparable! Our love came through regardless!"

As The Original Ancestry of the Gods became fully restored, memories flooded in from across the whole of time. Everyone remembered all things without judgment. Laughter erupted as a result of bringing all things into awareness in spite of the challenges and tragedies they had each experienced in the dream world once thought to be reality.

Luna was the only one who could not laugh. She stood breathless before Solar, unsure whether she had fallen into another dream or not.

"Perhaps, Luna, if I were to hold you in my arms and never let you go," Solar said, "you would realize this is not the same dream, after all."

ABOUT THE COVER ARTIST

Brigit Suslow is a photographer, graphic artist, and writer. She loves the creative process, engaging intuitively in many different kinds of expression through mixed media. Inspired by the imagination, she lives life in a dance, giving rise to images that playfully materialize and interact with her. She then gives them a voice, or an expression, that reveals the parallel realities of magical landscapes accessible to us all. Childlike, Brigit allows herself to be fully engaged in the world around her, never taking life's challenges too seriously. Her work is about taking a second look at life so the lightheartedness of the Soul can be discovered and reclaimed once again. To view her images, go to Flickr *"Dreaming into Reality"*: http://www.flickr.com/photos/brigitsuslow/

ABOUT THE ARTIST

Illustrator of images Inside of Book

Linda Lugo is a professional makeup artist, who uses faces as her canvas in the film industry. She shares the following, *"In the last few years, I began living my dream when I began painting faces on canvas as well. These faces brought to light special beings, which materialized and began to speak to me and share their message. It has given me the courage to develop my own "point of view", which I share with you in the illustrated characters brought to life in this story as well. I am thankful to have been a part of its unfolding. I hope my work will encourage you to follow your own dreams as I have. With Art Love, Linda."*

ABOUT THE AUTHOR

Formal Credentials

Sophia received her BA from Hunter College in New York City after completing part of her undergraduate credits at Harvard University in Cambridge, Massachusetts. She became an ordained Minister and Pastoral Psychologist after completing her MA and Ph.D from a theological college in Florida. After 25 years of passionate inquiry and research into the Soul, she refers to herself professionally as a *Dr. of the Soul.*

Informal Credentials

Sophia spent time in the Amazon Jungle and the Andes Mountains of Peru studying with shamans (medicine men) to learn about ancient healing techniques, for no Apprenticeship of the Soul can take place without learning how to heal oneself through direct Soul contact. She chose to study with shamans because they are experts in healing *Soul fragmentation, which takes place for everyone who incarnates on Earth.* It's part of the journey of the Soul that serves the education of innocence. Shamans refer to this malady as *Soul Loss,* while psychologists refer to this malady as *dissociation* or *dissociative disorders.*

Shamans look to the Soul and recognize that aspects of the Soul take leave when confronted by trauma. Psychologists look to the mind and believe that painful experiences can "split" the mind, when experiences, too painful to cope with by the conscious mind, drop into the subconscious to be forgotten as a way of escaping trauma. Shamans believe *Soul Loss* can only be healed by recovery of lost soul fragments. Psychologists believe *dissociation* can be healed (although not in all cases) by helping individuals *re-member—by putting themselves back together in the present once they have remembered what took place in the past.*

Sophia has also studied with Native Americans because they spiritually believe all of Mother Nature *is conscious.* This includes the existence of parallel worlds where nature spirits, power animals, and deities of the forces of nature can be contacted *at will.*

Sophia is able to read *The Akashic Records* (Soul Records) for individuals and look into *The Book of Life,* which details all of humanity's journey across time on Earth as a collective Soul experience. She refers to *The Book of Life* in the story as *The Divine Records of Consciousness.* By entering altered states, Sophia is able to access parallel worlds and realities where the Soul's journey can be tracked and known across time with extraordinary detail and understanding.

Loss of innocence became a theme common to everyone. By looking into *The Book of Life,* Sophia witnessed time and again that Souls began their sacred journey in a "fall" from grace that shattered their innocence and caused a splintering of the personality into a multiplicity of aspects. In four simple words, Sophia came to understand the Soul's *raison d'être* for existence—it is for *The Education of Innocence.* That reason is metaphorically explored in the story revealing one of the great Mysteries coveted by the ancients in the sacred Temples of old.

As importantly, is the final question that every Soul must answer, *"How does a Soul return to the vastness of its original Divine nature when so much has taken place across time?"* To know the answer, you must read the complete story to the end.

Contact Information

Sophia may be contacted about her classes, workshops, and educational programs involving *The Path of the Shaman, Holistic Practitioner of the Healing Arts, and The Masters of Living Light* Courses. She is also available for speaking engagements and as a consultant involving articles, film documentaries, and movies having to do with specialized information and phenomena concerning the Soul.

Please forward your inquiries to:

Sophia, Ph.D
Dr. of the Soul
Pathways to Soul Mastery
P.O. Box 5882
Pagosa Springs, CO 81147
www.pathwaystosoulmastery.com